ALSO BY TALIA HIBBERT

RAVENSWOOD

A Girl Like Her

Damaged Goods, a bonus novella

Untouchable

That Kind of Guy

THE BROWN SISTERS

Get a Life, Chloe Brown

DIRTY BRITISH ROMANCE

The Princess Trap

Wanna Bet?

JUST FOR HIM

Bad for the Boss

Undone by the Ex-Con

Sweet on the Greek

STANDALONE TITLES

Merry Inkmas

Mating the Huntress

Operation Atonement

Always With You

THAT KIND OF GUY

Ravenswood Book 3

TALIA HIBBERT

Nixon House

For the readers.

ACKNOWLEDGMENTS

This book, like most, took a village. Thank you to Jhenelle Jacas, Rosa Giles, Adina Taylor and Ellen Baier for your support. It will never be forgotten. Thank you to Em Ali for the sensitivity reads, and for being my friend. Thank you to Zahra Butt, Kia Thomas, and Xan West for invaluable critique. And thanks, as always, to my family, who kept me fed and watered while I cackled at my desk and typed nonstop for days at a time.

CONTENT NOTE

Please be aware: this book contains depictions of emotional abuse and mentions of unwanted sexual encounters that could trigger certain audiences.

CHAPTER ONE

ZACH WAS FURIOUS, and it felt good.

He bent over the anvil, laser-focused, a vicious energy burning through his bloodstream. This was his molten world of metal and flame, where his anger was acceptable, even reasonable. Here, it gave him strength. And so, at work, where no-one he loved could see, he became a god of war and rage. The hammer in his hand was an extension of his body, the sweat rolling down his spine was a scream of encouragement, and watching iron bend to his will was cool oxygen in this sweltering space.

He worked. He worked. He worked. Until his phone vibrated in his pocket, the alarm dragging him back to reality. It was time for a break. Time to face the real world for a while and become the safest version of himself: cool, cocky, *calm*. Mustn't forget the calm.

Outside, the early spring sun was choked by dull, pale clouds. He took a gulp of sharp Ravenswood air, clean and crisp even here, on the small town's tiny industrial estate.

Then he pulled out his phone and fired off a text to his mother, the same one he sent three times a day.

Did you take your meds?

A few minutes later, her reply came through.

...I have now! Relax, darling. I always remember eventually. :)

More like she always checked her texts eventually. He rolled his eyes and flicked through his notifications. The online forum he'd been lurking in for months now continued to be active, especially his favourite thread: Demis for DC, a place for demisexual members to discuss all things DC related, for no particular reason other than a love of nerdery and camaraderie.

Zach had learned a lot about demisexuality since discovering this forum for ace and arospec people. Had *felt* a lot, too, reading about others' experiences while he grappled with his own. Now he knew for sure that he was demisexual, a discussion about comic books was clearly the perfect place for him to slide in and make some... internet friends, or whatever they were called. Friends like him. Friends who got it.

But he was still too nervous.

Zach sighed and put his phone away. A breeze bit at his cheeks, ruffled his hair, made the sweat beneath his overshirt feel clammy and cold. He pulled off the shirt and swiped at his brow, wandering toward the low brick wall at the edge of the lot. He knew what he was waiting for, or rather, who: Rae. His morning ray of sunshine, full of smiles and fantastic stories.

From the corner of his eye, he caught a flash of movement, a hint of colour. His mouth hooked up into a smile, though the expression didn't come as easy as it used to. Ma's illness was under control, and the depression that had swallowed him whole was under control, too, but Zach still felt distant sometimes—like a faint photocopy of himself. Still, for his friends, he tried.

But it turned out, the person walking toward him wasn't exactly a friend. Not anymore. And it certainly wasn't Rae.

Callista Michaelson was all graceful movement and bold contrasts: pink coat, blue eyes, hair like summer wheat, topped off by a genuine, beauty pageant smile. He hadn't seen her in ages, but once—before Ma's diagnosis had rearranged his life—she'd been someone he knew. He wasn't sure he knew her anymore.

Still, he leaned lazily against the wall and gave her his usual grin. "Hey, Cal."

"Hey, Zach." She stopped and mirrored his posture, her arm coming to rest beside his. Familiar mischief lit her gaze, and she ran her fingers playfully over his wrist. His stomach tightened, and not in a good way. He'd slept with Callie three times, back when he didn't understand himself. Before he'd vowed to stop hurting himself on other people's lust. Before he'd abandoned his twisted attempts to seem 'normal'.

For her part, Callista liked decent guys who gave decent orgasms, and there weren't many to choose from in this town.

"What are you doing out here?" she asked, arching a brow toward the grim facade of the forge. "Is Daniel being a nightmare again?"

"He keeps to himself, these days," Zach said dryly. "I

think he's on thin ice with daddy." That was the trouble with men who had the world handed to them: someone could always take it away. Daniel Burne, town sweetheart and bona fide human shit stain, was learning that the hard way.

"Then why are you out here in the cold wearing that?" Callie's eyes slid over the thin, white vest plastered to Zach's torso with sweat. She didn't seem to mind the view.

He resisted the urge to put his overshirt back on. "Gets hot in the forge."

"I bet." Her fingers climbed higher and higher on his arm, gliding over the art inked into his skin. Her touch felt more like the slow creep of a spider. He tried not to flinch. It was funny: people used to call Zach a freak, a weirdo obsessed with comic books and cartoons. Now he wore his heroes on his biceps in greyscale, and women like Callie called him a *hot nerd*. Whatever the fuck that meant.

At least there was no confusion over what *this* meant: the look in her eyes, the tease in her touch, white teeth sinking into her plump lower lip. Shit. Rejecting a woman really wasn't his idea of fun—but he'd made himself a promise, recently. One designed to break his habit of handing out *Yes*es he didn't mean. Zach had sworn to himself that he wouldn't sleep with a woman again unless he really, truly wanted her. No exceptions. "Cal," he said, catching her hand. "I, uh…"

She smiled and pulled away. "No?"

Relief. "No."

"I hear you're saying no to everyone, these days."

Which wasn't like him, hence the gossip. There was a

question in Callie's eyes, one he'd seen a thousand times before. Briefly, he considered answering.

You see, a while back, I thought my mother was dying, so I had a come-to-Jesus moment and explored the sexuality I've always tried to ignore. I am now unapologetically demisexual, which means no more sleeping with women I don't want just because it seems like I should.

Of course, she probably wouldn't know what *demisexual* meant—he hadn't, for a long time—and the thought of defining it made him want to take a three-year nap. So he kept his mouth shut.

After a moment, Callie let it go.

"Well," she said brightly, "I'm glad I caught you, anyway."

For a moment, he thought, *Caught me?* But she kept talking, so his mind moved on.

"I have a problem, Zach," she said, shooting a glare behind her—where, around the corner, Ravenswood's only mechanic had set up shop years ago. "I've been down here once a week for months, now. *Months.* And bloody *Joe* still can't fix my car properly."

Zach knew Callie well enough to realise she was exaggerating. Still, he nodded sympathetically. "What's up?"

"Well, if only I knew!" She threw up her hands. "First, it's a coolant issue, then it's the head gasket, then, actually, no, it's an electrical fault. Honestly, we need a new mechanic around here. You should've taken over. You were always so good at that stuff."

Yeah, well, necessity was the mother of every skill Zach had. Growing up poor with a busy single parent and a missing older brother had led him to learn a lot of practical shit at a very young age. The hard way. And those skills had never been allowed to fade, because once someone identified you as useful, they'd always be around to... well, use you.

Callie was giving him this hopeful, lip-biting look that might've made him dizzy, if he was allosexual—if he developed attraction without an emotional connection. But he wasn't, and he didn't. Gorgeous as Callie was, she didn't make him feel a damn thing below the belt. What he *did* feel was a familiar tug in his chest, that nagging pull he always experienced when faced with someone who needed something. It was an urgent whisper he couldn't ignore: *You're the only one people can rely on. That makes it your duty to help.*

"I'll take a look at the car for you," he said. He had a job, a sick mother, and a life, but sure, why the fuck not? Somehow, in the middle of all that, he'd fix Callie Michaelson's car—even though he hadn't seen her in a century.

The uncharitable thought, so unlike him, brought a slight frown to Zach's face.

Callie didn't seem to notice. She clasped her hands together and beamed, "Oh, I knew you would! You are such a sweetheart." Then she flung her arms around his neck, which must have been uncomfortable, since there was a brick fucking wall separating their bodies. But she did it anyway.

She left pretty quick after that, which was, frankly, a relief. It took Zach a few deep, careful breaths to ease the prickling discomfort Callie had left behind, but he managed. He'd been managing more and more, lately.

Once he was calm, he loitered for a few more minutes, knowing his break was over, hating that he was behind schedule, but oddly eager to see Rae. For some reason, after that high-pressure exchange, he was starving for another woman's absent-minded smile. And eventually, his patience was rewarded. She came.

He heard her before he saw her: that slow clip of booted feet, accompanied by the gentle pad of heavy paws. Then they rounded a corner and came into view: Duke—a huge, fluffy beast who claimed to be a dog but was clearly part bear—and Duke's human. Rae.

She wandered closer, more tugged along by Duke than actually walking, her dark eyes distant as she stared into space. She was dreaming up stories, as always, and this one must've been good, because she had a crooked little smile on her face. The left side of her mouth tilted up; the right side barely moved. He'd always assumed that had something to do with the three dark scars that swept across her temple, over her cheek, and along her jaw.

And, speaking of cheeks—hers were reddened beneath the brown sugar of her skin, as was the tip of her nose. She wasn't wearing a big, wool coat like Callie; just jeans and a jacket way too thin for this early spring morning. She was cold. He never did like to see Rae cold.

So he called, "Hey. Would it kill you to put on a scarf, or something?"

She blinked, focusing on him. Deep smile lines fanned from the corners of her tip-tilted eyes, and a corresponding warmth flared inside his chest. "Piss off, Davis," she said cheerfully. "You're practically naked, yourself."

"Don't act like you're complaining." He paused, just to

enjoy the hell out of her derisive snort. "Anyway, I spent all morning in a forge. What's your excuse?"

She was beside him now, only the bricks between them. Her arms rested alongside his, just like Callie's had, but she didn't touch. "There's nothing wrong with my outfit, you unrepentant nag. I'm supposed to be the old lady around here."

"Old lady." He rolled his eyes, indignant. "Shut up."

Duke chose that moment to rise up on his hind legs and give Zach some love over the wall, his tongue lolling happily. His tiny, teddy bear eyes twinkled like dots of midnight. He might as well have said, *I'm here too, you know.*

"Morning, mate." Zach sank his hands wrist-deep into thick, chestnut fur.

"Shameless," Rae muttered. "He's absolutely throwing himself at you. Where's your pride, Duke?"

"Don't ask, don't get," Zach said.

She gave a low, dry chuckle that was music to his ears. Rae never took him seriously. It was his favourite thing about her.

And his second favourite thing—the reason he'd hung about waiting for her and made himself late—was her mind. By which he meant, obviously, her stories. "You got anymore drama for me?" His tone was hopeful, almost wheedling, but he didn't really care. It had been days since the last installment; he wanted to know what was going on in Rae's fantasy world of witchcraft and betrayal.

But she shook her head, frowning slightly. "Nothing new today. Sorry." She sighed, and the worry in her voice pricked something protective in him. "This book isn't coming easy."

He'd never heard her say that before. Of course, they weren't exactly life-long friends: his brother's girlfriend had introduced them last summer, which felt like forever ago, but wasn't. Still, the idea of his daydreamer struggling with stories seemed... wrong.

He leaned closer, narrowing his eyes like clues might be written beneath her skin. He didn't find anything, but for a moment, he caught her scent on the breeze: lemon and sugar pancakes. Zach breathed deeper. He loved pancakes. "Writer's block?"

She wrinkled her nose. "I don't believe in writer's block."

For some reason—maybe the prim way she said it—he chuckled. She was so fucking cute, sometimes, and she didn't even know it.

She tutted at his laughter, pointing a finger at him. "Positive words, positive mind! Or... something. My dad used to say that. Don't call it writer's block, is my point. You'll jinx me."

"Sure, yeah." The words might be more convincing if he could stop laughing.

"Oh, shut up. Someone should get you a muzzle. *I* should get you a muzzle. What do you think, Duke?" She looked down at her mammoth dog, whose head was level with her waist. And Rae wasn't a small woman.

"Duke would never muzzle me," Zach said.

"Don't be so sure," she replied archly.

Duke gave Zach a beady stare that seemed to say, *I am a loyal hound who will support his mistress in any endeavour.*

9

Zach rolled his lips inwards and contented himself with a smile. "So, what are you gonna do about your not-writer's-block?"

"I don't know. Sacrifice a goat?"

"Wow. Harsh."

"Desperate times call for desperate measures. My mind is anchored on dull, boring Earth, and I really don't like it here." She was smiling, but it wasn't her usual quirk of amusement; there was something thin and worn about it. She turned her head and the wind teased her hair into a flag of bronze and brown ribbons, shot through with whispers of silver. If she were a painting, she'd be titled something artsy like *Wistful* or *Wanting*.

"If your mind's anchored," he said slowly, "then something must be weighing you down."

Just like that, her faraway gaze was sharp as a scope and locked on him. For a second, she looked breathtakingly unhappy, so painfully vulnerable that it shook him to his bones. Then she blinked, flashed a one-sided smile, and the moment passed.

Maybe everyone on earth was hiding something massive inside them. He had the anger he didn't want and could rarely release. And Rae, apparently, had sadness. So much fucking sadness.

He'd never noticed before now.

Clearly, she hadn't wanted him to, and still didn't. She avoided his gaze as she said, "I'm just nervous about something. Work stuff. It doesn't matter. I'm taking up your break, aren't I?"

He wanted to say no, but that would be a lie, so he said nothing at all.

She gave him a wry smile. "Go on. Duke and I need to get home."

But I don't want you to go. Not until I figure out how to make you smile for real.

"If you ever want to talk about the… work stuff," he said carefully, "you should call me."

She rolled her eyes, all light-hearted amusement. "I'm sure. Let's pour some wine and have a DIY therapy session."

"Rae."

But she was already walking away, Duke trotting loyally beside her. Opportunity gone, then. For now.

"Wait," he called. "Just—will I see you tonight?"

She paused, shooting a look over her shoulder. "I don't know. Maybe."

"You should come." To the pub, he meant, for their group's unofficial Friday night drink. "When you don't, I'm surrounded by couples."

"Poor baby," she snorted, and left.

RAE HAD HEARD on the small-town grapevine that once upon a time, not so long ago, Zach Davis had been… well. Sexually prolific. She'd never seen him in action as the town sex god—apparently, he was now retired—but she'd bet he'd been fucking magnificent. He could certainly seduce her with the crook of a finger. She'd pay good money just to run her tongue over the fine map of raised veins on his thick forearms.

Then again, Rae was horribly sex-deprived, so perhaps

that didn't mean much.

By the time she and Duke got home, she was still over-heated by the memory of the man's smile. Zach Davis, barely clothed, was an atomic weapon. He looked like something out of a book: twelve years younger than her and ten times hotter, all broad shoulders and rough hands and subtle, effortless flirtation. Since he was practically a fictional character, he was safe to salivate over. The lust she felt towards him barely counted: they were friends, and he was the epitome of delicious impossibility.

He was also a complete sweetheart.

Thank God she hadn't buckled under the force of his quiet concern back there and spilled her guts. What would she have said—that her debut novel had been nominated for a prestigious award, and it was making her miserable? That she'd agreed to sign copies at an amazing fantasy convention, and the thought filled her with dread? That she was so anxious she couldn't write a word, all because she was about to spend a weekend working and sleeping in the same hotel as her ex-husband?

"No, no, no," she murmured to Duke, leading him into the kitchen. "Because that would be pathetic. And Ravenswood Rae is not pathetic."

But that was the problem: at the Burning Quill convention, with Kevin and his new wife swanning about, she wouldn't *be* Ravenswood Rae. She'd be Kevin's Rae. Abandoned Rae. Sad, pitied Rae. And the thought made her want to vomit.

It was time to think of other things.

She filled her baby's massive water bowl, set it down

before him, and asked, "You felt Zach's chest, right? Is it heavenly? Is it like a big, sexy slab of concrete?"

Duke gave her a look that said, *You're sick,* and lapped up his water.

She stepped out of the splash zone, chuckled to herself, and sat down at the kitchen table. But when her phone dinged with a new text message, her smile collapsed like a deflated soufflé. It was her mother. Oh, joy.

Marilyn: If you'd put as much effort into your marriage as you put into whining, you wouldn't have lost Kevin in the first place. Please grow up, darling. I worry for you.

In the space of ten seconds, Rae's stomach turned to lead.

She squeezed her phone tight—so tight that her fingers paled and the touchscreen display took on a strange, rainbow cast. Her pulse pounded in her ears, and her blood seemed to prickle in her veins.

She'd woken up especially anxious that morning and had messaged Marilyn about the convention during a moment of weakness. But really, what had she expected? Maternal advice, reassurance, support? "Idiot," Rae muttered through bloodless lips. "Absolute idiot."

This was all *feelings* ever got her. From the sour, murdered love between Kevin and her to the toxic, twisted thing between her and her mother, Rae should know by now that seeking comfort came with a price.

She loosened her grip on the phone and pushed her tongue against the scar on the inside of her cheek, her private talisman. After a few deep breaths, she typed out a response.

I didn't lose him, I left him.

No. It sounded defensive, and Marilyn thought Rae was weak for leaving Kevin, anyway, and... Rae sighed and tried again.

I'm not whining, I just

No.

I put plenty of effort

Delete. That would only cause an argument. In fact, any response that wasn't obsequious and self-flagellating would cause an argument, and Rae's stomach was already churning at the thought of her mother's call. She could almost hear the quiet, razor-sharp words couched as straight-talking concern, draped in affection like sheep's clothing. Ugh. She didn't have time for this.

Something heavy and warm landed in her lap. She looked down to discover that Duke had abandoned his sloppy rehydration-fest to come and see her. Rae set her phone aside and slid from the chair to the cold kitchen floor, wrapping her arms around her monster of a dog. His nose snuffled, wet and supportive, against her neck.

"I know what you're going to say," she murmured. "If we didn't talk to Mother at all, she couldn't bother us." Easier said than done, though. Easier said than done. Forty long years, and part of Rae was still waiting hopefully for her mother to change.

Sometimes, she hated that part of herself. And sometimes she needed it.

Taking a deep breath, she pulled herself together and muttered, "You know what I want? Wine."

Duke huffed disapprovingly.

"Yes, I realise it's early. Don't judge me."

Today was just one of those days.

CHAPTER TWO

EVEN RAE'S ill-advised day-drinking didn't awaken her hibernating creativity. She spent the rest of the day grappling with her own mind and staring at the words 'Chapter Four' on her computer screen, waiting for something to happen. Nothing did. By the time evening arrived, she had two options: take a break, or throw her bloody laptop out of the window.

The laptop had been rather expensive.

She arrived at the Unicorn before anyone else and snagged their usual table on the gently heated patio, Duke stretching out by her feet. A dozen judgemental eyes followed her every move, as if she'd stripped off her clothes instead of simply sitting down—but after months in Ravenswood, Rae was used to that. She made the achingly ordinary, upper-middle-class residents twitter like birds. New in town. Mysterious scars. Divorced and rolling in cash.

After a day of frustration, she felt like behaving badly.

A long, languid stretch drew back the sleeves of her jacket, and the Cartier bracelets stacked on her wrist caught the light. They were a reminder of her previous life, gifts she hadn't gotten around to removing because it would require a literal tiny screwdriver—but no-one else knew that. The scandalised looks increased. Good.

Most of the time, she hated being stared at—but here in Ravenswood, where she had some wild, Cruella de Vil reputation built off rubbish and assumptions? It was hilarious. It felt like a game. It felt like being a protagonist. Here, she enjoyed being outrageous.

But when she left this small town behind for Manchester, for the convention, for the world that Kevin ruled—it wouldn't be the same. Her newfound confidence would vanish like a gown at the stroke of midnight. She'd be sad and self-conscious and...

She couldn't bear it. She really fucking couldn't.

Thankfully, her phone buzzed just in time to cut those moody, panicked thoughts short.

Hannah: Beth just lost a tooth and swallowed it. This might take a while.

Rae chuckled softly and tapped out a quick reply. Hannah Kabbah didn't nanny her boyfriend's adorable kids anymore, but she'd taken to mothering them like a duck to water—which surprised exactly no-one. Rae assumed that the second couple in their little group, Ruth Kabbah and Evan Miller, would also be late. They usually were, and Rae didn't blame them: if she had to watch a man like Evan get ready, she'd be late all the time, as well.

So. Deliciously. Late.

"Penny for your thoughts." The voice was low and warm, like sunlight through the clouds. Zach.

She looked up to find him looming over her, fully dressed—unfortunately—and handsome as ever. He wore black jeans and a white shirt, like an echo of his jet-black hair and pale skin. His eyes were like that, too: winter-frost irises surrounded by a blue-black ring. His gaze was the kind of exhilarating cold that burned.

She pulled herself together and said primly, "My thoughts are not fit for public consumption."

His fine, expressive mouth curled. "Now you're just driving up the price." He dragged a chair closer to her, sitting with the sprawling grace reserved for tall men who knew every inch of their bodies. For a moment, she salivated over the pretty-boy definition of his jaw and the tiny mole above his eyebrow. Then she remembered that the mole was on his left side. Which meant he'd just gone out of his way to sit on her *right* side.

Her fingers itched to flutter over the scars there, but she curled her hand into a fist and lifted her chin. Rae always wore her hair pulled back for a reason: she refused to hide. And anyway, Zach never stared, or studied, or dissected her scars with a guilty, sliding gaze.

He simply looked.

"So," he said, shattering her thoughts. "Since we're alone..."

...Fancy a quickie in the bathroom?

"Any chance you want to talk about the thing that's not bothering you?" he finished.

Rae bit back a smile at her own wild thoughts and said, "No. And it's *not* bothering me." God, she was such a bloody liar. But, no matter how much she liked Zach, she couldn't pour her messy, bleeding heart out to him. It was too embarrassing. It was too vulnerable. The idea made her vaguely nauseated. With him, she was Ravenswood Rae, and that was how she wanted things to be.

He sighed dramatically, irreverent as ever, and raked a hand through his hair. At least ten pairs of covetous eyes drank down the sight, but he seemed oblivious. "Come on, sunshine. You're really going to deny this face?"

Oh, for heaven's sake. "It's for your own good."

He cocked a brow. "Because...?"

"Someone has to tell you no once in a while."

His grin was slow and sexy and clearly delighted. He leaned closer, the electric force of his presence crackling over her skin. "You don't think I hear it enough? Why's that, Rae?"

This was the part where she said something almost flirtatious and definitely outrageous, and he fell about laughing, and she felt ten feet tall. That was how they worked. Only, tonight, with the weight of everything crushing her, she suddenly didn't have the energy. She opened her mouth, but nothing witty sprang to mind, and she was tired of working for it. Of working for everything. She tapped her tongue against the inside of her cheek and shrugged.

Zach shot her a frown, confusion with an edge of concern. "You're really upset, aren't you?"

She reached down to stroke Duke, avoiding Zach's gaze. "Don't be ridiculous. About what?"

"I don't know."

She straightened. He reached out and took her hand. A

jolt of electric awareness crackled through her, inconvenient and uncontrollable, her nerve endings alive with pointless anticipation. She tried not to fall out of her chair, or faint, or float away like a balloon. Inappropriate lust: twice as buoyant as helium. That's what the newsreader would say, during the human interest segment on Rae's mind-blowing spontaneous flight.

Zach leaned in, his voice low in a way that made her stomach dip. "Seriously. Talk to me. Please?"

She blinked like a bamboozled chicken, which was appropriate, because she *felt* like a bamboozled chicken. "It's... I'm..." *I'm fine* is what she meant to say. But his *hand*. His big, broad hand with its calloused palm, holding hers so gently. And the frown on his face, so disarming with its obvious concern.

All that worry, just for her. She marvelled at the way her life had transformed. As a child, she'd hidden sadness by whatever means necessary, knowing her mother would take it as a personal insult and punish her accordingly. With Kevin, Rae's negative emotions were evidence that she considered him a terrible husband—no matter how many times she tried to explain that it was about work, or something she'd seen on the news, or just a bad fucking mood.

But here was Zach, asking about her feelings as if he wanted to help. As if they were solely hers, but he'd happily take the burden. As if he was mining for gold, because the opportunity to understand her was that precious.

Or not. She'd always had an overactive imagination. Rae opened her mouth, knowing she should brush him off, suspecting that she might spill a secret instead. He had an unnerving ability to tease out the things that made a person most vulnerable.

Thankfully, she was saved by the sound of Hannah's voice, dripping with amusement. "Zachary. Leave the nice lady alone."

Just like that, Zach was no longer serious. He shot Rae a look that lasted a second but seemed to say a thousand things. Then his hand left hers and he was himself again, so wonderfully scandalous, no-one would ever think him capable of caring.

"Hannah," he said. "Baby. Sweetheart. Love of my life. You came." He looked at the man standing behind her, a leaner, meaner version of Zach covered in tattoos, and scowled. "Oh. You brought him."

"Fuck off," Nate Davis grinned. He grabbed his brother's shirt, dragged him to his feet, and the two men hugged like they hadn't seen each other in a century. In reality, they'd probably seen each other yesterday. Still, Rae wasn't complaining. Double the Davis equalled double the hotness.

Ignoring their antics, Hannah turned to Rae. "I'm so glad you're here." She bent down to pet Duke gingerly. Probably didn't want to get fur on her fabulous wool skirt. "I didn't think you'd come."

For a while, neither had Rae. She tried not to look shifty. "Why?"

"Because, aside from the Beth situation, you've been ignoring my texts all day," Hannah said sweetly.

"Ah, yes. So I have. Well. As you know, I've been very—"

"But Nate saw you walking Duke through the old meadow this morning." Hannah's smile turned even sweeter. "So I'm certain you're not about to say that you were stuck at your desk, phone-free."

"Stop bullying Rae." Nate appeared behind his girl-friend, pressing a kiss to her cheek. "She can ignore you if she wants."

"Well!" Hannah gasped. "Of course she can. She has free will, doesn't she?" With the kind of grace Rae would never achieve, Hannah sank into the nearest chair and arranged her long skirt and countless braids effortlessly. "The thing is, there are sensible ways to exercise one's free will—such as eating cake—and then there are silly ways to exercise one's free will, such as avoiding one's best friend."

"I wasn't avoiding you," Rae corrected. "Honestly. So dramatic."

At which point, Ruth and Evan arrived, saving Rae from Hannah's narrow glare.

Ruth was a tiny, grumpy woman wearing a Hulk T-shirt and a pair of loose trousers that seemed to be pyjamas. Evan was a cheerful, blonde behemoth who looked at his girlfriend as if he might easily be persuaded to kill for her. Rae still hadn't decided if she was absolutely sick of them or horribly jealous. She was leaning toward the latter.

"Evening, you lot," Evan said, and pulled out Ruth's chair for her. She looked at him as if he'd just yanked off her glasses and thrown them onto the street. He arched a brow. She pursed her lips. He flashed the sweetest smile Rae had ever seen on a man.

Ruth sighed, sat down, and said to the table, "Yes, hello,

etcetera. Pointless greetings accomplished. Now, let's get on with it, shall we? Drinks and conversation, please."

Across the table, Nate pointed at Ruth. "This is why I like you."

"Really? I thought it was because you're in love with my terrifying sister."

Nate grinned. "I'm glad someone else admits she's terrifying."

The usual banter began, and Rae smiled a little, just to herself. Her fingers wound through Duke's fur again as she studied the misfit friends she'd found in this gossipy little town. There was Zach, of course, the town's resident charmer. Hannah, the prim and pristine childcare expert with a criminal record. Nate, the tattooed, widowed, single dad who'd once been Hannah's employer. Evan, all sweet and gorgeous and manly in a way that made sensible folk lose their minds. Tiny, prickly, introverted Ruth, whose autism made the ignorant feel uncomfortable, and whose lack of patience for bullshit made the guilty feel awkward.

And, of course, Rae couldn't forget herself. That *gauche divorcée*, as she'd heard one old man tell his wife at the supermarket just last week. She was considering putting the phrase on a T-shirt.

The beer garden was close to full despite the cool evening air, so it was impossible to miss the attention their group garnered. The flick-knife looks from two middle-aged women in the corner, with their £300 Barbour jackets and rapid whispers. The hard jaws and low mutters of three young men to the right, who nursed their beers like baby bottles and glared mutinously. But it wasn't all bad. There was also a group of giggly women in the corner who'd nodded at Ruth as she'd come in. And then there was the sweet, older couple—the man wearing a cap that read CLARKE'S PIPES and the woman in a shiny, blue wheelchair—who sent over encouraging looks like proud parents.

This town had its ups and downs. So far, the ups were worth it.

"So," Hannah said, clapping her hands. "We're all here."

"You know what that means," Zach piped up.

Rae smiled blandly at him, shaking off her introspection. "The ritual sacrifice begins?"

"The *inquisition* begins," he corrected. "You have sacrifice on the brain, woman. I'm starting to worry." Then he steepled his fingers under his chin, his usual grin replaced by a serious stare. Gravely, he began. "You know my stance, ladies and gentlemen. Before the night goes any further, we have a problem to solve. A tongue-twister in our midst. Rae and Ruth. Ruth and Rae. They're practically the same name. It's too confusing."

From her place further down the table, Ruth snorted. "They certainly are not. They have entirely different vowel sounds. The body of each word is fundamentally—"

"*Way* too confusing," Zach went on. "Something's got to give. And I have the perfect solution."

Evan—long-suffering, eminently reasonable, and somehow Zach's best friend—sighed. "Mate. You do this every time. She's not going to tell you."

"Shut up. As I was saying, something's got to give. Rae..." Zach turned to face her, flashing what he obviously considered to be his best and most charming smile.

Unfortunately, he was right.

"Tonight will go much more smoothly if you tell us your real name."

He was trying to cheer her up, and she knew it. Adored him for it. This wasn't a new topic; ever since Zach had learned that Rae's first name wasn't actually Rae, he'd been on a mission to find out 'the truth'—which he usually said with as much dramatic emphasis as the voiceover on the trailer of a Hollywood blockbuster. Since Rae's real name was truly terrible, he'd be waiting a long bloody time. But she rather enjoyed it when he asked. His frustration was delicious.

His attention was even better. Sweet and rich.

She maintained a purposefully bland expression, just to irritate him, and said, "My real name is McRae."

He arched a brow. "Stop being smart. What's your *first* name?"

"If the issue is confusion—if Rae is too similar to Ruth —why don't you just call me McRae?"

Zach narrowed his eyes and actually *growled* a little bit. Her vagina became a fountain. Of champagne. "Come on, sunshine. Take pity on me. What's your name?"

"Susan," she said. "What's everyone drinking? I'll get the first round."

Zach gave her an exasperated look. "You don't need to do that. Why do you always do that?"

She ignored him.

"I'll have a G&T," Hannah said, rising to her feet. "But I'll come with you. You can't carry everything on your own."

24

"Your name is not Susan," Zach declared, as if no-one else had spoken. "It's not."

"You're right. It's Sarah. Ruth, what'll you have?"

"Lemonade," Ruth said. "Zach, I know Rae's name. It's Natalie."

"Nah." Evan smiled, crossing his muscled arms behind his head. "It's Kate. You ladies want a hand?"

"We should be good," Rae said.

"Then I'll get a beer. Thanks, Kate."

"Her name isn't Kate," Zach snapped.

Nate smirked, flicking his brother's ear. "You sure about that?"

Zach threw up his hands, a reluctant grin spreading over his face. "Fine! Act like you don't want to know. Fuckin' traitors."

Rae shook her head and led Hannah inside toward the bar. But something made her turn back at the last second, and she caught a glimpse of Zach through the swinging patio doors. He was talking to Duke. Really, properly talking to her dog, the way only Rae did. And she could guess what he was saying.

I bet you know her name, don't you, boy?

"Hey. I'm sure that dog's a great conversationalist, but I'm gonna have to drag you away."

Zach bit back a smile, gave Duke one last scratch between the ears, and turned to face his older brother. "Yeah?"

There was something careful and considering in

25

Nate's eyes. He drummed his fingers against the table, and the swallow tattooed on the back of his hand seemed to fly with the movement. Finally, he asked, "How are you?"

It was a question they'd repeated regularly, purposefully, ever since Nate's return to Ravenswood. Getting to grips with Ma's illness had been a shitstorm. Of course, having Nate back home for the first time in years was one hell of a silver lining.

"I'm good," Zach said, and it was the truth. He felt more like himself than he had in... forever. Ma was doing better on her new medication, Nate was on cloud nine with Hannah, and Evan was across the table right now murmuring to Ruth like a lovesick sap. Everyone was happy, except, possibly, for Rae—but he was determined to fix that.

There was just one niggling worry at the back of Zach's mind: his own quiet, growing anger. It was heavy and secret and pointless, and no-one wanted to deal with it, least of all him—he didn't even know where it came from, because he refused to explore it. Zach Davis wasn't an angry person. He was cool. He was chill. He was easy. He made other people feel good. So this burning, teeth-gritting frustration would fade if he ignored it long enough. It had to.

But Nate didn't look convinced. With a weirdly shifty look around the patio, he leaned in close and lowered his voice. "Hannah says everyone's talking about you."

Zach arched his brows. "Well, if Hannah says so..." He wasn't being sarcastic. Hannah knew everything. She was the town crystal ball—or a very nosy woman with Machiavellian tendencies. One of those.

Nate nodded. "You remember the night we got Ma's new diagnosis?"

As if Zach could ever forget. If discovering his mother had a dangerous chronic illness wasn't memorable enough, there was also the part where he and Nate had gotten wasted and finally talked about all the heavy shit they liked to avoid. Like the past. And death. And depression. And...

"You said you weren't interested in sex anymore," Nate went on. "But you're better now, right? Except, according to Hannah the All-Knowing, you still... aren't. What's up with that?"

Jesus Christ, this fucking town. "You know," Zach said mildly, "I'm not in love with how much you two know about my sex life."

"Yeah, yeah. I'm serious here. Are you okay or not?"

Zach took in the harsh line of his brother's brow, the worry in his pale eyes, and felt a flash of guilt. A few months back, on that messy, drunken night of confessions, Zach had wanted to tell his brother what he was learning about himself. He'd wanted to say, *I'm not what everyone thinks I am. I don't experience attraction the way you do. I've been pretending this whole time.*

But he'd still been unsure, back then, still been confused, so he'd lied. Just a little. Just to test the waters. He'd acted like his sexuality was a strange new phenomenon instead of something he'd been avoiding his whole life, and Nate's supportive response had been reassuring.

Now it was months later, and Zach was confident in

his identity—but for some reason, he still hadn't come out to his brother.

For a moment, he felt a flare of temper at the fact that he even had to. After all, Nate had never come out to *him*. Nate had never sat him down and said, "Hey, sometimes when I see a nice arse or a pretty smile, I get this lurch of sexual attraction, so I wanted to let you know that I'm straight and allosexual." So why the fuck did Zach have to sit *Nate* down and say, "Hey, attraction doesn't work like that for me because I'm demisexual"? Why?

The anger was irrational, so Zach crushed it and focused on what mattered. His brother thought he was hiding something, and technically, he was: Zach Davis, Ravenswood's notorious man-slut, was actually a bullied, ostracised little nerd who'd grown up so self-conscious about his demisexuality that he'd slept around for years to overcompensate.

Just the memory of it made him sweat. Thank God he was himself now.

He should probably let his brother in on that fact. Evan, too. But the beer garden of the Unicorn didn't seem like the best place to discuss it, so Zach settled for clapping his brother on the shoulder and looking him in the eye. "Listen. I swear to you, I'm okay. We can talk about this later. We *will* talk about this later. But you don't need to worry about me."

Nate stared at him in silence for a moment, clearly searching his face for something. He must've found it, because he nodded and relaxed. "Good."

There. Everyone was happy. All was right with Zach's world.

Until Nate knocked him on his arse all over again. "So when are you and Rae going to get it over with?"

Zach frowned. "Uh...?" Then his brother's meaning sank in. "Wait—as in—wait—you don't think—?"

Judging by his steady, slightly amused stare, Nate did indeed think. Shit.

Zach swallowed hard and shook his head. "No. Me and her, that's not happening."

"Okay," Nate snorted. "Why the hell not?"

Zach rolled his eyes. "You know what your problem is? You want everyone coupled up."

"No. But I think you're into her, and I see why. Rae's smart like you. She writes those books—they're exactly the kind of shit you like. She's funny. She has a great dog."

At their feet, Duke opened one beady eye as if to say, *You're damn right she does.*

"And she's..." Nate waved a hand over his face. "Striking."

For some reason, that word irritated Zach. He pried his back teeth apart and said, "You could just call her pretty, you know." Maybe he sounded pissed off, but he was sick of the way people looked at Rae. Like she was a few scars surrounded by a person, instead of a person with a few scars.

Nate gave him an odd look. "She is pretty. But striking is better."

Zach pushed out a breath, nodding sharply. Of course Nate wouldn't use a word like *pretty*. He was a photographer obsessed with people who were visually interesting. "Right. Yeah. Whatever. She's great, but it's not like that."

Nate arched a brow. For some reason, that slight

29

movement made Zach want to smack his brother's face off.

Instead, he took a breath and told the only truth he knew. "I'm not into Rae."

"Not to be that guy," Nate said, "but... I think you are."

"Yeah. Just like, once upon a time, you thought I was into Hannah."

A rueful smile. "Okay. Fair point."

Zach's spike of alarm faded. There was no need to panic over his brother's mistake. He'd know if he was sending Rae mixed signals, right? He'd made it clear that they were just friends, right?

Of course he had. With Rae, he didn't need to worry about crossed wires, come-ons and awkward rejections—so he didn't need to worry about hurting her.

Which was good. Because he was suddenly really fucking disturbed by the idea of causing her pain.

Nate finally let it go, and they dragged Evan and Ruth away from each other and into the conversation. A few minutes later, Hannah and Rae reappeared with drinks. The sun set, and the laughter rose. The night grew colder, but none of them felt it. Hours ticked by and Zach grinned until his cheeks hurt. It was good.

Someone else got the second round, and the third. On the fourth, he found himself heading to the bar with Rae beside him. As they waited for the freckly sixth-form kid to pull their pints and pour their spirits, he leaned against the polished wood and studied Rae's face. Bright eyes, snub nose, lips half-curved like she was remembering a joke. She was tipsy, which was typical for a Friday night. Her alcohol tolerance was adorable.

She caught him looking and her smile faded. "What?"

"Your hair's curling."

She sighed, blowing out her lips like a little kid. "I hate spring."

"What does it look like? When you don't straighten it."

"I don't straighten it," she told him. "This is a blow-out. I—" She paused as her phone buzzed loudly to life. When she dragged it out of her back pocket and checked the caller ID, all the colour and comfort drained right out of her. She lost her happy, relaxed air in an instant.

Something viciously protective unfurled in his chest. "What is it?"

"Nothing." She lowered her hand, but she was still clutching the phone like it was a grenade she wanted to throw. And she didn't decline the call.

"*Who* is it?"

"My mother," she said.

That left him speechless for a second. When he regained the use of his voice, he wasted it with a pointless question. "Your mother makes you miserable like that?"

She scowled. The phone finally stopped ringing. "We've fallen out. It's nothing." But then the phone buzzed again, and her *face…*

"Rae," he murmured, with no idea what to say next. He just needed to catch her attention, to get between her and the phone that had frozen his sunshine. But she didn't seem to hear him, so he said again, louder now, "*Rae.*" His hand caught her wrist.

She looked up at him, her gaze shuttered. "I have to go."

He stared. "What?"

But she was already pulling away, breaking his grip, hurrying through the crowd toward the front doors.

"Hey," the bartender said from behind him. "That'll be—"

"Hold those for me, would you?" He followed Rae without waiting for an answer.

She was outside, a few paces away from the smokers, her gaze distant and her hands pressed against the brick. Like she needed to feel something against her skin just to remind herself she was still there.

He felt like that sometimes.

He approached her slowly, the way he would a wounded animal. She stiffened when she saw him, but she didn't turn away. Instead, she took a breath, wrapped her arms around herself, and said, "Sorry. I just needed some air."

"You don't have to apologise," he murmured, coming to stand beside her. They leaned against the wall together, both staring up at the sky, and he waited to see if she'd explain.

She didn't. "You're alright, Davis."

The comment surprised a laugh out of him. "Just alright? Damn."

Her lips twitched into a smile. Her eyes seemed bigger and darker than usual, slamming into him like a touch— like an exploration. "You don't hurt people. You help people. I've noticed that."

He didn't know if he was meant to answer. Her gaze still burned sensation over his skin, but her words floated, directionless, between the two of them, as if she was thinking aloud.

A second later, she went on, her sentences meandering tipsily. "You're a good friend. A real good friend. I can trust you with some things, can't I?"

Trust me with whatever's tearing you up inside. "Yes. You can." She nodded and remained silent. Apparently, that conversation was over. But he didn't want it to be, so he thought fast. "One more round, and everyone will be leaving. Nate's babysitter gets off soon."

She sighed. "These nights always end too early."

"Ours doesn't have to," he said. "How about we don't go home?"

She turned to stare at him, her tongue peeking out to wet her lips. "What?"

"When everyone leaves, how about we don't go home? You, me, and Duke. We can roam the streets terrorising pensioners, or something. It'll be fun." *And I'll drag your secrets out of you if it's the last thing I do.*

"Oh. Right. Yeah." She hesitated for a moment before that sweet, one-sided smile curved her lips. "Two trouble-makers and a dog running around in the dark? Isn't that how horror films start?"

"Nah. It's how adventures start."

"I see." Her right cheek plumped, as if she were pushing her tongue against the inside. "In that case, let's do it."

CHAPTER THREE

RAE WASN'T DRUNK, exactly. She was drunk, *perfectly*. That final round had tipped her from level two of intoxication —Excessive Sensitivity—to level three: Excessive Joy. Her mind was a shimmery blur that made everything warm and brilliant, even though it was actually night-time and the world was black-and-streetlight-orange.

At Ravenswood's play park, the shapes of swings and climbing frames cast odd shadows across the spongey, child-safe floor. But as Rae approached, Duke trotting happily on her left, Zach strolling along on her right, she didn't care that the park looked like the scene of a possible haunting. They were having an *adventure*.

That delightful fact expanded in her chest like a balloon, obliterating the last of her sadness. She said aloud, "I never would've done this before."

Though it was mostly dark, she felt Zach's gaze on her. He didn't ask what she meant by *before*. Instead, he said, "What? Gone to the park at midnight like a reprobate?"

"I didn't use to do anything like a reprobate."

"That sounds boring."

Oh, it had been. "I didn't have a dog, either."

There was a pause. Then he said, "What, ever?"

"No." She stopped walking for a moment to run her fingers through Duke's lovely fur. He was her lovely boy. She lovely, lovely, loved him.

"You never had a dog? In your life?"

"No." She started walking again.

"But you love dogs." They passed under a streetlight, and Zach's frown was illuminated for a few seconds—just long enough to remind her that he was gorgeous when he was indignant.

"My mother is allergic," Rae explained. "Well, she's not, but when she doesn't like something, she says she's allergic."

"Interesting tactic," he said dryly.

"And then, when I left home, I moved straight in with Kevin."

"Kevin?"

"My husband." They'd reached the park. She tried to pull the gate and misjudged its weight, stumbling a little as it swung half-open.

Zach caught her, steadied her, his massive chest against her back and his hands practically burning through her clothes. The contact tugged at something deep inside her, something hot and expectant and eager, as if he'd grabbed her arse instead of her upper arms. Rae liked men and Rae liked sex, but the way Zach turned her inside out without even trying...

She was starting to think she should do something

about it.

"Your ex-husband," he said, and grabbed the gate, holding it open for her.

She blinked as she and Duke walked through, reckless thoughts scattering on the breeze. "What?"

"He's your ex-husband. Kevin. Not your husband."

"Oh, right. Yes. Well." She cleared her throat. What were they talking about, again? "He doesn't like dogs. He's very focused. He has, this, you know." She stabbed her hand through the air, straight ahead, eyes narrowed, because that was what she thought of when she thought of Kevin. Like the thrust of a blade. "He's *focused*. And dogs are a responsibility that detracts from focus. I said I'd look after them, but he said when there's a dependent in the household, it affects everyone. So I never had a dog."

"How long were you together?"

"Twenty-two years. Then he, uh, knocked up his assistant."

Zach choked, wheezed, spluttered. "*What?*"

Oops. She hadn't meant to say that, but she was Ravenswood Rae, so maybe it wasn't a big deal. Zach certainly wasn't staring at her with horrified pity or anything like that. No; he looked outraged, actually, so outraged that she found herself grinning in response.

And so outraged that it felt easy to talk about. "Ridiculous, isn't it? I mean, first—what a fucking cliché. Second —*pregnant*! He got her pregnant! And I wasn't even allowed a dog! Hypocrisy, thy name is Kevin." She wandered over to the park's little roundabout and sank onto the wooden platform. "It's okay, though. Now I have Duke. Do you want to know something sad?" Because she was beginning to think Zach could handle a little sadness, that it wouldn't make him stiff and sympathetic.

He looked slightly dizzy, his eyebrows practically lost in his hairline, but he nodded slowly. "Hit me."

"I like Duke so much more than I ever liked Kevin. I mean, I hate Kevin, because he's a slimy, traitorous liar. But even before that—before I found out about the affair, I mean—I didn't feel good around him the way I feel good around Duke." *Or the way I feel around you.*

"Yeah," Zach said softly. "That is sad." But he didn't sound sad; he sounded absolutely furious, and looked it, too. His mouth was a hard line and a muscle ticked at his jaw as he stared daggers at the ground. She imagined burning, ice-blue knives sinking into the floor. That wouldn't do. The kids would arrive tomorrow to find their park a jagged mess of wounds that never bled, and she knew just how much trouble *those* were.

So she patted the roundabout she'd sat down on and said, "Duke. Play."

Duke's tongue rolled out of his mouth like a red carpet and he gave a little hop of excitement. He threw himself onto the platform with so much enthusiasm, she felt the structure shake beneath them.

Zach was clearly alarmed by the sight of a 200lb dog lounging on a children's roundabout with all four legs in the air as if waiting for a belly rub from the heavens. "Uh... What's he doing on there?"

"Just watch." She'd ruined the adventure, babbling about Kevin, so now she'd make everything fun again. Holding on to the red-painted bars with one hand, and Duke with the other, Rae used her legs to push off. The roundabout started to spin, slow and heavy at first, then easier as they gained a little momentum. She didn't go too fast, though. Duke didn't like it too fast. When she got the speed just right, his tongue lolled some more, and he tipped his head back in an expression of doggy joy. She watched him and laughed, the sound snatched away by the wind as they spun.

That same wind brought Zach's astonished chuckle to her ears. He was slightly blurry around the edges now, and he looked like night turned into a man: pale as moonlight with that silky, pitch-black hair and those hypnotic eyes. His smile was a gorgeous kind of danger. No wonder so many people got lost in him.

He was a bad boy fantasy with a dirty mouth and a bleeding heart: sweet, sexy, achingly gentle. He'd be gentle in bed, too, wouldn't he? Not with her body, which craved something else, but with the tender, vulnerable part of her that had only ever been with Kevin. Zach was the rare sort of man who would care enough to make the first time easy. She should explore that fact, sometime.

The idea made something inside her leap like a flame.

"Duke likes this?" he asked, his smile disbelieving and delighted.

"He does," she confirmed, already slowing the roundabout. The alcohol in her stomach sloshed ominously. The roundabout came to a stop, but Duke whined for more. He sounded like Chewbacca. She scratched between his ears and tried not to be sick. Maybe spinning around like a five-year-old hadn't been her smartest idea of the night, or the week, or even the year. She needed to get off this wobbly platform.

She stood up and her world turned black.

"Woah, woah." Zach grabbed her, his arm an iron bar around her waist. She heard Duke's worried bark, felt the warmth and weight of him pressing against her legs. He was trying to prop her up because he was a good boy.

"I'm fine," she said unconvincingly, except this time it was true. Her vision prickled back to life and the dizziness faded. She tried to push Zach away, but she might as well have pushed a brick wall. He was immoveable.

"Are you that drunk?" he asked, worry threaded through the words. "You only had—"

"I started early today."

"What? Why?"

"But I'm not that drunk. I have POTS."

Apparently convinced she was steady, he stepped back. She tried not to miss the feel of him, that reassuring solidness. "What the fuck is POTS?" he demanded.

"It's a circulation thing. Mine is fairly mild. Sometimes, when I stand up, my heart beats too fast and I get dizzy." She usually rose slowly, so she wouldn't drop like a sack of potatoes. Except she was preoccupied and, let's face it, wasted, so she hadn't.

Zach shook his head, a smile playing at the corners of his mouth. "Okay. Got it. But you know what? You and me, we're going to sit right here. Just for a little while." Clearly, POTS or not, he knew she was drunk as hell. His arm came around her waist again, pulling gently, and a moment later she was sprawled in a heap on the playground, Duke licking her shoulder happily. Zach sat beside her with his face tipped up to the stars and his thigh pressed against hers.

Well, *pressed* was an overstatement. There was some slight contact, perhaps. But she felt it so intensely, he might as well have slapped her in the face with his dick.

"You seem sad lately," he said, which certainly distracted her from inappropriate horniness.

She sighed dramatically. "Maybe I'm always sad. Maybe I'm a nihilist. We're all going to die, the earth is just a doomed chunk of rock, and my mother never loved me." There. The best lies were always technically true.

Zach turned away from the stars to face her. If this conversation were a duel, the care in his eyes would be a canon. "Hey. We're friends, aren't we?"

She feigned reluctance. "I suppose."

He snorted and bumped their shoulders together. "Talk to me, sunshine. Might help."

It absolutely would not help. There were so many things she hadn't told him, or anyone—things that didn't fit the character she played in this town. The breezy, bitchy divorcée gleefully spending her husband's money while simultaneously giving not one flying fuck about the man. She liked playing that person. The longer she inhabited the role, the more real it felt. In fact, she'd started to believe it *was* real.

And then the call had come—the award and the invitation—and she'd been forced to face facts. She might not love Kevin anymore, but he still had the power to affect her life and fuck up her choices, just like he always had.

Her voice was choked when she finally confessed, "I'm angry."

Zach's reply was careful. "About?"

She opened her mouth, closed it, and shook her head.

"I don't think I want to have this conversation." And she couldn't. She *really* couldn't, because she'd promised, she'd sworn, and it was pointless anyway.

He must've heard something desperate in her voice, because he stopped pushing. "Alright. Fair enough. What do you want to do?"

Now that was a damned good question.

Rae had decided a while ago to always choose herself: to write whatever her heart desired; to move somewhere slow and pretty and get a big old dog; to make friends who were kind to each other, whose interests weren't carefully curated to make them look smarter or more cultured than they actually were. Hadn't she done those things? And hadn't it gone pretty fucking well? Yes and yes. She was Ravenswood Rae and she chased whatever made her feel good—so what was one more reckless risk?

The alcohol in her blood whispered, *Nothing.* Its persuasive hum was low and languid, like rolling hips or limbs tangled together beneath warm sheets. She raised a hand toward Zach, tentative but determined, and traced a finger over his jaw. It was harshly defined, a sharp contrast to his smiling mouth which always curved like a fine, sickle moon. Only, he wasn't smiling now. He'd gone utterly still, as if she'd frozen him in time. That wouldn't do. She wanted his sarcasm and his laughter and his flirting, so she swung a leg over his thighs and straddled his lap. The action seemed to bring him back to life.

"Rae..." His hands settled at her hips, disappeared. Closed around her wrists, disappeared. Finally, he curled them into fists, as if he couldn't figure out where to touch her. "What—uh, what are you doing?"

She shrugged. "Seducing you, maybe?"

He choked a little bit. Was that a good sign? She didn't know, since she'd never seduced anyone before. She needed the practice and Zach was a close friend with boundless bedroom experience and a smile she could almost trust. He laughed like the first day of spring after a long, cold winter. He made her feel soft and pure and *right* inside. He'd be... he'd be her training wheels.

She tried to share that well-reasoned speech with him, but all that came out was, "Pretty sure you're great in the sack."

This was the part where he laughed, or teased, or offered to make her *absolutely* sure.

He didn't.

How the hell had this happened?

Zach was caught between outright panic and sheer disbelief. He'd brought Rae to the park to interrogate her about emotional shit, yet somehow, she'd ended up in his lap. Did he produce *I'm up for it* pheromones or something?

She fidgeted impatiently, staring down at him while he quietly lost his mind. What was the polite thing to do in a situation like this? In the past, he'd solved these sorts of problems with his dick, but these days he was giving the poor guy a break. Which meant he'd actually have to be diplomatic or something. Shit.

Rae smoothed curious hands over his chest as the silence stretched between them. Her eyes widened as if a thought had just occurred to her. "Is it weird being so built? Are muscles *heavy?*"

Ah—he'd forgotten she was absolutely smashed. His panic faded a little. He laughed, grabbing her by the waist and lifting her off him. "You're so fucking wasted." That was the problem, right? She didn't actually want to sleep with *him*. She was just drunk and horny, so her boundaries had dissolved.

Or maybe not, because she didn't take the hint. She reached for him again, beautiful and breathless in the dimly-lit shadows. "Come home with me."

He didn't want to say yes, but he would hate to tell her no—to see her wince or shrink away from him, to watch as injured pride and hurt rose like a wall between them. Maybe he should just go along with it. One last time. He'd done it before, after all, and for people he liked a hell of a lot less. For a moment, he teetered on the precipice. Even raised a hand to touch her. But then, through the haze of old habits, purifying anger shone bright.

Zach stiffened. Scowled. Asked himself one question.

Why the fuck should he?

Rae was a grown woman; she wasn't going to die if he turned her down. And Zach deserved better than forcing himself into sex just to save a friend's ego. Jesus, what was he, a participation trophy? He didn't want to do this, so he wouldn't. The world would have to keep on turning without his fucking dick.

He scrambled to his feet, shaking his head. "No." He should say more to soften the rejection, but anger still pulsed at the back of his mind. It wasn't directed at Rae, or even at himself—it was directed at a world that had made him think saying *Yes* was a gentlemanly obligation. That performing hetero-masculine, always-available bullshit mattered more than he did. Because who ever heard of a man saying no?

Fuck that.

Rae stood too—slowly, and without any ominous wobbles. "Because I'm drunk?"

Please don't make me explain this. His jaw tight, Zach strode to the park gate, opening it for her and Duke.

She walked through with a sunny smile. "Thanks. Anyway, I'm really not *that* drunk—but we could wait until tomorrow if you're worried."

He followed her out of the gate and onto the field, hands shoved in his pockets, the glittering night suddenly dark and oppressive. He didn't know what to say. He didn't know how to stop this train.

"I'm always free on Sundays," she said, like they were discussing brunch. "I know you're often busy, but I'm not asking for a marathon. I'd just need you to pop my cherry." She snorted at her own words.

He paused, staring at her. "I don't think that means what you think it means."

"Oh, my God, Zach, I know what it means." She laughed and kept walking, or rather, weaving. "I don't think I'm explaining this very well. I meant my post-divorce... oh, never mind. I just need to get it over with, you know?"

No, he didn't know. She wanted to have sex with him, but only to get it over with? What a bloody charmer. Zach took a breath and bit out, "I'm not fucking you, and it's not because you're drunk."

She raised her eyebrows, all interested surprise, like she couldn't quite grasp that the town bike would ever turn a woman down. Unsurprisingly, that pissed him off even more. He was over here twisting himself in knots about her feelings while she acted like he was a foregone conclusion—and not even a pleasurable one. His temper surged.

He stopped walking again and looked her in the eye, just to make sure she really got the message. "I'm saying no—now and tomorrow and next fucking week—because I don't want to. Is that so hard to understand? Or do you think I sleep with anything breathing?"

"Oh." She stepped back. It was the tiniest movement—barely even a real step—but it hit him hard. Then she lifted her chin and said tightly, "No. I don't think that at all. For one thing, I consider myself better than just *breathing*."

Oh, fuck. He inhaled sharply. "Rae, that's not what I meant. I swear it isn't."

Her gaze skittered away from his. She looked like she was about to dig a hole in the grass with her bare hands and curl up inside it. Like his words had slapped her and the dizzy, drunken light in her chest had been snuffed out.

"I just—" He grappled helplessly for words. "I just meant... no."

"It's fine," she said softly. "It's my fault. I mean, I think I just harassed you." Her hollow laugh was a good effort, but not quite good enough. "Gosh, I really am drunk. I'm sorry. I'm so sorry."

His heart sagged. He reached for her, but she jerked away.

"You don't need to make me feel better." This time, her smile was slightly more believable. "I messed up, and I know it. I'm a big girl." An awkward silence hovered before she added, "I'm going to head home, okay?"

"I'll walk you."

"I have Duke, so—"

"I'll walk you," he repeated.

She set her jaw and nodded.

Their journey to the park had been tipsy and sparkling with laughter. The journey to Rae's house was dark, tense, swollen with things left unsaid. Zach couldn't keep his eyes off her, couldn't make his mouth open, couldn't figure out a way to say, "You're beautiful, you know," without making it a consolation. He replayed his own words and cursed the angry panic that had made him harsh. He was never harsh. He *hated* harsh.

He wondered if, after tonight, Rae would become another friend he used to have.

When they reached her house, he blurted out, "I'm sorry," a last-ditch effort to save the relationship he was certain had just crumbled.

She frowned at him, clearly confused, and asked, "For what?"

That was… unexpected. He didn't quite know how to answer. *For not being easier. Not being nicer. Not bending over backwards for you and hurting myself to do it.*

But he didn't want to apologise for any of those things. And she didn't let him. After a pause, she said softly, "Goodnight, Zach."

And then she went.

CHAPTER FOUR

By THE TIME Monday morning rolled around, Zach still wasn't sure how to fix the mess of Friday night. He couldn't forget the stricken look on Rae's face as she'd clipped out, *I consider myself better than just breathing.* Maybe he should've told her the truth: that he was off sex until he could be sure he was doing it for the right reasons. Or a deeper truth: that she was lovely, she just didn't do it for him, but then, not many people did.

He could've told her about his first love, the one he'd known for a year before desire even occurred to him. Or the ex who'd barely been on his radar until one drunken night when they'd shared their deepest, darkest fears. He could've explained that there was a key in him, one that only turned when he *knew* someone down to the bone, down to their secret self.

But he'd been way too surprised to corral his thoughts, and then, all at once, he'd been angry. Now here he was, pounding away at the forge, wondering what it would take to keep all this temper locked up where it belonged. To stop it bleeding out into his relationships and ruining everything. So far, he hadn't come up with a decent answer.

From behind him, a voice shouted, "Hey. You want to ease up on that iron before it's drowning in cut marks?"

Zach blinked, his tangled thoughts fading into the background, reality coming into sharp focus. Fuck. His muscles were screaming, his chest was heaving, and he'd pretty much beaten his work into oblivion. He pulled out his ear protectors and turned to find Evan in the doorway, eying him with obvious concern. And once Evan was concerned about you, you were doomed. He'd turn up at your house with homemade apple pie until you cracked and spilled your inner turmoil everywhere.

See, Evan was a genuinely nice guy. As rare as a fucking unicorn. And for some reason, he thought Zach was a nice guy, too. In truth, Zach was a messy fucker who resented his own compulsion to fill in other people's gaps but couldn't make himself stop. He was also in a foul mood, so instead of thanking his friend for the save, he just grunted.

Evan arched a brow. "That Monday morning feeling, huh?"

"Yeah," Zach lied. "Fuck Mondays."

Evan's lips twitched into something like a smile. It was the only hint that he saw right through Zach's bullshit. He'd never be rude enough to say so. "Don't you usually take a break about now?"

Zach wanted to say he'd lost track of time, except he never lost track of time. He set alarms and reminders and made schedules. If he was late it was because he'd decided to be. He'd already texted his mother today, adding a smiley face to the message because she'd spent the weekend prodding him about his mood. Obviously, an emoji would throw her off the scent. Once that was done, he'd turned off his usual alarm, because he hadn't wanted to wander outside and wait for a woman who wouldn't come.

When he didn't answer, Evan nudged, "You going or what?"

Zach sighed. Hesitated. Made a decision he'd probably regret. "Yeah, I'll head outside. Need to cool off." *Need to see just how bad Rae and I fucked up a good thing.* Maybe freezing his balls off waiting for her would kick-start his brain and he'd finally figure out how to set things back to normal. Right now, he had a little speech drafted in the notes app on his phone. It started like this:

You're funny and beautiful and someone should be fucking the life out of you. But I'm not that guy.

Yeah. He wasn't doing too well.

"Maybe I'll come with you," Evan said. "See why you love loitering outside so much when we have a perfectly good, very warm break room. With tea."

Zach straightened, stamping down the alarm he couldn't show. "Uh, yeah. Okay." *No. Not okay. Stay in the fucking break room and drink your fucking tea. Read my mind. I'm begging you.*

There was a heavy pause before Evan laughed, shaking his head. "You should see your face, man. Relax. I know you go out there to meet Rae."

Zach tried not to look too relieved. "She's telling me a

story. We'd have to start from the beginning to catch you up." It wasn't technically a lie. When Rae had stories to tell, she shared them.

"Oh, that's what it is?" Evan grinned. "A story?"

"Yep."

"Right," he said mildly.

"It is."

"I hear you. Just a story. Nothing to do with the way she makes you smile."

"Oh, for—" Zach snorted, shoving Evan's shoulder. "Have you ever heard of friendship?"

"I have. Me and Ruth, for example, were very good friends for quite a while."

Zach sighed heavily, pinched the bridge of his nose, and tried to control the amusement in his voice. "Piss off out of my way, would you?"

"Pissing off." Evan strolled down the corridor with an irritating smirk on his face.

Allosexuals, Zach was starting to realise, were fucking obsessed with attraction.

HE WAITED TEN MINUTES, then decided that she wasn't coming. A minute later, she arrived.

No absent-minded wandering today; this morning, Rae walked with purpose, Duke marching ahead of her like a bodyguard. She looked different, too: her dreamy, faraway eyes and lopsided smile were replaced by a grim mouth and a nervous gaze. The dark scars on the right side of her face were bolder than usual, or maybe her skin seemed paler. His heart twisted; his mind eased. Maybe she missed him too. That must be it, right? She'd come to find him, to fix things.

She wasn't going to disappear because he couldn't give her what she wanted. And he was so relieved, he could die.

She came to face him over the wall, silent and wary. Duke, as always, rose up to give Zach some love. He responded with the required amount of fuss, but he couldn't seem to drag his eyes away from Rae. She hesitated, then shoved a plastic tub against his chest.

He held it up, looked inside, and found... "Brownies?"

"To apologise." Her voice was quieter than usual. "Friday was a bit of a nightmare, wasn't it? And I wasn't sure what to say, except I'm sorry and here's some sugar."

"Good tactic. I'd have done that, too, only I can't bake for shit." He put the tub on the wall and tried not to smile too much. It didn't feel right when she still looked all tormented. But he was really fucking happy, glowing with it, humming with it like he'd never been. The feeling was weirdly intense. "I'm sorry, too. I was a dick. I'll buy you some donuts."

Her lips curved, and she pressed her eyes shut for a moment. Maybe she was like him, and she hadn't realised just how much this friendship meant until they hit an iceberg. She opened her eyes and said, "You really don't need to, but if you're offering...strawberry jam?"

"Hell yeah."

Warmth lit her gaze. Those eyes of hers could go from midnight to sunlight in a blink. "I think we've got a deal, Davis."

"Good." He leaned in closer, lowering his voice, though no-one was around. "I don't like it when we're not okay."

Her expression softened. She leaned in too, and whispered, "Neither do I. Zach, about the things I said—"

"We don't have to talk about this."

"But I want to explain. I really do."

She looked so guilty. He knew the feeling. If she was in the grip of that uncomfortable burn, he'd help her wiggle out of it, no problem. He'd listen to whatever she needed to say. "Alright."

She nodded and set her shoulders, as determined as a soldier on the frontlines. As if saying this might just kill her, but she had to anyway. "I was drunk, obviously, and I got it into my head that… well. I haven't had sex since my divorce, and I thought the first time should be someone I knew, someone safe. Because it was only ever Kevin. That's all."

It took him a moment to figure out what she was saying. "You've never—?"

"I was a teenager when we met." The words stumbled over each other, rushed and embarrassed. "Sometimes it seems like a big deal."

He nodded slowly to cover the clamour of his thoughts. So, not only had Rae's arsehole husband thrown away decades of marriage, he'd cheated on a woman who'd only ever been with him. Classy. So, so classy. But there was a silver lining to this confession, too, Zach supposed. Rae had wanted to use him, yes—but it sounded like the whole thing had come about because she trusted him. And for some reason, that was enough to soothe the jagged, painful edges left over from Friday night.

"The truth is," she went on, calmer now, "you were right. I've been in a terrible mood lately, and it's because I know I'll see Kevin soon. There's this whole thing that I should be happy about, but he's ruining it without even trying. Actually, I'm *letting* him ruin it." She gave a wry laugh. "Sorry. I shouldn't dump all of this on you."

"It's fine. It's good. I wanted you to talk." He lifted a hand to touch her, as natural as breathing, but something brought him up short. Maybe it was the memory of her fingers grazing his jaw—the look in her eyes, the hitch in her breath, and the *Oh, fuck* moment when he'd realised what was happening. Suddenly awkward, he ran his hand through his hair instead.

Rae's lips twisted into a rueful smile. She knew what had just run through his mind. Turned out, things weren't quite fixed between them yet.

I should tell her.

Tell her about his sexuality, when he hadn't even told his own brother? He couldn't want to do that, not really. It made no sense.

"Listen," he said, looking over his shoulder. "This sounds like a shit storm of epic proportions, and I need to get back to work, so we should catch up later. You want to come over tonight and talk?"

She arched a brow. "To yours? I don't even know where you live."

"Sure you do," he said cheerfully. "I'm in the old white house by the main road."

Rae let out a burst of laughter, then sobered when he didn't join in. "Wait, seriously? You live in the haunted serial killer house?"

"It was only one murder. And yeah, I do. Rent's great."

She stared. "Jesus take the wheel. I am not stepping foot in that creepy, creepy place. You can come to me."

"Chicken."

"I'm black. Black people die first in horror films, which is why we don't put ourselves in the paths of demons."

He snorted. "Whatever. I'll come over around seven?" *And I might share something I've never said before. Maybe that's what you do for me. You make everything easier, the way I do for everyone else.*

She was already leaving, Duke bringing up the rear. "Yes. Bring donuts," she called over her shoulder. Her smile burned away his doubts.

RAE HAD SPENT all weekend marinating in rejection. She'd really rolled around in there, letting the memories soak into her bones like an extra layer of protection. If someone bit her, she'd taste like *Who the hell do you think you are?* She'd taste like *Get over it, you're embarrassing yourself.* She'd taste like the look on Zach's face when he'd rejected her as clearly as humanly possible because she couldn't take the fucking hint.

Jesus, what had she thought? That he'd automatically be gagging to sleep with her, like it was a benefits package that came with his friendship, and she just had to make a request? Alcohol and horniness had rotted her brain, clearly. In fact, there'd been a moment after she arrived home that Rae had honestly thought she might... cry.

Clearly, she'd drunk even more than she'd realised.

But she was stone-cold sober now and supremely over it, since the offer had meant nothing in the first place. And, just to make sure Zach knew that—just to emphasise how unimportant and purely physical the whole proposition had been—Rae was going to behave *completely* normally around him.

Starting right now.

It was evening, and he was here. He'd shown up with a sweet smile and damp hair, wearing jeans that adored his thighs and a T-shirt that worshipped the breadth of his chest. She'd offered him a beer, and he'd noticed the dead spotlight in her kitchen. Now he was changing it for her, because he was that kind of guy.

His T-shirt was riding up. While he fiddled with the light, she held a torch and tried to ignore the eye candy. She'd already ogled him enough, and she wasn't a pest or a bad friend... but it turned out she *was* highly susceptible to wanton gorgeousness, because she couldn't tear her gaze away. He was a carefully carved slab of marble with those sharp, diagonal lines at his hips that acted like blinking arrows. Those lines had no sympathy for the plight of a woman hopelessly in lust. *Hey,* they said, *look down here. Lower.* She resisted, focusing on the faint trail of dark hair that dusted his abdomen. But that was pointing downward, too.

This was a conspiracy. Zach's body was out to get her, and she wanted to be caught.

No. Nope. Bad Rae. We've been through this. Zach didn't want her. She didn't mind. For the sake of their friendship, she had to stop being weird.

"There we go," he said, climbing off her dining chair. "Flick the switch."

She did as she was told, and the kitchen glowed to life, every spotlight present and correct. "Thanks. You didn't have to."

"This is the kitchen where you make fantastic brownies. I definitely had to. By the way, I want some more."

"I bet you do." She rolled her eyes and grabbed her lemonade. She was avoiding wine for the rest of the month. "You're lucky I baked at all. I hate doing things for men."

"Men, specifically?" He followed her into the living room, sips of beer interrupting his smile. "Why's that?"

"I suppose I'm bored of it. Life will do that to you." She sank onto the sofa beside Duke's curled up bulk. He was snoring like a sledgehammer, each breath whacking at her heart in the best way possible. She kissed the top of his precious baby head.

"You know Duke's a man, right?" Zach pointed out, sprawling into an armchair.

"Duke's a dog." She paused, cocking her head. "Hmm. Actually, I see what you mean."

"Hilarious." He was trying to sound sarcastic, but the twist of his mouth said he was fighting a smile. He thumbed the neck of his beer bottle and her mind showed her something: Zach, maintaining eye contact, burning her with that blue fire, while he slid the neck of the bottle into his sinful mouth. She shifted awkwardly against the cushions, trying not to roll her hips. *Stop that.*

Her mind switched things up. Now Zach was standing over her, cradling her face with one hand, parting her lips with his thumb and easing the bottle into *her* mouth. Jesus. She made a mental note to book a date with her vibrator. Clearly, she'd been neglectful.

"Speaking of dogs," he said, dragging her back to reality, "tell me about this thing with your ex."

Ah, Kevin. A bucket of cold water when she needed it. This was the most useful he'd been in years. "I've been invited to a convention. It's this annual event in Manchester, over the bank holiday weekend, for fantasy authors and readers. The Burning Quill."

Zach didn't seem to recognise the name, which made sense; as far as Rae could tell, he was a casual fantasy fan, more of a sci-fi guy. Still, he said, "They invited you, huh? Ms. Big-Shot author." His smile was all pleased and glowing, like he was proud of her.

She sipped her lemonade demurely and admitted, "I've been nominated for an award, too."

"*What?*" Now he was openly excited. "When did that happen? You been keeping secrets, sunshine?"

She grimaced. "I haven't really let myself enjoy it. It's like a solid-gold cloud lined with shit."

"Because of your ex?" And now his expression darkened. She caught a glimpse of fury in his eyes, like he was ready to crack skulls, but trying to hide it.

Sometimes she wondered what else Zach hid. The thought intrigued her more than it should.

She sank back into the cushions and said, "He hasn't done anything wrong, if that's what you're thinking." *Not recently, anyway.*

"Except for the part where he cheated on you after twenty-two years together?" Zach said mildly.

57

"Good memory." She pointed at him. "But that doesn't matter. We don't care. We actually hate him for other reasons."

That didn't help Zach's skull-cracking expression. "What reasons?"

"Private reasons," she sniffed. "Here's my problem: he'll be at the convention. He'll probably win an award. He'll bring Billie—"

"Billie?"

"The new wife. The assistant."

Zach wrinkled his nose. "Do we hate her?"

Rae shrugged. "She's not the one who vowed her fidelity to me, so no. We are exhausted and ambivalent."

"Alright. So, he'll be at this thing, and he'll bring Billie."

"Yes. And everyone will look at me like I'm a big, sad, abandoned sack of poop. I'll feel awkward and defensive and I'll hate myself for letting him ruin my weekend. I can already see it happening. I'm already pissed in advance." *I wish I didn't have to go alone. I wish I had a friend there.*

I wish I had you.

Zach gave her a strange look. "I had no idea that you... Well, to be honest, I kind of thought you were impervious to judgment and all that shit. I don't know why. It just never seems to bother you."

Of course he'd think that. After all, when he was around her, it was true. But for some reason—maybe because she'd already hit rock-bottom embarrassment with him on Friday night—she found herself correcting his assumption.

"Sometimes it feels like there are two of me. There's me after the divorce, the person I am here. The person I want to be. Here, I don't care what people say or think—I honestly don't. But then, when I'm not here, I become the old me. Kevin's me. Because the people I used to know look at me differently, and..." She obviously couldn't explain it, because the words tumbling from her lips made no sense. Her voice grew quieter as she finished. "No-one pities the real me, the person I am here. But in Kevin's world, that's all anyone ever does. And it makes me feel like someone else."

Zach's gaze was so tender, so soft and understanding, that looking him in the eye made her feel naked. And not in a sexy way. "I get it," he said, nodding slowly. "I'm sorry, Rae."

"Don't be. I'll get over it." That was what she did, after all. She got over things. She'd gotten over Kevin's betrayal, she'd gotten over Zach's rejection, and she'd get over the nightmare that this convention promised to be.

"I didn't realise he was an author, too," Zach said. He studied his beer bottle with narrowed, thoughtful eyes. "Your ex, I mean."

Something resentful flared inside her, a volcano that had been dormant for months. "He's *the* author. I'm just his wife." Even though she'd been the one with the dream. Even though he'd never picked up *Lord of the fucking Rings* before the day they'd met in that old library, when she'd told him to impress her. Even though...

"You're not his wife," Zach reminded her. "You're Something McRae. Hey, what's your name again?"

She smirked, amusement chasing the bitterness away. "Nice try."

He clicked his fingers. "It's on the tip of my tongue. Jennifer?"

"No."

"Melissa?"

She sighed like she wasn't loving this. "No."

"Uh..." He pulled out his phone and squinted at the screen for a second. "Amanda?"

"What, do you have a list on there?"

"Yeah." He waved the phone. "The 100 most popular baby names in 1979. I've done my research."

She couldn't help it. She burst out laughing, so loud that Duke cracked an eyelid and looked up at her like, *Do you mind?*

Zach sighed. "I take it I won't find you on this list?"

"Oh, honey. The only list my name has ever made is my mother's list of sins."

"It can't be that bad."

"It's not," she said honestly. "It's straight-up ridiculous."

"Now you're just teasing me."

"Kind of like how you teased me with those donuts."

"Nope." He stood. "I brought the donuts. Hang on."

She waited while he disappeared into the hall, presumably in search of the jacket he'd hung up by the door. He came back with a brown paper bag that he presented with a flourish.

She raised her eyebrows, opened the bag, and pulled out a rock-hard, blackened ring. "Um..."

"I thought I'd try making my own, like you do. Unfortunately," he said, all grave solemnity, "turns out I still can't bake for shit."

This time, her laughter was the high, helpless kind that

signified imminent pants-wetting. Nothing had ever been funnier than big, strong, handsome Zach standing there with his bag of shitty donuts.

"Hey, what if you're hurting my feelings?" he protested. "I worked really hard on these. I was hoping you'd try one."

She threw one at him instead.

It bounced off his chest, and he grinned. "Ungrateful."

"I gave you the best brownies ever," she said, "and this is how you repay me?"

"Oh, come on. Isn't it the thought that counts?"

"No. It's the sugar, carbs, calories."

He shook the bag hopefully. "Pretty sure my donuts have all that."

"And the *taste*," she added.

"Charming." He flopped down beside her, his weight jolting the cushions, his presence jolting her heart. Duke opened one eye again and shot her a warning look. *Hands to yourself, woman. I mean it. I will guard you against your own foolishness, if necessary.* She imagined him grabbing her arm gently between his massive jaws and leading her into a cold shower. What a good boy.

"These were actually my third try," Zach told her with an air of confession.

"Maybe your kitchen is cursed," she suggested. "Maybe the serial killing ghost is sabotaging you."

"It was just one murder! And I don't have any ghosts."

"What you have are balls of steel, living in a place like that," she muttered.

"I'm thinking of buying it."

She spluttered, unable to keep the disbelief out of her voice. "Are you taking the piss?"

"Property is an investment," he said, his tone all studious and sensible and therefore disturbingly sexy. "The price is unbelievable. I should take the plunge."

"But you haven't, because your gut knows that place is evil. Don't buy it."

"I have to buy something soon," he shrugged. "It's in my five-year plan."

Um, what? Record-scratch. Pause. She gaped. "You have a five-year plan?"

"I have multiple five-year plans. A new one every five years." He winced. "But I'm a little behind, because..."

He didn't have to say it. Rae had heard whispers about Zach almost losing his job a while back. He'd taken a ton of days off before Nate moved up here to help with their mum. The idea that he could've been sacked for taking care of a sick relative—never mind his *mother*—made her fingers tighten around her glass. She shifted away from the topic. "You're twenty-eight. So when you say *multiple* plans, I'm assuming you mean two."

"Three," he corrected, then looked thoughtful. "Or four."

"You're telling me you were making these plans as a kid?"

"It's what I do," he said, like it was no big deal. "I had shit to handle. I always have shit to handle."

Something twanged beneath her breastbone. She felt herself get all soft and sympathetic. "Zach..."

He flashed her a look. Might as well have said *Don't* out loud. "There's something I wanted to tell you."

"What a smooth change of subject."

"Shut up." He tugged one of her little plaits. As usual, she'd braided the front of her hair off her face. His eyes eased over her scars for a second, like a touch.

No, not her scars—just her. He was looking at her. Always.

"Let me talk," he said. "It's about Friday night."

She screwed her face into what must be a highly unattractive expression. "Are we still on that?"

"Yes. Right now, I'm blurting out a big speech while you listen."

She started to smile, but then she saw the tightness of his jaw and realised he was nervous. "Oh. Okay."

"It's not a big deal."

"Okay."

He met her eyes. "So, do you know what *demisexual* means?"

CHAPTER FIVE

WHAT A WAY TO BEGIN. *Do you know what* demisexual *means?* But it was part of the plan, and Zach couldn't deviate from the plan. He'd thought it all through so carefully, from his opening line to the fact that he would tell Rae before anyone else. She'd be his trial run. He'd decided that, if he had to face an ignorant meltdown from someone he cared about, he'd rather not start with his fucking brother.

But, as he waited for Rae to respond, he started to think she wasn't a great first choice, either. He should've told a random old lady at a bus stop, or something, just to get used to the conversation. And, maybe, to get used to negative reactions. He could handle just about anything, so long as he knew what to expect. Right now, he had not a fucking clue what to expect.

After a pause, she said carefully, "I think I do." Her eyes seemed darker and more direct than ever, two patient black holes sucking the air out of the room.

He wasn't surprised. She knew all kinds of shit. It was one of the many ticks in the 'for' column of his *Should I Come Out to Rae?* project.

"As far as I'm aware," she went on, "demisexuality is an orientation on the asexual spectrum. Demisexual people only experience sexual attraction toward those they've formed an emotional bond with. Does that sound right to you?"

Like she was checking her explanation hadn't offended him. So, she'd already figured out what he was going to say. That was another tick he'd put in Rae's 'for' column: she was smart.

"Yeah," he said. His voice came out too rough, so he cleared his throat. "Yeah. That's about right. I figured out a while ago that I'm demisexual—I mean, I knew from the start, but I didn't realise it was, uh, an official thing. And I wasn't exactly okay with it. Which is why I slept around a lot." He gave her a wry look. "You might've heard about that."

She bit her lip and looked mildly tortured, which he enjoyed more than a gentleman should. She was real fucking cute when she felt guilty. "You know, I really don't care about that stuff."

"I know."

"Are you okay with it now?" She looked at him like, if he wasn't, she'd drag him off for lessons in self-love.

"I am," he assured her. "Honestly, it wasn't like I hated myself or anything. I just didn't get it, and then, when I was starting to..." He trailed off with a frown, because this story wasn't necessary, and he didn't know why he'd started to tell it. Sharing details like that wasn't part of the plan, mostly because no-one wanted to hear them.

But Rae kept watching him, like anything that might come out of his mouth was vital. Like she had all the time and inclination in the world. Fuck it. He shrugged off his hesitation and just kept going.

"I was an unpopular kid," he said. "Giant nerd. Obvious target." He'd been lanky and pale with milk-bottle glasses and an open love of comics, always daydreaming and drawing weird shit in the back of his notebooks. It hadn't really mattered, at first, because everyone was terrified of Nate, and no-one would touch Zach if it meant facing his big brother's wrath. But then Nate left, and it had been open season.

Rae cocked her head and smiled. "You? Seriously? Mr. Tall, Charming and Handsome?"

"Aw, shut up. Back then I was just awkward. But during the summer between school and sixth form, I started labouring—you know, for extra money, to help out at home. And I had a growth spurt around the same time. So, when summer ended, I, uh, I looked like this."

"I see." Judging by the expression on her face, she really did see. Zach hadn't, not for a while. He'd been baffled, then slowly, tentatively hopeful when the kids who used to tease him had suddenly wanted to talk. When girls who'd never looked at him twice developed a fascination with his Batman rucksack. And when one of those girls had asked him out, he'd said yes, because... well, because she was nice, and because that was what people did.

"I got a girlfriend," he said. "She was lovely. But, eventually, she wanted to have sex—which is when I realised that I didn't."

"How'd that turn out?" Rae's voice was gentle.

His mouth twisted into a rueful smile. "She thought there was something wrong with her."

"I'm starting to see where this is going."

He snorted, unsurprised. "Am I that predictable?"

"You're that sweet. Even when you shouldn't be."

Something about the way she said it, with this deep, undying appreciation, made it seem like an actual compliment instead of a laughable character flaw. His smile felt real all of a sudden. He laughed, surprising himself. Rae made things easy like that.

"I slept with her, obviously. It made her happy, so I kept doing it. I think that's how it all started—how I wound up sleeping with a shit-ton of people I wasn't even attracted to. But a little while back I realised that it mattered, and it was doing something awful to me. I just wanted to be... myself. So, I stopped. Better late than never, I guess."

"Definitely." She put a hand on his shoulder, and he met her eyes. She looked so serious, like she needed to hammer this home. "You should be proud of yourself, you know. Changing learned behaviour is hard. And brave. Even when you want to."

He nodded. "Thanks."

"And I'm sorry, Zach. So sorry that you ever had to go through that. I mean—that you did things you didn't really want to do. That's... That's never okay."

He covered her hand with his own and squeezed.

Murmured again, "Thanks, Rae." The phrase didn't reflect even half of the bittersweet gratitude swirling inside him.

"Well," she said, "thanks for telling me. Trusting me, I mean." She smiled slightly, leaning back and sipping her lemonade. "Gotta say, Davis, I'm flattered."

"I bet." He rolled his eyes, but sunlight radiated from his chest. What had he been nervous about, anyway? He barely even knew anymore.

But then she hesitated, flashing him a wary look, and something inside him tensed. They weren't quite done here. Rae paused, then took a deep breath. She seemed to be searching for just the right words, and once she found them, they came out steadily. "I want to ask you something. But you don't have to answer, okay?"

Ah, shit. "Okay." *Please don't ruin this. Please don't ask me some bullshit—*

"What I did on Friday night. The way I didn't really take no for an answer. Did that trigger you?"

Her tone was so neutral, so calm, so utterly focused on Zach. There was no subtext, no pressure to answer one way or another. That fact, combined with her even bothering to ask—with her understanding that an experience like that *could* trigger him—meant so fucking much.

"That night was... a lot," he admitted. "But, honestly? I'm okay."

She bit her lip. "I'm so sorry."

"It's fine. A lot of the stuff in my past, I've worked through it."

"But I—"

"Hey." Now it was his turn to put a hand on *her* shoulder. "Listen to me. You didn't know, but now you do. You fucked up, you get it, you apologised. I don't want to dwell on it anymore. Alright?"

She nodded slowly. "Alright. But just so you know, that won't happen again. And if I ever fuck up do something that makes you uncomfortable..."

"I'll tell you," he said softly.

She smiled and whispered, "Thanks."

"While we're doing this," he added, "sorry if I was a little overzealous about... about turning you down."

She winced. "You kind of had to be."

True.

"Anyway, there's really no need to apologise. I'm an adult. I've been rejected before."

For some reason, he found that difficult to believe. "By who?"

"Kevin," she said easily, then slapped a hand over her mouth. Her eyes widened, her cheeks darkened. She mumbled behind her palm, "Oh dear. That sounded rather pathetic."

He dragged her hand away from her face. "No, it didn't. Kevin's got the sense of a rock, and nothing you say or do could ever be pathetic. You're a fucking superhero."

She swallowed, her gaze fluttering to the tattoos on his arm. "I take that very highly, coming from you."

"You should." He meant it. He'd never meant anything more in his life. He'd also never been more pissed off in his life. "Fucking Kevin. I bet he's an ugly little toad."

"He's quite handsome, actually," she said, sounding aggrieved.

"Of course he is. They always are."

"And Billie's very pretty. They suit each other."

"Don't act like you're not beautiful. You know what you need?"

She didn't respond—just stared at him with a stunned expression that made him play his words back. *Don't act like you're not beautiful.* Well, she was. But he had no idea why he'd mentioned it when they didn't usually discuss that sort of thing. His face heated slightly.

Finally, she re-hinged her jaw and said, "Um, no. What do I need?"

"You need to beat him at his own game. If he's bringing his pretty wife, get yourself a pretty boyfriend."

She laughed and lifted her glass of lemonade. "I need wine when you're like this."

"I'm serious." He wasn't, and they both knew it. But this game was chasing the shadows from her eyes, so he'd play it forever. "When's the convention? How much time have you got?"

"A few weeks. You think I should hunt down a date?"

He shrugged. "Why not?"

"Waste of time," she tutted, clearly fighting a smile. "I don't even like men."

Oh, for God's sake. "Best bullshit I ever heard. When we walk into a room it takes you thirty seconds to clock every hot guy in there."

She gave an outraged gasp, eyes wide, lips half-curved into a reluctant smile. "That is not true."

He waited.

"Fine! It's true. But looking at men and dating men are two very different things—and trust me, I have no desire to date anyone. Ever."

The words seemed to echo with finality, like she'd just

cast a terrible spell. Zach paused, taken aback by the vehemence in her voice. Was this an aftereffect of divorce? It would make sense. He wanted to ask, to push, to figure out exactly why the thought of romance made her narrow her eyes and speak like a peal of thunder. But the look she speared him with said loud and clear: *Don't.*

So he didn't. "It'll be a means to an end. We'll get you on Tinder or something."

"Ugh. I predict sad or disgusting dick pics and other forms of harassment."

"I'll be your Tinder manager. Let me vet the messages and delete the dick pics for you, madam. What are friends for?"

"You're ridiculous." But she liked it. He could tell by the look on her face; that wild, reckless amusement lighting her up. She pursed her lips thoughtfully. "It *has* occurred to me that maybe I should bring a friend. For support. I suppose your idea is just a more extreme version of that." Her expression changed, embarrassment creeping in. "Is it weird that I'm actually considering this?"

He blinked. Unexpected, maybe, but... "Who cares if it is? Weird can be good. Weird can be great. Would it make you feel better to go with someone who had your back?"

"They wouldn't need to have my back," she admitted. "All I want is fewer pitying looks. I really hate pitying looks." She stared into her lemonade like it was a crystal ball—and whatever she saw in there seemed to make her feel stabby.

"That's fair," Zach murmured. Growing up in a gossip-hungry town like this, with a single mother and a disappearing brother, he knew a few things about pitying looks himself. His dad had run off with a beekeeper, for Christ's sake. He'd felt the acid burn of strangers' sympathy for too many years to count. He didn't want Rae—proud, brilliant, accomplished Rae—to feel a thing like that, especially when she should be high on her own success instead.

And that was it. Maybe he'd been joking before, but now he was deadly serious. "This is a solid plan," he said. "You're doing it."

She sighed. "I don't think so. It seems kind of—"

"If you say *pathetic* I will force-feed you my homemade donuts."

She pressed her lips together and held up both hands.

"Good girl."

Her mouth never stayed closed for long. "I am twelve years older than you."

"And I'm an expert in pissing you off."

"Fuck you." She rolled her eyes and grabbed his beer. She'd done it a million times before, but for some reason, he couldn't look away when she pressed her lips to the rim. Her throat shifted as she swallowed. A voice in his head growled, *She's drinking my beer.*

No shit, Sherlock. Thanks for the running commentary.

She handed it back and said, "There's only one way this would work."

"What's that?"

"If you were my date."

THE SHOCK on Zach's face was so overwhelming it made

Rae physically cringe. She hurried to clarify. "My *fake* date. You know, for the... actually, no, forget it." She was being ridiculous. Again. Zach made her forget to corral the most fanciful parts of her brain, the imagination she usually poured into her writing.

But, to her surprise, he didn't stay silent or laugh awkwardly and change the subject. Instead, he lurched back to life and said, "Why?"

She blinked, taken off guard. "Uh... why what?"

"Why me?" He had a slight frown as he said it, like he was confused. Or focused. Or both.

She shrugged, drowning in her own self-consciousness but determined not to show it. "I like you. You're charming. You'll make the whole weekend less of a living hell. You're not some sleazy stranger who'd use the experience to try and get in my pants." Kind of like how she'd sleazily tried to get in his pants. Her cheeks heated. "And, really, there's no way I could get a real date."

His frown became a scowl. "Why the hell not?"

She blinked. "I don't know if you've noticed, but I have a slight problem with people."

"Problem being?"

"I hate them."

His laughter was incredulous. "What? No, you don't."

"Zach." She leaned forward. "When have you ever seen me talk to anyone but our little group?"

He opened his mouth, presumably to give her an example. But the example never came, because—as she well knew—there were none. He looked nonplussed, snapped his jaw shut, then said, "But you're so great with all of us."

Their friends, he meant. "Of course I am. Ruth and Hannah are amazing."

"And me and the guys are...?"

"Solid tens who don't get on my nerves too often."

"Oh, nice, Rae." He grinned like she was actually funny. She grinned back. They were sitting there smiling in each other's faces like a pair of bobbleheads. She couldn't help it; she supposed there was just something about him.

And the fact that he wasn't laughing in her face or running screaming for the door made her wild idea seem not-so-wild anymore. "I just remembered another reason why you should come."

He arched a brow.

"Because you're much better looking than Kevin, so he'll have an apoplexy. Not," she said demurely, "that I am concerned by such shallow and immature things."

"Oh, no way," he agreed, like he was calm about all this. "So... you really want me to come with you? As your, uh, fake boyfriend?"

She laughed, shaking her head. "It's silly. I know it is." But there was an equally silly seed of hope inside her, biting its lip and watching him with wide eyes.

That seed blossomed without permission when he put down his beer and said, "Let's do it."

She gaped. "You cannot be serious."

"Oh, I'm dead serious."

"Zach." She gave a high, nervous laugh. "I can't actually ask you to do that."

He shot her an amused look. "Don't come over all polite on me. You already asked. I'm saying yes."

"I... I..." She stopped, cleared her throat, and pulled

herself firmly together. "No. It's too much to ask. Obviously, I'd get your ticket and everything, but you'd have to share my room at the hotel, and you'd have to book Friday off work, and—"

"So, what you're saying here," he drawled, "is that I get to attend this convention, which sounds pretty fucking cool, sleep on fancy hotel sheets, see you win your award—"

"I'm not going to—"

"See you win your award," he repeated loudly, "and get time off work and good karma points. All in return for, what? Holding your hand in public and telling everyone how great you are? Wow, torture."

For some reason, her mouth ran dry at those words. She croaked out, "Is that your boyfriend routine? Holding hands?"

He shrugged, as if this were a reasonable topic. "Part of it, yeah. But attraction isn't about touching, not really. Not just that, anyway. Attraction is about energy." His eyes settled on hers, oddly heavy, almost hypnotic. "About the space between two people and how loud it hums. Hot looks that burn through busy rooms." His voice softened, sending a shiver through her. "This is one thing I know exactly how to fake. Trust me. No-one who sees us together will pity you."

Oh, she just bet. Even now, her breath hitched under his gaze. There was no doubt in Rae's mind that Zach could play the doting boyfriend dangerously well—so well, she'd completely forget it was fake. "It's not a good idea."

"It's a great idea. Look—I know how this shit goes. Not

ex-husband shit," he added, "but messy shit. Without some kind of buffer, you'll spend all weekend avoiding knowing looks and awkward questions. Hell, avoiding your fucking ex. I know you must have writer friends, or something like that—"

Her lips twitched, because she absolutely did not. She was too flaky to manage it.

"—but I can't stop feeling like..." He huffed out a breath. "Like you'd be alone. At the very least, you need someone to cheer when you win that award. Why shouldn't it be me?"

He asked the question like the answer actually mattered. She tapped her tongue against the inside of her cheek and tried to dredge up a decent response. It was difficult, not because there were none, but because a not-so-secret part of her didn't want to argue. It wasn't sensible or mature or especially clever, but she wanted to bring a fake boyfriend along to a work event her ex-husband was involved in. And, for reasons she couldn't bring herself to examine too closely, she wanted that fake boyfriend to be Zach.

But one thing still bothered her. "You're not doing this because you feel bad about Friday night, are you?"

For a moment, he actually looked thoughtful, picking up his beer and fiddling with the label. She held her breath. After a while, or possibly a lifetime, he spoke. "No. I'm doing this because I honestly think you'd do it for me."

That was what tipped her over the edge of Decision Mountain. She smiled, the knot of tension in her belly finally loosening, the heavy dread she'd carried floating away. "I'll make you brownies forever."

"You'd better."

"I'll tell you every story before I tell anyone else." Once she got around to writing them again.

He laughed and reminded her, "You already do."

"I'll owe you a thousand times over," she insisted. She'd never meant anything more in her life.

ZACH KNEW that helping Rae was the right decision because when he woke up the next morning, he still wanted to do it. She wasn't there in front of him, needing him, but he still had the desire to be there for her, which meant it was real—not a bad habit, not a compulsion, not an attempt to make himself indispensable. Just a friend plotting a mildly ridiculous scheme to help another friend. Just Zach being himself.

Helping Callie with her car that weekend didn't feel quite the same.

He didn't often give up his Saturdays, or rather, he didn't anymore. Once upon a time, offering the help his friends invariably needed had been part of his weekly routine. But since his mother's diagnosis, his world had shrunk to a hopeful, hopeless pinpoint made up of frantic family, and his friends had sort of... faded. Of course, Ma was better now—or coping, anyway—so here he was, just like the old days, freezing his balls off on Callie Michaelson's drive.

Well, no, not exactly like the old days. Before, he and Callie had been friends, so she would've asked him for this favour at the pub or something—instead of hunting him down at work like he was a bleeding gazelle.

Zach paused under the hood of her car, the uncharitable thought catching him like a scratchy tag in a new shirt. That wasn't really how it had happened, was it? She'd just been passing by. It had been pure chance. But as he bent over Callista's engine, hands busy, mind idle, it almost felt like his time was being spent for him. This favour was so much smaller than the one he'd happily offered Rae, but it felt a hell of a lot heavier.

Before he could dwell on that, a familiar, reedy voice interrupted his thoughts.

"Zachary Davis! I thought that was you!"

Enid Hutton wobbled toward him on her stick-thin legs, her threadbare cardigan flapping in the brisk wind and a big, steaming mug in her bony, wrinkled hands.

He dropped his wrench so fast he almost broke his own toe, then hurried over to take the mug. "Enid, what are you doing out here? Where's your stick?"

"Oh, bugger my stick. I can walk up the drive and pop next door without it, thank you very much." She glared grey-sky eyes at him and tutted, but when he offered his arm, she clung to it quite happily.

"You're supposed to use it all the time," he told her sternly. "Where's your grandson?"

"Never mind him." Enid flapped a hand as though the man she lived with was a mild irritation. "That's for you, my darling." She nodded at the tea.

Zach grinned despite himself. "Aw, Enid. You didn't have to do that."

"Well, Lord knows Her Majesty won't bother," Enid

snorted, rolling her eyes toward Callie's house. "She's sitting inside, wrapped up warm, while you sort her car out for free, isn't she?"

Zach took a sip of hot, milky tea before answering. "No use her standing out here and getting cold."

"*No use* is right," Enid muttered. "But it's lovely to see you, my darling. You haven't been round this side of town in months and months, now."

"Been busy. My mum…"

"I know, sweetheart." Enid patted his hand. "I suppose you weren't in the mood for any of Callie's lovely barbecues last summer?"

No, Zach hadn't been. Although, his mood might have improved if anyone had thought to invite him to those barbecues. Or tell him he'd been missed. Or ask if he was okay.

Or remember he existed at all.

"Thing is," he hedged, "I haven't seen Callie for a long time." Since his mum's diagnosis, actually. He hadn't seen a lot of people since then.

Enid's lip curled. "Fair-weather friends." She must have seen something in his expression—the dawning realisation, or the disappointment that followed—because she flashed him a too-bright smile. "But I'd better be going inside. I'll never hear the end of it if I catch a chill."

"Oh, yeah, of course. Let's get you in." Zach helped Enid down her drive, promising to leave the mug inside the kitchen windowsill when he was done. Then he returned to Callie's car and stared at the engine while his thoughts lurched around drunkenly.

Was Callie a fair-weather friend? Was she one of those

people who'd been happy to hang out with the eternally cheerful Zach, but couldn't be bothered with the stressed and depressed version he'd become after his mother's illness?

Had Callie come by the forge that day purely because she wanted something, and Ma was better now?

Not so long ago, the idea would have panicked him. Would've made him feel like the bullied, friendless kid no-one truly wanted around—or the boy people only bothered with because of the way he looked and the things he could provide. But for some reason, today, that feeling didn't come.

Maybe because, these days, he had people in his life who knew he was worth more than that. People who gave him everything he'd barely dared to hope for and made him feel like he deserved it.

Zach grabbed his wrench and got back to work, a weight lifting from his shoulders.

This would be the last favour he'd do Callista Michaelson.

CHAPTER SIX

TWO WEEKS LATER

THE HOTEL that hosted the Burning Quill Convention was incongruously business-y and boring. Everything—from the wide, minimalist front desk to the uncomfortable-looking chairs scattered about the foyer—was dark wood or dull, duck-egg blue. And Rae usually *liked* blue. Didn't matter. This place was awful. She'd already texted Hannah a million times, ostensibly to check on Duke, but her fingers itched to pick up the phone again.

Zach's massive shoulder nudged hers. She looked up and saw their reflections in the vast mirror above the check-in desk. Watched him bend toward her and felt his breath against her ear. "Stop freaking out," he murmured.

She gritted her teeth. "I'm not."

"You're glaring at thin air like you're ready to commit a murder. That little French girl behind the desk started stammering when we joined the queue. You have homicidal energy."

A smile snuck onto her face. "You're so dramatic."

"You're so nervous. Don't be. We're going to have fun."

She looked at him, the real him, rather than his reflection. His words were light, but he had the determined expression of a man on a mission. They would have fun because he would *make* it so. Zach really was the best candidate for this sort of thing—and, with those sleepy, blue eyes and that welcoming mouth, the worst.

On the drive up, it had hit Rae like a brick to the face that she and Zach would share a room for three whole nights. How the hell was she supposed to cope with that? Being trapped in the car with no means of escape or distraction from his sheer sex appeal had been difficult enough. She hoped the hotel room windows opened or they'd both suffocate in the fog of her lust. This physical attraction was bloody inconvenient, and honestly? It seemed to be getting worse.

"Yes," she agreed dutifully. "We'll have fun." It wasn't exactly a lie. Spending time with him: that would be fun. But acting like they were together, letting him shower her with casual affection and hot looks while knowing it was 100% fake? She had the oddest feeling she was going to hate that part.

They finally reached the desk and its French receptionist, a petite blonde with impressively fluttery eyelashes. Once, after the accident that scarred her face, Rae's mother had insisted she try eyelash extensions because *You need to make an effort, these days, darling.* They'd been irritating as fuck. Rae had pulled them all out and her natural lashes had been unintended casualties. An unattractive couple of months had followed.

This receptionist looked far too chic and put together

to accidentally yank out her own lashes—although she did seem slightly nervous around Rae. What had Zach said? *You have homicidal energy.* Despite herself, Rae chuckled under her breath. Zach caught her eye in the mirror behind the desk, and his own lips curved like he knew exactly what she was thinking.

"Bonjour sir, madame." The blonde—Céline, according to her badge—offered them a tremulous smile. "Name?"

Zach grinned like a shark. "Oh, yeah, Rae. Tell the nice lady your name."

She shot him a quelling look, then said calmly, "B. A. McRae."

He bent down to whisper in her ear again. "Chicken." He had no idea that every time he whispered to her like that, the intimacy of it destroyed her composure. He was turning her on like a tap. The scent of him, pure flame overlaid by something cool and green, like walking Duke through the woods just after dawn, made her dizzy and drunk and desperate.

She needed to control her reactions. If he ever realised how tragically in lust she was, he'd be horribly uncomfortable, and she'd have to throw herself into the Trent.

Céline clicked away at her computer for a moment, then looked up at Rae, arching perfectly plucked eyebrows. Yeah, yeah. What a name, blah, blah. To her credit, Céline didn't say a word, just tapped some more and said, "You're in room eleven-fifteen. Would you like one key or two?"

"Two, please."

The hotel was already rammed, convention-goers checking in, hanging about at the bar, or taking selfies in front of the banners decorating the foyer. Those banners, with their bold images of iconic fantasy covers, looked as out of place in the business hotel as the convention-goers themselves. Rae checked off types as she led the way to the lifts: excited influencers, antisocial writers, harried assistants, and speculative agents and editors wondering who they'd discover this time. Her own agent was here somewhere, but she was in no hurry to see him or anyone else she knew.

Concocting this ridiculous plan had been all fun and games, but now they were here, Rae knew it wouldn't work. How did you fake a relationship? She was forty years old, for Christ's sake. She didn't do shit like this. Zach could support her just fine while being exactly what he was: a dear friend whose loveliness occasionally— okay, regularly—made her melt. That was more than enough.

Muttering nervously under her breath, she hit the gleaming button for the lift. While she was distracted, Zach snagged her suitcase, biceps bulging as he lifted it along with his own.

"Give it back," she said, already resigned to the fact that he absolutely wouldn't.

His laughing eyes focused on the lift doors instead of her. Zach-speak for *This is not a debate.* "No. It's heavy."

"Which is why I should be carrying it."

"Shut up," he said. "Who lets his girlfriend carry her own shit? Kevins, that's who."

He was like a mugger, stealing her smiles at gunpoint. "Zach..."

One dark brow arched, deliciously arrogant. "Don't

pretend you're pissed. I always know when you're faking it. That's my specialty."

"Spotting fakes?" She cocked her head. "How ironic."

"Hey. Stay in character."

"I didn't say anything!"

"You're flirting with confession, sunshine." He looked around warily, like they were running from the mob. "You never know who's listening."

"Oh, for God's—"

The *ding* and slide of elevator doors interrupted her eyeroll. Fuck. A pair of men she recognised stepped out of the shiny chrome box, their eyes widening as they caught sight of her. It'd been years since she'd seen Mark and Ed Pike, brothers and cowriters with a love of cheap Scotch, loud conversation, and thoughtless, nasty 'opinions.' Mark was the elder, his fringe of dark hair being rapidly swallowed by a pink bald patch, his brow permanently furrowed. Ed, the taller of the two, still had a thick head of waves, along with green eyes so bright they could stop traffic. Those eyes were the only interesting thing about him. Both men were rather average in appearance—which would be fine, if they weren't convinced they were sex gods sent to save the planet with the power of their mighty wangs.

Rae nodded politely and attempted to scurry by. That, of course, did not fucking work.

"Hey," Mark said, pointing a finger at her. He'd chewed his nail almost to the quick. Maybe she wasn't the only writer who got nervous about weekends like this. "I know you. You're... ahhhh, I know it, I know it—"

"Kevin Cummings's missus," Ed supplied helpfully,

offering a tobacco-stained smile and a wink. "Haven't seen you in a while, love."

How was she supposed to reply? Should she snap, *I'm not Kevin's wife*, like it was a sore spot, and receive that *Oh, God, a hysterical female* look? No; she should just smile and say, all cool, *Actually, Kevin and I parted ways*. Was that a thing normal people said about relationships? *Parted ways?*

Dealing with your first ever breakup at forty was a special kind of torture.

Now she'd hesitated for too long, and she knew what happened when a woman hesitated with men like these: they'd sweep up the conversation like a broom, rolling her into their pile of social dust and muck, boring her half to death. She'd lose her patience and say something rude to make them piss off, and they'd wander away muttering about *Kevin's bitchy wife*. Kevin would hear about it later on and make one of those mild, detached comments he was so good at. The ones that seemed guileless but were sharper than a scythe. She would be shredded in her absence and hear about it three weeks after the fact. That was how it usually happened—and it would be even worse now they were no longer together.

Then, in the midst of her panic, she heard Zach's voice. "Actually, Rae's with me now." It was the kind of statement that could've sounded all macho ownership, but he turned it into a friendly update, a calm, no-big-deal correction. *Actually, they lowered the speed limit around here. Actually, Emily Bronte wrote* Wuthering Heights. *Actually, Rae's with me now.*

She officially changed her mind about everything. This

weekend was going to be just fine, and their fake relationship was inspired.

"Oh," Mark said. "It really has been a while. Alright, mate?"

Zach shifted all the luggage in a ripple of hypnotising muscle, shaking Mark's hand, then Ed's. She quietly fumed at the fact that no-one had shaken her hand, then remembered that giving a shit about the manners of men in general, and irritating, arrogant men in particular, was a waste of precious energy.

"So," Ed said in that drawn-out, leading way that meant an awkward comment was forthcoming. His gaze flickered to Rae's scars, and in that split second, she realised: it had indeed been a while. Maybe five years or more. Which meant she was about to be asked her least favourite question of all time.

With calm interest, as if this were an acceptable topic, Ed nodded at Rae and said, "That's a corker, eh? What the hell happened to your face?"

FIGHTING A FLARE OF WHITE-HOT FURY, Zach spoke through gritted teeth. "What the fuck did you just say to her?"

The brothers must have heard the murder in his voice, because, all of a sudden, they looked mighty alarmed. "Woah," Ed said, raising his hands like he was warding off a rabid animal. "Come on, mate. I didn't mean anything by it."

For some reason, that only made Zach angrier. Then,

through a burning barrier of rage, he felt a hand against his back. Rae's hand. Without noticing, he'd moved to stand in front of her. Her voice was like a distant song, a half-forgotten lullaby in the back of his mind.

"Zach. It's fine."

No, it fucking wasn't, but he heard the warning beneath her words. He breathed in deep. Exhaled. Then he stepped aside and shut his furious mouth, which was a good idea because his teeth felt like deadly weapons. Finally, he shot her a look. *Well? I stopped.*

Her answering expression was all amusement. The sight soothed him. If she could tease with nothing but the glint in those dark eyes, she couldn't be too upset. And if she wasn't too upset, he wouldn't have to sneak into Ed and Mark's room tonight for a bit of mild decapitation.

Still, he caught her hand in his, because that's what a boyfriend would do—touch her, ground her, make sure she was okay. Only, the moment he did it, his mind went blank. Palm against palm, fingers intertwining, hers long and fine and delicate. For no reason he could discern, it just... it fucked him up. Everything about him glitched. Like she was a plug socket and he'd just been shocked. Bright heat, a thrill of sensation, a slight jump to his heart, and he was staring down at her like he'd never seen her before.

Had he ever seen her before? She looked different, somehow.

Oh. The change must have something to do with her anger. She'd told him to calm down, but he saw what she was trying to hide: Rae was furious, calculating, and magnificent. Her smile was a bite. Her voice was a knife.

She turned to the brothers and said matter-of-factly, "I was in a bar fight."

The two men leaned back a little, as if shoved by surprise. "A bar fight?" Ed echoed faintly.

"Yes. A strange man made an unwanted, unnecessary and intrusive comment about my appearance, so I hit him over the head with a chair." Rae shrugged, rolling her eyes in a *What am I like?* gesture of self-deprecation. "It's all a bit of a blur from there."

Zach bit down on the inside of his cheek to stop from laughing. The brothers looked slightly stunned, then slowly irritated. They shared a grim look, and Ed said coldly, "Very funny. There's no need to get snippy."

"I know." Rae gave them a brilliant, one-sided smile. "But I so enjoy it."

With twin scowls and spluttering, disapproving huffs, they swept away.

"Oh, dear," Rae said, utterly serene. "We lost the lift." She shook her head and pressed the button to call another. Zach tried not to bubble over with laughter or admiration. It wasn't easy.

The elevator arrived with impressive speed, a sparkling, mirrored box made up of reflections. He got in and was treated to a thousand different angles of Rae's smile, a slight, smug tilt of the lips. She was pleased with herself, and he liked it. Something powerful crackled in her gaze, like a bonfire dancing in the dark.

It made him smile, too. "You know what that was?" he asked.

She raised her eyebrows in question as the chrome doors slid shut. "What?"

"That was Ravenswood Rae out in the wild."

Her eyes crinkled at the corners as she grinned. "Hmm. It was, wasn't it?"

"Oh, yeah." *You don't need me at all, you know.* But he was glad to be there, anyway. Then a thought occurred to him, souring his mood. "Do you get questions like that a lot?"

"Of course I do." She said it mildly, but her pleasure dimmed a little, her gaze shuttering.

He was pissed all over again, but for once, the emotion didn't feel dangerous. He didn't want to pour it, bruised and bitter, into manual labour, or to cut it off cold. He remembered the touch of Rae's hand against his back, the care and trust and connection in that simple movement, and he felt... balanced. Released from expectation. Like he didn't have to chain up his negative emotions and leave them in the dark just to keep her by his side.

He breathed in her sugar-and-lemon scent and let the anger pass.

Then he said, "That's fucked up."

"Yes. But it helps me figure out who's worth befriending and who I should write off immediately. I appreciate the efficiency of it all." She paused, turning to look at him. Her eyes were so intense, like whole worlds existed there in the dark. "You've never asked me about them."

Her scars. "If you wanted to tell me, you probably would. If it was important, you definitely would."

"No," she said lightly. "I mean, it's not important at all. But I never tell people important things, anyway. I don't know how."

Nothing about her expression said she was hurting,

but suddenly, he felt sure that she was—and he didn't like it. So, he raised a hand, and when she didn't pull away, he cupped her face. He was glad the awkwardness between them had faded over the last couple of weeks, because touching Rae was something he never wanted to give up. It always felt so easy, so right.

"If you want to share something," he murmured, "you start like this. *Hey, Zach, did I ever tell you about...?*"

She smiled softly and closed her eyes. Began with an air of release, as if he'd given her permission. "Hey, Zach, did I ever tell you about New Year's Eve three years ago?"

"No. Tell me."

Her smile widened, and he saw it reflected around them countless times. The sight tugged at something in him, something raw and vulnerable and unfamiliar. Probably because he could already tell that this would be a sad story—not tragic-sad, but subtle-sad, like the fact that she'd never had a dog before.

He couldn't stop thinking about that information, even weeks later. It had pissed him off royally.

"We had a party," she said. "Kevin and I. We were the *fun* friends because, you know, no kids. So, every year, up until that year, we hosted. That night, I passed out on the sofa, woke up at dawn, and had this bright idea—if I cleaned up the mess before Kevin woke up, he'd be really happy. He hated untidiness, and the house was my responsibility. I suppose I got a bit nervous. So, I stood up to move all of the empty bottles... only, I'd forgotten about my heart."

The smooth glide of the elevator became slow and weighty. They were almost at their floor, but if the doors opened and the world flooded in, this moment might shatter like glass. It took half a second for Zach to smack the emergency stop button. The lift jerked, then stilled.

Rae laughed, and he felt it, his hand still cradling her face. "What are you doing?" she asked, incredulous, delighted.

"Keep going. Finish the story."

She nodded solemnly, like she got him, even though he barely got himself. "I stood up too fast. My heart panicked, and I passed out and dropped everything. Then there was all this blood, shouting... It was a dramatic way to ring in the new year." She held up her hand and showed him something he'd never noticed before: fine slashes dissecting her palm, pale and shiny.

"Shit," he murmured. When she lowered the hand again, his gaze returned to her face—to the scar by the corner of her lovely mouth. He found himself asking, "Can I touch you?"

She didn't point out that he was already touching her. She didn't even ask what he meant. Just whispered in the shimmering silence of the lift, "Yes."

For some reason, that simple permission rung loud in his ears. He felt as if she'd set something caged between them free. A voice in his mind whispered, *We were meant to touch,* but the thought couldn't be his, so he pushed it away. Pretended he hadn't heard a thing, and swept an absent thumb over the fine line of Rae's scar.

She sucked in a breath.

He froze. "You okay?"

"Yes," she said quickly. "I just... no-one's ever really touched them before."

He didn't like that idea. Not at all. "Maybe it should be my job, then."

He only realised how the words sounded after they'd left his mouth.

Her eyes widened, and she stepped away, out of his reach. The minute he lost her skin, her softness and her warmth, the spell broke. He blinked hard and caught sight of his reflection, the faint flush on his cheeks taking him by surprise. What the hell was he doing?

Running his mouth and making Rae uncomfortable, clearly. He cleared his throat, searching for some kind of joke that would lighten the mood, but a staticky voice filled the lift, cutting him off. "Everything alright in there?"

Oops. He pressed the button on the control panel beside the speaker. "Yeah. Sorry. Must've leaned on something."

The response was a disbelieving huff. "Right." Then the lift surged back to life.

CHAPTER SEVEN

KEEP IT TOGETHER. That was all Rae had to do: keep it together, keep her distance, and avoid freaking Zach out the way she had at the park. It should've been easy, but by the time the elevator doors slid open, her heart was shuddering with the effort. She'd barely managed to pull away from him, had almost succumbed to the urge to step closer. When Zach touched her, looked at her, spoke to her with so much feeling in his voice, something inside her trembled. Unwieldy emotions and dangerous thoughts battled their way to the fore. If this wild and ravenous need was purely carnal, she'd deal with it, no problem.

But it wasn't.

She needed to get a grip. Zach had made it clear that he wasn't interested, and she had no desire to hurt him with her lust. She also had no desire to hurt herself with... with *feelings*. Rae shouldn't want a man this way. Not so personally, so specifically, like only Zach's hands and

Zach's smile and Zach's strength would do. That was something more than attraction. It was something she couldn't risk again.

They padded down the 11th floor corridor in silence, their footsteps muffled by the thick, grey-flecked carpet. When they reached their room, she fumbled with the key card, suddenly awkward and hyper aware of her body. Of the way it strained toward him, even when she was still. She shoved the feeling ruthlessly away.

Their hotel room was Boring Blue just like the foyer, all smooth and sharp and spacious—which was a relief, since Zach's presence felt larger than life. At least they wouldn't be squashed together like sardines, with nowhere for her secrets to hide. The furniture was all clean, dark wood, reassuringly business-like. There was a tea set, a decent TV, a huge double bed—

Oh. Shit. The huge double bed.

Zach dumped their luggage at the foot of that bed, staring at the plump white pillows and snowy sheets with a slightly stunned expression. She didn't blame him. In her head, a king-size had seemed vast enough to hold two very separate human islands. But now she compared the space to the breadth of his shoulders and wondered if she'd end up sleeping on top of him.

"Sorry," she blurted, because they'd never explicitly discussed this. "I—I didn't think this part through. The room was booked and then you were coming, and it was all so—"

"This is fine," he interrupted roughly. Then he cleared his throat, smiled, and everything was easy again. "I heard someone saying downstairs that the hotel's been fully booked for months. Plus," he winked, "I trust you with my virtue."

Rae huffed out a rusty, creaking laugh that did nothing to hide her discomfort and went to the window, running a frazzled hand over her hair. They had a stunning view of the grey, blocky office building next door. It was blessedly dull, bland enough to distract her from forbidden, shameful wants. Hopefully.

Zach appeared beside her, his wonderful hands safely on the windowsill instead of cradling her face like she was precious. Thank God. "So, what's the plan, Captain?"

She snorted. "Plan? Never heard of her."

"Colour me surprised." His voice was a warm mix of fondness and exasperation. It was no secret that preparation wasn't one of Rae's talents, or even one of her interests. Still, the last thing she expected was for him to say, all self-consciously casual, "Luckily, I printed out an itinerary."

She turned to face him. "I'm sorry. You did what?"

He whipped out a folder from somewhere. "Thought you might forget your schedule."

He knew damn well that she had never laid eyes— never mind *hands*—on a schedule. "Where did you get that?" she demanded, staring at the folder with horrified fascination. It looked so... official. Organised. Put together. She was starting to sweat.

"I checked the website," he said calmly.

"You did?"

"I did." He opened the folder. "And then I printed it out and highlighted all the shit we should go to. There's a colour-coding system, if you're into that. Actually, never mind. I know for a fact you're not into that." He thrust the folder at her. "Go wild."

She flicked through the pages and said faintly, "It looks like you already did."

She had the delicious pleasure of seeing the ever-confident Zach Davis look slightly nervous. He grunted, rubbing the back of his neck. "I like organising shit. I knew you'd be too busy to do it—"

"Incapable, more like."

"Your brain," he said seriously, "is full of more important things."

For some reason, those words hit her hard—maybe because she'd never heard anything like them before. Usually, it was, *Jesus, Rae, pay attention. Hurry up. Stop daydreaming. Can't you do anything useful?* The mental voice that repeated those barbs was a disturbing mixture of Mother's drawl and Kevin's irritated snap, a toxic cocktail that tightened her gut and hardened her jaw automatically. It was as if the two had joined forces to emphasise that the contents of Rae's head—the stories and fantasies and incandescent what-ifs—would never be important enough to make up for everything she lacked.

But, clearly, the things in Rae's head were important to Zach. He got it. In fact, it seemed like he got *her* at a fundamental level. Like he saw her in a way no-one had ever cared to before.

Her stunned silence must have gone on a little too long, because he said quickly, "We don't have to use this, obviously. You can throw it away right now, if you want. You know what you're doing."

"Zach…" She trailed off, shaking her head in disbelief. "I absolutely do *not* know what I'm doing. Ever."

He cracked a smile. "I know. But it'd be rude to point that out."

"Oh, and you're never rude," she muttered, but there was no bite to her sarcasm. She couldn't manage it. She studied the colourful pages, and for a moment, ridiculous tears prickled behind her eyes. He'd highlighted the signing she was booked to attend, the workshops she might be interested in. He'd written notes in the margins in his messy scrawl, like the sweetest spider on earth had crawled across the page on inky feet.

If we go to that breakfast, we can have a late lunch to fit this marketing workshop in.

Do you like this author? I recognise her name and I think you're the one who gave it to me.

She didn't have the words to describe what a relief this was—or rather, she did, but they were all too earnest and adoring. Setting them free right now, while she brimmed with ill-advised emotion, would be like striking a match in a room full of gas. For Christ's sake, all he'd done was print out a schedule and make some notes, except that *wasn't* all, because he'd done it for her—and the way that made her feel…

No. No. He's my friend. That's all this feeling is: just friendship and desire.

Yeah. Like books were just paper and ink.

Still, she pulled herself together and gave Zach a purely platonic pat on the shoulder. Then, for emphasis, she said, "Thanks, mate."

He arched a brow, maybe because her voice was

rougher than gravel, maybe because she'd just used the word *mate* for the first time in her life. "No problem. So, what's the plan?"

"This—" she tapped the folder "—is now, officially, the plan. We're already registered, so after we get settled in, we'll..." She consulted the newly christened Master Schedule. "We'll go down to dinner. I suppose it's a good chance to, er, mingle."

He chuckled. "You sound thrilled. I take it mingling is your favourite thing."

"Oh, yeah. For sure." She ignored his smirk and went to unzip her suitcase, dumping out the stack of books at the top. "I need a shower, but you should go first."

"If that's what you want." He paused on his way to the bathroom, running a hand over her pile of books. "So, this is why your suitcase weighs as much as a baby elephant. I should've known. Hey, what's—?"

"Nothing," she said quickly, snatching a heavy, silver-blue book from his hand. Of course that one would catch his eye. It was her favourite cover of all time, after all, with its iridescent colours, its delicate lines, its embossed lettering. Lettering that looked particularly beautiful on the author's name.

But, judging by the look of faint amusement Zach shot her, he hadn't noticed that last part. "You know, it's okay if you read sex books," he said dryly. "You don't need to hide it."

She scoffed, shoving the book firmly under her pyjamas. "*Sex books?* I'm assuming you mean erotica."

"Whatever you want to call it. I can't judge. I read Ruth's freaky comic, after all."

She paused, narrowing her eyes at him. She knew about Ruth's web comic, but sci-fi wasn't her thing, so she'd never actually read it. "What's freaky about Ruth's comic?"

"Three words," he said. "Alien desk sex."

Rae tried to process that for a moment, then decided it wasn't going to happen. "Take a shower, Davis."

He shook his head, chuckling at her expression. "Are you scandalised? You are."

"No," she lied. "I'm not."

"You're cute, sometimes, you know that?"

"Piss off."

"Real cute."

She glared at his retreating back until he was safely locked in the bathroom. Then she unpacked the things she needed tonight and shoved the rest of her suitcase into the wardrobe, including the hidden book she shouldn't have. When she was done, she flopped down on the bed and listened to the spray of the shower through the wall. Tried not to think about Zach standing under it. Counted the dots in the dot-patterned carpet and did *not* let her mind wander.

Fifteen minutes later, Zach walked out of the bathroom with dark jeans hanging low on his hips and a navy, collared shirt... in his hands. Which was, Rae reflected, both a useless and wonderful place for a shirt to be. He was humming to himself, but her mind was too scrambled to decipher the tune. She couldn't process sound *and* watch water droplets roll over his skin.

Of course, she shouldn't be watching the droplets at all, should she? Giving herself a mental slap, Rae tore her gaze away—and found his eyes on hers. Burning. Intense.

His absent humming stopped abruptly. For a heartbeat, the air seemed to crackle with electricity, like thunder might boom at any moment and shake them both to their cores. But the clock ticked, a second passed, and the tension vanished. She wondered if he'd felt it at all.

He turned his back on her, facing the mirror as he put on his shirt. "Sometimes I have no idea what you're thinking."

Thank God. "I was thinking you must be allergic to clothing. You seem to spend half your life barely dressed."

He snorted, buttoning up the shirt. Bit by bit, the carved brilliance of his body disappeared. She wanted to rip the fabric off his back and set it on fire, then do the same to every shirt within a five-mile radius, just in case. "I promise I'm not allergic. Just lazy. Er..." Something uncertain entered his voice, and she saw him frown in the mirror. "Does it bother you? Because—"

Oh, no. She wasn't about to make him feel awkward just because she had a sordid sort-of-crush. "It doesn't bother me," she said firmly, forcing a jovial laugh. Pretending he was Nate or Evan. "But you know how I get around muscles."

It worked. He chuckled. "Yeah, I know. You lost it when we saw *Aquaman.*"

Her cheeks heated. "I don't think I was that bad."

"Are you joking? I think you actually moaned a few times." He turned around, giving her a sweet, innocent smile. "It's okay if you came a little bit. I'm sure you're not alone."

She slapped her hands over her face. "You're so fucking annoying. I'm going to shower."

He laughed as she scurried away, blissfully unaware that she was just as into him as she was into Jason Momoa. On a physical level, obviously, which was the only level Rae felt anything. Ever. She spent the length of her cold shower reminding herself of that fact, scrubbing her skin clean and her mind free of Zach-related thoughts. By the time she'd wriggled into her outfit and slapped on some makeup, she'd all but forgotten the whole thing. She was too busy staring at her own reflection and thinking about what a twat she looked.

This was why she hated Events with a capital E. She never felt excited or sparkly enough, so she'd make up for it by dressing nice and jabbing herself in the eye with a mascara wand. Then she'd come face to face with the finished product and realise she looked like her usual dull self, playing dress-up. Her lipstick was too bright, she should learn to use concealer, her eyebrows were uneven, and now she was agonising over her appearance like she'd travelled back in time to her teens.

Rae had not enjoyed her teens.

She checked her watch, sighed, and unlocked the bathroom door. Zach was lying on his side of the bed, a mirror image of the way she'd waited for him to shower. He had the hotel brochure in his hands and appeared to be reading the list of amenities like it was fine literature. There was a slight wrinkle between his dark eyebrows and a silky-straight lock of ebony hair slashed over his pale forehead. For some reason, she couldn't stop staring at his socks, charcoal grey against the white sheets. He had big feet. She shouldn't be surprised.

"What'd you do in there?" he asked, turning a page.

"Sacrifice a—?" He looked up, and the words cut out like he'd swallowed his tongue. His brows rose, his gaze raking over her like she'd turned into an alien.

She swallowed, dredging up a smile. "Did I sacrifice a what?"

No dice. He remained silent as he studied her, though at least he'd closed his mouth now.

She shut her eyes and fingered the hem of her skirt. She'd meant for the cream swing dress to give her a sexy-smart dinner look, only it felt a bit too short. She'd gained some weight recently, so now her arse and belly took up fabric that her legs were sorely missing. *Sigh.* "Do I look ridiculous?"

"No."

Rae opened her eyes and checked his expression. Zach looked deadly serious. Emphasis on *deadly.* She relaxed. "Oh. Good. I don't often wear makeup—"

"You never wear makeup," he said. "I have never in my life seen you wearing makeup." He stood and crossed the hotel room in three strides, until he was right up in her space. His gaze settled on her lipsticked mouth and he huffed out a breath, nostrils flaring. He was in dragon mode. He'd start breathing fire in a second; then he'd catch her in the cage of his sharp teeth and fly her away to his lair. Maybe in a hundred years some knight would come to rescue her, and she'd say, *"Oh, sorry for the misunderstanding, but I actually like it here."* Then Zach would eat the knight alive.

"Your lips," he told her gravely, "are red."

She blinked. "Yep. That's, er, the colour they should be. Based on the lipstick that I, you know, applied. So. Thanks for the confirmation."

He didn't laugh. He didn't even tell her to shut up. He looked down at her body, his jaw tight. "Is this because of Kevin?"

The question was so unexpected, she thought she might've misheard. "Kevin?"

Helpfully, he added, "Your ex-husband."

"Oh, yes, *that* Kevin. I do get confused, sometimes." She rolled her eyes, irritated. "No, this is not because of Kevin. I thought I should look nice for dinner. You're wearing a shirt, for God's sake."

"I didn't want to embarrass you."

She opened her mouth, then closed it. The simple honesty in his voice had just knocked the air out of her.

Before she could formulate an answer, he added, "I didn't know you owned a dress."

"I own several, but why would I bother shaving my legs just to waste the sight on Duke and Mrs. Needham at the news shop?"

The joke, or maybe just her light-hearted tone, punctured his intense bubble. His lips twitched. A moment later, he chuckled under his breath. "Yeah. Fair point. Listen, let's do this again, okay?"

Um... "Do what?"

"This. The moment. I freaked out. But what's supposed to happen is, you come out of the bathroom and it's this whole reveal, and I say you look like Halle Berry or something. Yeah. Go on." He put his hands on her shoulders and turned her around, steering her toward the bathroom door. "Let's do this again."

She blinked, caught between confusion and slow, steady affection. "You want me to go in there and walk out again?"

"Yep. Not until I'm ready, though. Go."

She must be high after applying her makeup in a room full of deodorant fumes because for some reason, she went along with it.

A few seconds after she re-entered the bathroom, he called, "Ready."

Fighting a grin, she marched into the bedroom. He was sitting down, just like before, apparently reading the hotel brochure—but he clearly wasn't focusing on the words. Something lovely danced in his eyes and played at the corners of his mouth.

Slowly, he asked, "What'd you do in there? Sacrifice a sea sponge?"

"Seriously?" she snorted. "That's what you're going with? A *sea sponge?*"

"What else could you sacrifice in a bathroom? I considered saying *giant sewer rat*, but I didn't want to freak you out."

"Good call," she said dryly.

And, finally, finally, he looked up.

This was all pretend. He'd seen her five bloody minutes ago. Even so, his gaze bit into her like jumper cables and revved the hell out of her engine. He put down the brochure, stood, and said, "Something McRae, you look fucking incredible."

Laughter bubbled out of her. "*Something* again? You know, I think I like it."

"Lauren," he said, stepping toward her. "Charlotte. Amy."

"If only."

"Heaven. Angel. Divinity." His socked feet nudged her stockinged ones. His hands cupped her upper arms, and she felt an odd tension thrum through his body and shudder into hers.

"No," she managed to whisper, "but I'm glad you're thinking bigger."

He whispered, too. "Rae. You. Look. Beautiful."

"Thank you. And, Zach—I don't know what you were talking about, before, but no matter what you wear, you could never embarrass me."

He smiled that lazy-sexy smile. "I don't know about that. Next to you, most guys would seem lacking. And now you're wearing—Christ, sunshine, are those earrings?"

"Yep. I pulled out all the stops."

"Didn't even know you had piercings." He arched a brow. "Hey, want to know about my pierc—?"

"Nope. Let's go to dinner now." She whirled around, grabbed her shoes, and slid them on as she went. He followed her into the corridor, laughing all the way. The warmth between them filled her up like helium.

She shouldn't want anything else from him, not when he already made her so happy. But she'd always been a little bit greedy.

CHAPTER EIGHT

WAS it weird to fixate on the way a woman typed? Probably.

Ten minutes into the buffet dinner, Rae's face had lit up and she'd reached for her phone. "I'm sorry," she said. "I just got an idea. Do you mind if I write it down?"

Zach waved her on and watched her hands. He was well aware of the men around them studying her long, brown legs beneath the table; her mouth, red like a warning sign; the breasts her dress clung to so lovingly. But all he could focus on were those hands: the way she laced her fingers together at the back of her phone, creating a careful cradle. The thoughtful hover of her thumbs over each key, like the words she chose mattered, down to the very letter. Then there was her frown of concentration and the press of her tongue inside her cheek...

He blinked away, disorientated, as if he'd been staring into the sun.

Earlier, when she'd come out of the bathroom, he'd wondered for one wild moment if she wanted Kevin's attention. As a friend who protected her interests and hated her ex-husband in solidarity, Zach had been unnerved by the possibility. But he should've known better; these days, Rae lived for herself. Whether or not she saw it, felt it, believed in it all the time, she was Ravenswood Rae no matter where she went. He'd stay by her side until she grew comfortable enough to realise that, and it would be no hardship.

In the lift, she'd sent her reflection pleased little smiles that made his heart melt.

Now, she stopped typing and looked up. When their eyes met, she smiled and leaned forward, her feet nudging his beneath the table. She might as well have set him on fire. Just the slightest brush of contact, leather on leather, and his whole body thrilled to life like they'd never touched before. *Jesus.*

"Done," she said excitedly. "I'm not sure where that came from, but thank God it came at all."

Great," he croaked, still grappling with the sensations spiralling through him. "Lots of magical murder going on in your head, then?"

"Tons," she said with satisfaction. God, he liked her satisfaction.

"Do you want to rush through dinner, so you can go upstairs and write?"

"Oh, that's a great idea. If you don't mind. I should strike while my brain's being cooperative," she said, and went back to devouring her plate of tempura prawns like it was her last meal. Unsurprisingly, she finished before he could manage his steak, and got up for a second course.

Which is how Zach ended up alone at the table, chewing overdone beef like a cow with cud, while a swarm of eager men chatted Rae up by the fucking pasta bar. For some reason, he found the sight profoundly irritating.

A guy on the table to his left leaned over, smiling beneath a bristly, white moustache. "That's the missus, eh?"

Zach grunted.

"She's impressive, that one," the man said.

It was true, and it sounded complimentary, so Zach grunted again. Thank God for the food in his mouth. Without it, he might've said something rude like *Fuck off and leave me to my creepy staring.*

The poor guy seemed to get the message, anyway.

Rae now had a serving spoon in her hand, but she couldn't reach the chicken arrabiata because she was still surrounded by men. Older men with grey hair and gravitas who were probably successful writers with brilliant minds like hers. She seemed to know most of them, and she looked happy enough, so he couldn't interrupt. Which was fine. She deserved to be fawned over. He, as her friend, was glad. The tight, hot feeling in his middle was a very pure and platonic kind of pleasure.

Eventually, she grabbed some pasta and left her adoring fans in the dust. For the next hour, she sparkled like champagne while Zach grew dull beside her, hovering helplessly over his own body, watching himself be grim and difficult. He didn't know what was happening, and he couldn't seem to control it. Still, forcing smiles and seeming fine had been his coping mechanism for years, so he tried his best.

It wasn't enough. When they finished dinner, Rae stopped him on the way to the exit. In the shadow of a sharp, potted fern, she rose up on tiptoe to whisper in his ear. "Hey. Are you okay?" Her palm lay over his heart, fingers splayed, searing through his shirt.

He touched her lower back, just to steady her, but it felt like the one place on earth his hand was born to rest. All the edgy tension rippled right out of him, and he exhaled through the dizziness of the change. He'd been not-okay, but now he was just fine. Like magic.

He was starting to irritate himself.

"Don't worry about me," he murmured. "I'm sorry I'm being so..."

She arched her brows and waited, forcing him to finish the sentence.

He sighed. "Sorry I'm being so quiet. I think I ate too much."

Her laughter was incredulous. "You could eat a truck-full of pizza, and it wouldn't be too much."

His lips twitched. She wasn't wrong.

"It's okay to be in a bad mood, you know. I don't need you to entertain me all the time." She gave him a considering look with those pretty doe eyes. Her hesitation tasted like icing sugar, like care. "I like being around you, Zach. Even when you're not performing. Okay?"

Honestly? He felt like she'd just whacked him over the head with a two-by-four. This was the sweetest concussion of his life. "Okay," he said, and meant it. His hand at the small of her back felt electric.

She smiled. Then she turned away, and her expression changed. Drooped. He followed her gaze and found the cause: at the centre of the dining hall, a group of adults cooed happily as a golden-haired toddler stumbled across the floor. Then a beaming, equally golden-haired woman came along to sweep the kid up in her arms. The toddler squealed and laughed and clapped its pudgy hands. Rae looked like she'd been teabagged by a ghost, her expression caught between shock and horror.

Zach didn't want kids, so he'd always assumed Rae was childless for the same reason. Now he wondered if he'd been way off.

"Hey," he said, grabbing her hand, clutching her limp fingers tight. "You good?"

She blinked a few times, like a robot rebooting. "I'm fine," she breathed, and she did look better now. "I was just... surprised."

He nodded dubiously. "It is pretty late for a kid to be up."

"No," she said. "That's—that's Kevin's son."

Now *Zach* probably looked like he'd been teabagged by a ghost. "What?"

"That's Kevin's son. It looks just like him. And the woman holding him is Billie." She nodded again, as if talking it through had made her certain. "They must have brought him to the convention."

"Why the fuck would they bring a toddler to a convention?"

"Maybe they couldn't get a sitter."

"I thought your husband was rolling in it?"

There was a flash of familiar fire in her rakish, one-sided smile. "Maybe he wanted to make this a family affair. He likes attention. Oh, God, everyone's noticed me." She stiffened. The fire flickered, went out.

"No, they haven't," Zach lied, sliding an arm over her shoulders, dragging her into his side. Despite his words, curious eyes crept toward them, two by two. The room seemed to be holding its breath, wondering how Rae would take this. He felt her crumbling against him with sheer embarrassment, and suddenly, he was desperate to fix it.

"They're all staring at me," she hissed.

"They've been staring all night. You're beautiful."

Laughter bubbled out of her, sharper than it should be. "I'm lurking in the shadows, spying on my ex-husband's baby."

"Actually," Zach said, "we're lurking in the shadows because you look like dessert."

She tipped her head back to frown at him in confusion. He couldn't help himself. He kissed her snub little nose.

She sucked in a breath, and he felt like she'd taken it directly from his lungs. That was how they worked: she acted, he reacted. Or maybe it was the other way around, a cycle that had started without him noticing. He didn't know. He didn't *want* to know; he just wanted to make things better. This was exactly the kind of disaster he'd come to help with, after all.

He wrapped his arms around her and spoke into the fall of her hair. "I'm about to fake-boyfriend you."

After a moment, she relaxed against his chest, flashing him a familiar smirk. "Is that a verb?"

"It is now." He grazed a kiss over her cheekbone. Lips, skin, pressure. He'd done this a thousand times—not with her, but then, it shouldn't really matter that it was with her.

And yet, it did. The way the tension slid out of her body, the way her fingers tangled in the fabric of his shirt, the way she stared at his mouth when he was done... it all mattered.

"Is this what fake-boyfriending is?" she whispered.

"It's a process," he told her solemnly, and kissed her forehead. He could hear his own pulse and it was frantic.

She smiled a little. "This isn't bad."

"Glad to hear it. Tell me when to stop."

"You don't need to stop."

The TV screen of his mind glitched, flashing a fantasy he wasn't prepared for: Rae, under him, begging him not to stop. Then the glitch vanished, and it was back to his regular programming.

He swallowed, then kissed her jaw. She gave a soft, helpless moan that was doomed to live inside him forever. He'd never forget it. He'd be at the supermarket in fifteen years' time trying to choose a flavour of ice cream, and out of nowhere he'd remember Rae moaning because he'd kissed her fucking jaw.

"Oh my God," she muttered, stiffening in his arms, her gaze skittering away. She was embarrassed. "I'm so sor—"

"Don't." He nudged her chin until she looked him in the eyes. And then, finally, he kissed her on the mouth.

He hadn't exactly planned to. They hadn't even

discussed this. He'd been waiting for her to bring up Physical Fake Boyfriend Boundaries, but she never had, and now... here they were. He started carefully, his lips gliding over hers, testing, asking—but soon enough, a seething, potent *something* spilled out of him, turning the slight touch intense. He felt as if he'd shoved her against the nearest wall and hiked up her skirt. Kissing her like this, barely breathing her in, was making him shake. He just hoped to God she wouldn't notice, because he didn't know how to explain it.

The way she kissed him back was dizzying. She was careful, too, her lips slow and curious, like a question. *Is this what we're doing?*

He increased the pressure, his hands tightening around her hips. *Yes. This is what we're doing.*

Her tongue barely touched his, sweet and slick and sexy as fuck. *Okay. I like it.*

That's when things spiralled out of control.

She was hot, liquid, molten. She pressed herself against him, and he shocked himself by feeling the opposite of nothing. He felt everything, all at once, without an ounce of bloody warning, and wondered how he hadn't seen the signs. He raised a hand to cradle the back of her neck and grew rapidly addicted to the feel of holding her in secret, private places. Places no-one else could touch. He wanted to run his unworthy palms up her thighs, to trace a finger down the column of her spine, to sweep his thumb over the dip of her navel. He settled for pushing his tongue deeper into her mouth. She tasted of wine in a silver cup, of cool, clever steel. She kissed like she was starving, and it made his chest cave in. He'd feed her. Of course he would. Whatever she wanted. As long as what she wanted was him.

He didn't realise he was hard until delicious pain shot through his body. His jeans were throttling his cock. Devouring his fake girlfriend with an audience of Way Too Many hadn't made him hesitate, but a public erection felt a little too far and a lot too teenage. He meant to break the kiss gently, but in the end, they came up for air as if they'd been drowning. They stared at each other with matching wide eyes, and he wondered if they had matching thoughts. Maybe. Because she looked shocked, and he sure as shit *felt* shocked.

He was into Rae. Who knew?

And what should he do about it?

The most obvious answer was nothing. Reasons piled high. They were friends; he was here to support her; she'd specifically invited him because he wouldn't make it weird or try to get in her pants. And anyway, she'd already offered, and he'd said no, which meant he'd fucked his chances, and—

And earlier, in the elevator, when he'd touched her without an audience, she'd turned away.

The memory was a timely reminder that their mind-blowing, world-altering kiss had been nothing but performance—to her, anyway. Everything between them was fake, except for their friendship, which was a different kind of everything. So Zach dragged himself from dizzy, *oh-fuck* heaven back down to depressing earth, where Rae was breathing heavy in his arms.

He frowned, studying her face. "Is your heart okay?"

"That's not how it works," she told him, then hesitated.

"Actually, I'm not sure how it works. I never finished the NHS pamphlet."

Helpfully, worry ruined his hard-on. "Rae."

"What? I get along just fine."

"*Rae.*"

She rolled her eyes, but there was something mischievous about her mouth. He had a feeling she was being difficult on purpose, as if bickering would defuse this thing between them. It did. He was grateful. They untangled themselves, and it was almost like nothing had happened. He kept hold of her hand for the benefit of the audience he'd forgotten.

The baby and Billie were nowhere to be seen. He watched Rae carefully, but she didn't even look for them. She had faraway eyes, like she was dreaming up different worlds.

He was glad she wasn't dwelling on the kiss. That was for the best. Because if she'd felt that lurch of attraction, too, and if she tried to touch him in private, he might ask for something she'd never offered. Something close and silent and strong, skin-to-skin in the dark, all intimate secrets and whispered confessions. And she would tell him no.

"You still want to go upstairs?" he asked.

She didn't answer. Her tongue ran over her lower lip, and his heart shivered.

He squeezed her hand. "Rae."

"Hmm?" She blinked back to life. "Oh, sorry. What?"

"Upstairs?"

Ah," she said. "Yes. I need to write."

Zach nodded, tugging her toward the elevators. Her

plans complemented his perfectly, because he needed to log into his demisexual forum and search for discussions tagged, *Oops, I'm suddenly attracted to my friend/fake date. Please help.*

Or maybe he could start his own thread with that very question?

No. No. Not yet. He had too much to think about. Such as the very painful truth currently weighing on his shoulders.

He'd just kissed this woman with everything he had, down to his fucking soul. And she would never know it had been real.

UPSTAIRS, Rae typed her own version of lorem ipsum and tried to remain cool while Zach sat beside her, the sheets pulled up to his waist, his bare chest gilded by the sultry lamplight. After fiddling with his phone for half an hour, he'd taken out his contact lenses and put on honest-to-God horn rimmed, tortoiseshell glasses. Then he'd started reading some sci-fi novel like the sexiest nerd she'd ever seen. Even if he hadn't ruined her with his mouth in the middle of the dining hall, the sight would have scrambled her brain.

But he had. He *had* ruined her, without even trying—so utterly that, an hour later, she still had to remind herself to breathe. She also reminded herself that he'd been performing. That the hard press of his erection against her belly, that jutting steel she felt the ghost of even now, was simply a physical reaction to stimulation. It didn't mean a damned thing, because he'd made it crystal clear that he didn't see her that way. She could never let herself forget it.

"How's the writing going?" he asked after a while, and her cheeks heated.

"Fine," she said tightly. It wasn't exactly a lie. She couldn't focus at the minute because he was suffocating her with sexiness both past and present, but the knot inside her mind had started to unravel the moment they'd arrived in Manchester. Ideas were flowing fast now, dripping steadily like blood and wine did in the venomous world of her imagination. It was as if coming here and facing her fears had already set her worries to rest. As if she were one of her own heroines, trapped in a vicious court, proving her strength to herself with every inch of control she took.

Tonight hadn't been so bad, after all. Largely thanks to Zach.

He removed his glasses and closed the book, marking his page with a finger. "Do you want to talk through anything?"

This was a habit of theirs, one she still couldn't believe she'd fallen into. Discussing ideas with Zach, telling him stories before they made their way onto paper, helped Rae think. And yet, every time, a warning siren sounded at the back of her mind: *You can't trust him with that.*

She did her best to ignore that siren. There were all sorts of things she couldn't trust Zach with, but her work wasn't one of them. "Maybe tomorrow," she murmured. "Right now, I think I'm ready for bed."

"Me, too," he agreed, and his smile knocked her on her arse.

They packed up and turned off the bedside lamps. The room's gauzy curtains let in hints of city light, so she could see the outline of Zach's body beside her. He was a forbidding, shadowed landscape, a mountain she shouldn't want to climb. But she did want to, in more ways than one. During that kiss downstairs, the man she'd always thought of as emotionally safe had plucked at something tender and possessive in her chest. It was sickening, not to mention gravely alarming. If she'd developed feelings for the twenty-eight-year-old friend who'd firmly turned her down, she was going to be *very* displeased with herself.

Rae sighed, a self-indulgent, gusty huff that she really, really enjoyed.

Then Zach murmured, sounding much too alert, "You awake?"

Shit.

She considered lying, then remembered that lying would still reveal she was awake. Playing dead, like Duke sometimes did when it was time to visit the vet, seemed beneath her. In the end, she cleared her throat and said, "Yes."

The sheets rustled. There were a few violent dips in the mattress, like a bedtime earthquake, and the shape of Zach in the dark transformed. He'd rolled over. Now they lay side by side, staring holes into each other, and she felt the ghost of his breath against her cheek. She could smell the mint toothpaste they shared, too. Every exhalation caused a zing up her spine and a flutter in her belly, which was rather inconvenient, all things considered.

"You okay?" he asked.

"Are you?" she shot back, like it was a trick question.

He huffed out a laugh and she imagined him shaking his head at her prickliness. "Relax, Rae." Easy for him to say. He wasn't coping with doomed lust 24 hours a day. "I wanted to ask you about what happened after dinner."

The silence that followed was short but heavy. She panicked and wondered if he could secretly read minds. Maybe her thoughts were getting so out of hand that even he, after years of hiding his power for his own protection, could no longer feign ignorance. She was preparing a speech about how he could trust her not to sell his story to the papers, or report his existence to the government, when he finally spoke.

"Are kids... a difficult subject for you?" There was a wince in his voice, like he thought she might burst into tears.

Oh. No mind-reading powers, then. Thank goodness for small mercies. "No," she said, then added, since people always wanted to know: "I don't have any kids because I've never wanted them."

"So, you're not emotionally gutted by the sight of Kevin Junior, or anything?"

She wrinkled her nose. "You may find this hard to believe, but I am a woman who does not regret being childless."

"I just wanted to make sure. But no, I don't find it hard to believe." He didn't sound like he was lying.

Still, she narrowed her eyes suspiciously at the outline of his head. "Why not? Most people do."

"Probably because I don't want kids either."

"Ha," she barked, and remembered a similar conversation in another life. Earnest eyes behind sharp spectacles and words she'd worried she might never hear. "That's what Kevin said, and look. You'll change your mind." About everything. She knew that well enough.

Mildly, Zach asked, "How many people told you that you'd change your mind?"

Rae opened her mouth, then shut it. Blinked. Finally, she tutted, "Stop that."

There was a smile in his voice. "Stop what?"

"Making sensible arguments."

"I can't help it," he said. "I have so much sense."

She laughed, but the sound was brittle because she was still on edge. She could feel him beside her, heat and weight and aching presence, and she couldn't shake the worry that he must be able to feel her too—a mass of unrequited lust and seething need and something deeper, more vulnerable, horribly emotional. Something she couldn't bring herself to face head-on.

Silence fell, so she closed her eyes and tried her level best to sleep. But then Zach spoke again. "Another thing. About the kiss…" He trailed off for a moment, leaving a yawning gap of possibility between them. Then he said, "I'm sorry."

Everything in her tensed. Sorry? As in, *I'm sorry, but I know you're obsessed with me? Sorry, but you're freaking me out, and I'm leaving tomorrow before this goes further?* Like helium leaking through a pinpricked balloon, she squeaked, "For what?"

"For kissing you like that. Without asking."

The breath rushed out of her lungs. *Oh.* "It's fine," she said. "If I hadn't wanted to, I would've told you."

He shifted uncomfortably—guiltily, she realised. "Well, you couldn't really shove me off in public without blowing our cover."

This really must be bothering him, because he used a phrase like *blowing our cover* without milking every ounce of its ridiculousness.

"I didn't need to shove you." She reached out, meaning to pat him reassuringly, but then she remembered that he was shirtless and she was desperate for him. She lowered her hand. "If I'd pushed you even slightly, or hadn't kissed you back, or been stiff or uncertain, you would've stopped. Wouldn't you?"

"Of course I would."

"But I grabbed you and stuck my tongue down your throat instead. We're good."

He exhaled. "Okay. If you're sure. You *can* be mad at me, if you want."

"Zach."

"Okay, yeah." She heard the smile in his voice, and he was back to his usual devil-may-care self. "So. Boundaries, everybody's favourite thing. Let's talk."

She supposed it was about time, wasn't it? She hadn't even thought about this stuff, but of course he'd have his shit together. "You're the one who's helping me, which makes you the potentially vulnerable party." When he snorted, she pursed her lips and forged on. "You go first."

She felt him shift, saw mountains move in the dark, and imagined him shrugging those massive shoulders. "We already hold hands and shit like that, right?"

"Right." She fidgeted beneath the blankets. Wondered what would happen if she did something mortifying while they slept, like hunting down his body heat and curling around him the way she sometimes curled around Duke.

"Then there's kissing," Zach said, all studious and distant. If he'd put on his glasses and started lecturing her on the etymology of the word, she wouldn't have been surprised. "Did you mind what we did tonight? I mean, is it something we could do again, or would you rather not?"

He spoke carefully, like each word had sharp edges he needed to keep an eye on. She wondered if he was worried that she'd liked it a little too much.

She should take kissing off the table, but she was weak, so she said, "We can do it again if necessary."

"You sure?"

"I am."

"Then we need to do something about this wall."

She faltered, blinking through the darkness. "Uh... what wall?"

"The imaginary but very sturdy wall you put between us the minute we left the dining hall." He sounded faintly amused, mildly exasperated, and beneath it all, concerned. "You're freaking out, right? You don't need to. It was just—"

"I know," she interrupted, because she couldn't bear to hear him say it out loud. *It was just pretend.*

There was a pause. Then, quietly, he asked, "Where are you?"

"What?"

His meaning sank in just as his warm, rough hand came to rest tentatively on her shoulder. He skated his fingertips down her arm, caught her wrist, and pulled her hand toward his face. Then, without warning, she felt his teeth sink gently into the meat of her palm. She sucked in a breath and pressed her knees together while the bite tingled its way through her body, heading directly to her nipples. Teasing, tightening, torturing.

She choked out, "What are you doing?"

"You're all stiff like you think I'm gonna bite. So, I bit. Now relax."

Was her breathing too fast? Was her heartbeat too loud? Could he tell her clit was already aching, her pulse thrumming hard between her thighs? She wasn't sure. She squeaked something unintelligible and tried to seem unaffected.

He laced their hands together and murmured, "See? This is fine. Same as always."

Yeah. As always, I want to jump you.

But there was something new, too: a burning desire to curl up inside him and make all that sweet strength her home.

"Okay?" he asked.

"Okay," she lied.

He drew her closer. She might as well have been a spare pillow, for all the effort he put into it: just a few gentle pulls and they were a breath apart, his arm around her waist.

He kissed her knuckles in the dark and spoke with

iron in his voice. "Nothing is going to change between us. This weekend will not fuck anything up."

How ironic. She'd just been thinking that everything had to change and this weekend would fuck them up.

"We're gonna be the way we've always been," he said, like it was an incantation or an order to the universe. "Nothing's awkward," he told her. He was telling someone, anyway. *"We're* not awkward. Are we?"

"No," she said quickly. "No, Zach. We're perfect." It was mostly true. *He* was perfect, anyway. She wished she could tell him so.

"Then let's go to sleep."

She shouldn't have been able to obey. But maybe his words really were a spell, and maybe they sank into her skin, because all of a sudden, this situation didn't feel awkward at all. Lying beside him, touching him, felt... good.

She lay safe and warm in the cage of his arms, falling asleep to a reassuring thought. *This is not what love feels like. It doesn't hurt nearly enough.*

CHAPTER NINE

ZACH WASN'T SURPRISED to discover that Rae had honest-to-God fans.

They lined up in front of her decorated table, buzzing with eager excitement, clutching books to be signed and sliding awed looks her way when they thought she wasn't looking. He watched with a sappy smile on his face as a woman with dangerously pink cheeks squeezed her newly-signed paperback to her chest.

"I just loved *Blood Court* so much. Incredible, absolutely incredible. I can't wait to read the rest of Myra's story!"

"Oh, well, thank you," Rae said, all sweet and flattered. He could tell she was tempted to curl into an embarrassed ball under the onslaught of praise—but she didn't, because she was way too professional and completely badass.

"And your hair is so amazing," the woman beamed. "You look like a princess."

"Oh. Um…" Aaaand, Rae was officially broken, or at

least rebooting. "Thanks," she finally croaked, patting her head self-consciously. "Really, thank you."

He'd thought that *princess* thing a few times, himself. She always wore her hair down in the back and braided at the front, strands of grey sparkling at her temples. Zach had his suspicions about why she did it—but he wanted to know for sure. He wanted to know everything about her.

"Do you think she's okay?" The voice came from his left, where Rae's agent, Neil, had been hovering like an anxious genie for the last five minutes. "I feel like I should be around more, but she's technically done this before—or seen it before—on a much higher level, and I have a lot of clients here today..."

Zach let the lean, balding man shove out his worried, halting speech, hands wringing and frown deep. The guy was worn out and gentle like your grandpa's favourite chair, and for someone whose job—as Rae had explained —involved being an author's negotiator and protector, he sure did hesitate and bite his lip a lot. But then, Zach supposed, tons of people set aside their personal qualities in order to be good at their job. Neil probably managed to seem hardcore when it was time to talk contracts or whatever.

"She's fine," Zach told the older man, partly because it was true and partly because the guy's darting, rabbity eyes were starting to make even Zach nervous. "She knows exactly what she's doing. You can focus on the others."

"I just like to make sure everyone's taking rests," Neil winced.

"I've got it."

The older man paused, turning his dark eyes on Zach

in a moment of unnerving focus. "Do you know, I'm sure you do." Then he gave a mournful sigh and was back to his usual self, like that second of intensity had been a hallucination. "Well, alright then. I'll be off. Perhaps I'll see you at lunch."

"Yeah," Zach nodded, and Neil hurried away. Then Zach abandoned his post—a chair he'd dragged to the corner by Rae's stand—and went to see his girlfriend.

His *fake* girlfriend.

She finished saying goodbye to another reader, and he bent down to whisper in her ear. "So, you're kind of a big deal."

She snorted. "No."

"Yeah. Drink this." He put a fresh bottle of water by her poor, curled-up signing hand and kissed her cheek.

She rolled her eyes at him, then smiled at the next person in the queue. "Sorry. I'll just be a second."

The reader, a kid with waist-length braids and her own copy of *Blood Court* ready to be signed, nodded happily. Rae uncapped the water and took greedy gulps. Zach tried not to stare too lustfully at the delicate bob of her throat with each swallow; a lot of the influencers at this event were teenagers, and the way he wanted to look at Rae wasn't particularly PG.

When she put down the water, he waved a cereal bar at her. "You've signed a million books already. Your hand must be killing you."

She shrugged, unwrapped the bar, and took a bite. Nodding at the commotion across the vast hall, she said, "I'm nothing compared to the big names."

"Good thing I'm not comparing you to anyone. I'm here for you, and so's this huge queue of readers."

She bit her lip on a smile and looked away, pleasure sparkling around her. His body flooded with happiness in response, as if reassuring Rae was his life's purpose.

That morning, he'd opened his eyes to see her face and been hit with a bolt of contentment. Then he'd spent way too long staring at her in the dawn light, trying to convince himself that these feelings were nothing to worry about. Nothing he hadn't experienced before with every other woman he'd been genuinely attracted to.

But he didn't think that was true.

The emotions surging to life inside him were too intense to face head-on. All he could do was take glimpses from the corner of his eye, and feel their warmth, and know that he didn't want to dismiss them just because they complicated things. In the end, he'd devised a simple solution: right now, he would be whatever Rae needed. Because she deserved it, and because, for this weekend, she'd asked it of him. The rest, he could deal with later. He'd figure it out, probably when he was back at work next week pounding a lump of metal into art.

She finished the cereal bar in record time and tapped his nose with the empty wrapper. "Hey, daydreamer."

"Says you," he smiled.

She smiled back, so suddenly it took his breath away. "Thank you for this. No-one's ever—" The words cut out abruptly, as if they'd been snatched back. She frowned like her tongue had gone rogue and snapped her mouth shut with an audible *click*.

"No-one's ever what?" he demanded.

"Nothing." She turned away from him. "I should get back to work."

She meant that last part; he had no doubt. But that didn't make it any less of an excuse. "Tell me."

Her glare made him want to smile because it said she was still with him, irritated but easy rather than stiff and distant. "No."

"Tell me, or I'll tickle it out of you upstairs."

"Oh, piss off," she muttered, the glare sharpening. "I was just—I was just going to say—" The words had jagged edges, as if she physically couldn't manage them. But in the end, she pushed past it, chin up, eyes dark with determination. "I was just going to say, no-one's ever really looked after me before."

The words, quick and quiet, silenced him utterly. He hated everyone who'd failed her so thoroughly that she was moved by a fucking cereal bar and some water. He was desperate to *really* look after her, not just for an audience but every damn day, as if he had the right. But most of all, he wanted to touch her. Kissing her would be ideal, except he didn't feel like he had a valid excuse. There was no reason to fake-boyfriend her right now, not to that level.

He wanted to do it anyway.

She shrugged and added airily, "Of course, I suppose that's what you're here for."

The words sounded wrong coming out of her mouth because five seconds ago she'd been nervous and embarrassed. Zach shot her a hard look. She must realise that *this* wasn't part of the performance—that he just cared about her, for Christ's sake. But her gaze avoided his with impressive determination, so, clearly, she preferred to ignore that particular fact. Perhaps she found tenderness easier to take if it was disguised as something else.

Alright. He could do that. He could ease her into being looked after.

Since it was his *job*, Zach kissed her forehead before straightening. "Go on. I know you're dying to get back to work."

And she was. She flashed him a grateful smile, then turned to the girl with the braids and said, "I'm so sorry."

"It's fine," the girl chirped, rushing up to the table. "Is that your boyfriend?" She lowered her voice, but Zach still heard her as he walked away. "He's so handsome."

"He is, isn't he?" Rae murmured, and she almost sounded... *dreamy*.

He bit back a smile. At least his face was good for something.

CONVINCING ZACH TO attend an afternoon panel without her wasn't easy, but in the end, Rae managed it. The discussion of complex magic systems sounded fun, but she knew herself well enough to realise that she was overwhelmed by the busy day so far. She needed to lie down like an old Victorian lady. She also needed a couple of hours away from Zach, because trying to convince everyone that they were together, while subtly showing him she knew they really *weren't*, was starting to depress her.

But when she reached their shadowed, still-messy

room, she didn't feel relieved or relaxed. Instead, she was de-energised, like a flower taken out of the sun. She told herself it was tiredness, and her ever-weary body allowed the white lie. She'd slept wonderfully last night, but she could always—*always*—use a nap, so she peeled off her clothes and dumped them on the back of a chair. Then she thought, *Fuck it*, and added her bra to the pile. She'd wake up before the talk finished, and dress before Zach came upstairs.

She wove the length of her hair into a rough braid, searched through the mountain of pillows for her silk scarf, and came up empty handed. It must be around here somewhere, but she couldn't be arsed to find it right now. Wearing nothing but her knickers, she stumbled into bed.

Before her eyes could slide shut, Rae grabbed her phone to set an alarm—and discovered five missed calls from the usual suspect. Anxiety shot her comfortable tiredness out of a cannon. She knew she'd ignored maternal criticism one too many times, lately—and nothing made her mother nastier.

Her notifications displayed the first few words of a text message.

Marilyn: I don't know what...

Rae could finish that sentence without any prompting. *I don't know what I did to deserve such a cruel and selfish daughter.*

She set her jaw and deleted the text without opening it. Then she re-opened the message she'd received that morning, one that had made her smile all day.

Hannah: This animal of yours is a big baby. What have you been doing to him?

It was accompanied by a picture of Duke lolling around on the floor, his tongue flopping like a flag, Zach's niece and nephew brushing his long, chestnut fur. Rae stared at the image until her heart slowed, her nerves eased, and tiredness crept in again. *There.* She'd replied to Hannah earlier, so she put her phone away and settled into the bed's plush embrace.

Christ, she missed her dog.

But at least these sheets smelled like Zach. Before they'd left for breakfast that morning, Rae had hung a sign on the door to tell Housekeeping there was no need to clean. She'd thought of it as saving the staff some work, but now she wondered if her subconscious had quietly planned this: sneaking upstairs to curl up in the pure peace that was her fake boyfriend.

She really wouldn't put it past herself. It seemed like every time she laid eyes on Zach, she stumbled treacherously closer to the edge of... something. One of these days, she would trip and fall. And then where would she be? Up shit creek, that's where. Because they were just friends, he didn't want her, and, while she probably *could* trust a man again, she saw no reason to bother. It certainly couldn't end well.

But that didn't stop the smell of him from lulling her to sleep, and it didn't stop her from dreaming of him, either.

Rae's skin was warm, kissed by sultry ocean air, shadowed within a cool, marble hotel room. She was on holiday. She was with Zach, tangled up in white sheets. He leaned over her, that lazy smile lighting up his blue eyes. He ran an ice cube over her sweltering skin, and she gasped. He followed the cold, wet trail with his warm, wet tongue and she moaned. He bit her hip the way he'd bitten her hand last night.

Rae's eyes flicked open like a doll's and she stared up at the ceiling, panting, lust shaking through her. She knew exactly what she wanted, and she was close enough to sleep to let herself take it. Her legs splayed open, and her hips rocked as if searching for something. She licked her fingers, shoved a hand into her knickers, and touched herself. Parted her swollen folds with desperate, decisive movements and thought about the way he'd kissed her, the way he'd crushed her to him. Last night in bed, he'd only touched her arm, but she massaged her clit and imagined his hand gliding between her breasts, over her belly, easing beneath her underwear. Imagined watching his knuckles shift through the cotton as he worked her, his murmured praise hot and breathless in her ear. Her pussy tightened, her mouth opened on a gasp—

There was a slow, quiet *click* as the hotel room's door opened.

Shit.

She yanked her hand out of her pants, squeezed her knees together and bit back a whimper of wild disappointment. Precious seconds from orgasm, but now her heart raced for another reason entirely. Fuck, fuck, fuck. She battled free of the sheets and leapt guiltily from the bed just as Zach rounded the corner and set eyes on her. Only when those eyes widened did Rae remember that she was essentially naked.

And then, like a terrible cherry plopped on a disaster sundae, black crept in at the edges of her vision. Too fast. She'd stood up too fast.

Oops.

ZACH WATCHED Rae close her eyes and catch herself against the wall, her splayed fingers brown and vulnerable against the harsh, white paint. He swallowed a curse. He'd researched POTS a while ago and confirmed everything she'd said: it was a circulatory condition that caused dizziness and fainting, one that *could* be mild enough for a person to ignore. It could also be life-changing. Clearly, Rae dealt with her condition just fine, but his heart skipped a beat every time hers fucked around.

He moved toward her, but she gritted out, "Don't. I've got it."

So he stepped back, calmed down, and finally noticed that she was fucking naked. His mind blanked. Was she—? Was this—?

That night in the park, she'd made the first move and said she was seducing him, slightly embarrassed but bold as brass all the same. He'd thought that was his one and only chance, the missed opportunity of a lifetime. Maybe he'd been wrong. Maybe the growing charge between them had electrified her too, and she'd decided to try again. The idea took him by the throat, his senses short-circuiting. Just like that, he was made up of precisely two elements: the words, *She's right in front of you,* cycling hot and frantic through his mind, and the bittersweet pain of his instantly aching cock.

He was about to blow at the thought.

Then her voice carved through his dizzy fantasy. "For God's sake, Zach, close your eyes."

Understanding buried him like a pile of bricks. *Ah.* So, this whole thing was an accident after all, and here he was, apparently staring. In reality, he could barely see her, but he closed his eyes anyway. Didn't help; her image was burned into his brain. She was all outlines and shadows, courtesy of the thin, tightly drawn curtains: her arm slapped over her soft, sweet breasts, the edge of one dark nipple peeking out. The rippling curve of her belly and the prim, white V of her underwear, which made his mouth run dry. Fuck.

He tried to say, "Sorry." His voice was so rough it probably sounded like an alien language.

"What are you doing here?" she demanded, like she suspected he'd installed spy cameras and purposefully barged in as soon as she was undressed.

"I came to fetch you for dinner. It's been five hours and you weren't answering my texts."

"Five hours?" She sounded shocked, then resigned. "Oh. Yes. I meant to set an alarm, but I..."

Something in her voice, the sudden flatness, made him frown. "You what? What happened?"

"Nothing," she said. "I fell asleep."

Maybe he should let it go, but the fact was... "You're kind of a bad liar. Did you know that?"

She spluttered for a moment, and he grinned, imagining her outraged expression. Then she shocked the smile right off his face. "And your dick is hard. Did you know *that?*"

Uh, yeah. He couldn't fucking miss it. But he'd been praying to God that she would. Christ, could this get anymore Perverted-Peeping-Tom? Prying his back teeth apart, he muttered, "Sorry. It's not—I'm not—"

"I know," she sighed. He heard her move around the room, felt something—a tension, a crackle in the air—that suggested she'd just walked past him. "I promise, you don't have to say it again. You're not attracted to me, and so on and so forth, and I really don't know why I mentioned—"

His eyes popped open. "Wait."

She was on the other side of the room, now, dragging a T-shirt off the back of a chair. Presumably still naked, but Zach kept his gaze on her face. Because he thought he'd just heard something unbelievable in her voice, and he wanted to read something wonderful into her words, but to be sure—really sure—he needed to see her eyes.

Right now, they were dancing away from his like butterflies.

"Rae," he said slowly, taking a step toward her. "Correct me if I'm wrong, but I had this wild idea that you didn't care if I was attracted to you or not."

Her jaw shifted. "You're right. I don't." But she still didn't look at him.

"Of course not. Because, when you asked me to come home with you last month, it was purely practical. Right?" He watched her closely, because he knew her, and because his instincts urged him to push. Just this once. *Please.*

She finally met his eyes, chin raised, gaze defiant. "I meant what I said that night."

Perhaps her iron tone should've put him in his place, but he was feeling reckless. If it gave him a chance at her, he'd be reckless forever. "What if I told you," he said, taking another step toward her, "that I'm attracted to you?" *Would you want me still? Just to help? Or the way that I want you?*

She stilled. He saw her shock, and then, blissfully, the slow dawn of her pleasure. Surprised, uncertain, but unmistakably there, like the first golden rays of sunlight. "Oh," she murmured.

"Yeah."

She looked at the bed. It was a sudden, quickly aborted turn of the head, but he caught it, and followed—and noticed that the sheets were a tangled mess. His mind flashed back to the moment he'd first walked in, casting a curious new light on certain events. Like the way she'd leapt up so fast she'd made herself dizzy. If she hadn't wanted him to see her naked, why had she *left* the sheets instead of hiding under them?

The possibilities hooked into his flesh, teasing his tortured cock until it hurt. His voice was a growl when he asked quietly, "What were you doing before I came in?"

She stepped back, toward the bed, even though he hadn't moved. And she didn't try to put on her clothes. "Nothing."

"Nothing?"

"Sleeping," she corrected.

"I told you, love. You're a terrible liar."

She inhaled, her eyes fluttering shut. "And what

happens if I tell you the truth?" When her eyes opened again, they were gentle and hopeless at the same time. "All I can have is sex—*just* sex. But you've had enough of that. You've been *hurt* by that. I won't hurt you, Zach, and I won't use you. Not ever."

His breath caught in his chest. His heart stuttered for a moment, and when it started again, it felt like it was beating for her. Those words, those eyes, the protective note in her voice—careful, she was being so careful with him.

And with herself, too. *All I can have is sex*, she'd said. Not, *All I want*.

"You don't need to worry about me, sunshine," he told her softly. "I want this. I want you." When he'd made his promise—when he'd sworn never to touch anyone he didn't honestly desire—he'd wondered how he'd know for sure that the moment was right. But he shouldn't have worried. The feelings he had for Rae were about as easy to miss as the fucking sun. She illuminated him.

Sadly, his words didn't do the same for her. Panic flashed over her face and she stammered "You do? But, Zach, what does that—? I adore you, I do, but I can't—I can't be with—"

Maybe she was going to say, *I can't be with anyone*. Maybe she was going to say, *I can't be with you*. Either way, he couldn't stand to hear it, so he cut her off. Tried his best to soothe her, because seeing Rae afraid did something awful to his insides. "Don't freak out. I'm not asking for anything you can't give. We're friends, remember? We care about each other. Attraction can come from friendship." It wasn't a lie. Attraction *could* come from friendship for him, and that was where his need for Rae had started.

But friendship wasn't where it ended.

He watched as she exhaled sheer relief, as her tense shoulders relaxed and her jaw softened. Watched, and kept going. "This won't change anything. It's safe," he murmured. "We'll call this... we'll call it a favour, okay?"

Because it was becoming painfully obvious that Rae couldn't handle anything more than that. And he had a few infuriating ideas as to why—but right now wasn't the time to interrogate her. Right now, all he wanted was to make her feel good. To prove that the people she cared about weren't all just waiting to hurt her. And that daring to want things wouldn't always end in punishment.

Maybe if he showed her often enough, she'd start to believe it.

"A favour," she repeated under her breath, like the words were an incantation. "As friends. I can do that. We can do that. As long as you promise me—you have to promise me—do you really want this?"

Zach's chest ached. Rae was so distrustful of tenderness that she couldn't bear to feel it, couldn't admit to more than basic lust—yet it was him she worried about. "I promise. Now, don't ask me again, or I'll start to think you don't trust me."

She didn't laugh at the gentle joke. Didn't even crack a smile. She looked so lost standing there, teetering on the edge of something indefinable, something he couldn't see. And then, in the space of a breath, she changed. Transformed. Became solid and certain again, as if she'd made a decision.

Her chin rose, and her mouth softened, and her words slid out like a delicious tease. "You want me," she murmured, a confirmation rather than a question.

More than anything. But he couldn't say that out loud. He was cool, calm, collected. "Yes."

Her lips curved into a wicked smile, and it was the sexiest thing he'd ever seen in his life. Slowly, she moved closer to the bed, challenge in her gaze. An answering heat rushed through him, just like that, as if she held the key to his desire. Right now, it felt like she did.

Her voice low, she asked, "Tell me something, Zach. What do *you* think I was doing in our bed?"

So they were back to this. What a fucking question. And the way she said *Our bed...*

He released a long, shuddery breath as his mind went into overdrive. Lust shoved his words, his hopes, out into the world without an ounce of finesse. "I think you were lying there, touching yourself, thinking about me." He paused. *Deny it.*

She didn't.

"Hand in your underwear, just—" He broke off, his own hands curling into fists. He was desperate to reach for her, but resisting temptation felt just as good as taking. Better, even. "I bet you were dying to come, weren't you? But you couldn't. I interrupted."

"You have such a filthy mind." She didn't sound unhappy about it.

Satisfaction rolled through him as he stalked across the room towards her. She backed away, as if she were cornered, but no-one who saw the look on her face would ever believe that. She let him see the need she refused to name, let him drown in it.

Which made it so easy, when the back of her thighs hit the bed, to set his filthiest thoughts free. "Sit down and spread your legs for me. I want to see you come."

CHAPTER TEN

THE WORDS HUNG between them in the shadowed quiet of the hotel room. Despite her bravado and her sheer, pulsing need, Rae knew that if she held out her hand, it would shake. This moment felt dangerous. Touching a man she cared for like this could only end in tears.

But she told herself firmly that, under these circumstances, it was safe. A simple favour between close friends, nothing more. Nothing that could burrow into her heart and soul, make itself a part of her, then disappear one day and leave her bleeding out. This was her secret moment of divine rebellion, her heart hidden safely under lock and key.

She hoped.

Zach watched her with eyes turned midnight by their blown pupils, his pale cheeks flushed and his mouth soft and sensual. The way he looked at her felt more intimate than a hand between her thighs. She sat back on the bed, but it felt a little bit like swooning. All his burning intensity was making her dizzy. He'd come to the convention as her fake boyfriend, but right now, he was so achingly *real*.

And safe, she reminded her barely dormant panic. *No matter what, this is safe.* That was his word, after all, and she was grateful for it.

Rae knew that, for Zach, desire signified a deeper connection. An emotional one. So, when he'd admitted to wanting her, she'd worried for a second: would he expect a new relationship to form between them? The kind of relationship she was too afraid to offer?

Now, she knew that worry had been ridiculous. Arrogant, even. Friendship was important to Zach, and theirs had become so deep that he'd developed an attraction. That was it. That was all. The feeling didn't have to be romantic. It *wasn't* romantic.

And if that fact had disappointed her, just a little bit—well. No-one ever had to know.

"Now," he murmured, "are you going to give me what I want?"

I'll give you anything you ask for as long as it doesn't hurt.

She couldn't quite bring herself to peel off her underwear—it felt too vulnerable too fast, even though the rest of her body was already exposed. So she left the cotton in place, leaning back on her hands, drawing up her knees and spreading her legs wide. But the action dragged her mind from emotional worries to physical ones. Sleeping with someone new for the first time could so easily go wrong.

Take now, for example: Zach probably assumed she was wet as a lubed-up porn actress, but she wasn't. She rarely ever was. So, did she pause proceedings to explain that? Would he stop and ask her? Would this be horribly awkward with someone she hadn't already seen naked twenty-thousand times?

Apparently, the answer to all those questions was *No*. When Zach saw the dry V of fabric between her legs, all he did was groan—long and low and deliciously tortured, like the sight of her physically hurt. He certainly didn't look crestfallen or confused by the fact that she wasn't a waterfall. In fact, he closed his eyes for a moment and bit his fist. He *bit* his *fist*.

Then, after a harsh breath, he opened his eyes and murmured, "Fuck, I like that."

She licked her lips automatically—not nervously. "What?"

He took a step closer, his gaze trained between her legs. "Plain white fabric, so tight over your pussy. You're all prim and soft and swollen. Show me."

"I—I'm—" She was too breathless to get the words out, too dizzy to know what she even planned to say. *I'll do whatever you want? I'm already falling apart for you, and I wish I didn't know why?* She was thinking in nonsense circles. She was, she was, she was.

"Show me." His voice was hypnotic, his breathing heavy. He sank to his knees at the edge of the bed, as if to get a closer look.

She hooked a finger under the edge of her knickers, pulled them aside, and showed him.

"Ah, Rae," he breathed. "Look at you. Spread open for me like you need it."

"Don't," she blurted, even as her heart pounded and desire zipped over her skin.

145

He tore his gaze from her pussy, arching a brow. "Don't what?"

"Don't... don't say those things." She wasn't used to it. She couldn't bear to hear it from that wanting mouth and in that gravel voice.

"Why not, love?"

She couldn't answer.

"You don't like it?"

She swallowed.

"You do. You like it."

Too much. And what was the point of pretending she didn't? Only, she couldn't say it. She was mortified enough already. She just nodded.

His smile was sunshine after a storm. He slid both hands into his back pockets, which made his broad shoulders seem even broader, and said, "You should touch yourself."

The word *should* caught hold of her. "Why?"

"Because you want to."

It was difficult to argue with that kind of logic. Somehow, Rae found herself spreading her legs wider. Leaning back on one hand and slipping the other into her knickers. He couldn't see as much anymore; she'd stopped holding them aside. But he watched the veiled motion of her fingers beneath the cotton like it was something he couldn't bear to miss.

"Yeah," he murmured. "Like that." His frown was agonized. His eyes fluttered shut for a second—then he snapped them open again, like he couldn't miss a moment. He wet his lips as she traced a finger up and down the plump folds of her labia, again and again. "Is this what you do," he asked, "when you're alone?"

When I'm alone I think of you.

"This is how I start," she found herself whispering. It sounded like a shout.

He drifted closer, so close—too close. She was too hot to handle, her pussy tightening desperately, the tension in her chest leaping like a flame. The idea that he might touch her landed somewhere between panic and need—but his hands were still in his pockets, behind his back. Hidden. Contained?

"You like to tease yourself?" he murmured.

She nodded, a moan stuck in her throat.

"Then what? What's next?" As if this were a guided tour. A tutorial. *How Rae Gets Off.*

Without a word, she made the torturous path of her fingers smaller, tighter, a harsh circle centred over her clit. Even through her underwear, he seemed to know exactly what she was doing. He bit his lip, and Rae decided she'd never seen anything so fucking sexy in her life. Which was ridiculous, because she'd seen plenty of sexy things— things involving actual genitals as opposed to this guy's fucking mouth.

But God, what a mouth.

"Do you always do it in bed?" he asked. "In the dark, when you're half-asleep? Do you have a routine, Rae, or do you make yourself come whenever you feel like it?"

Breathless, she demanded, "Why do you want to know?"

"Why do you think?"

She couldn't answer.

"Do you use your fingers?" he whispered. "Or something else?"

"I have a vibrator." Now, why the fuck had she said that?

But his reaction was somewhat unexpected. If she'd considered his smile dirty before, it was absolutely filthy now.

"Yeah? Is that how you tease yourself? Do you run it all over your pussy?" Zach leaned closer, his breath hot against her inner thigh, his whisper pure decadence. "Do you hold it tight over your clit, sweetheart? Until you come? Or do you oil it up and slide it inside that pretty cunt?"

"I..." She gasped as a spark of desperate sensation ripped through her. She was too close. She should stop. Instead, she rubbed herself harder and faster and said, "I put it inside me, but I keep..."

"You keep strumming that little clit, too," he breathed.

She meant to say *Yes*, but it was strangled by a moan— because he finally touched her. Nowhere indecent, nowhere scandalous. He rose up on his knees and slid an arm around her waist; that was all. He took her weight. She leaned back against the steel band of his forearm. Watched as he brought her freed hand to his mouth and sucked slowly on her first two fingers.

Fuck.

A thousand fireworks popped and sparkled inside her, breathless desire fluttering in her stomach. His lips slid down to her knuckles, his tongue gliding between her fingers. The sight and the sensation combined to unravel all of her control. She thought wildly that he'd lick her pussy just like this, *just* like this...

He released her fingers—more's the fucking pity—and reached between their bodies. She jumped slightly as he tugged her underwear aside, his knuckles grazing her sensitive skin. Even that light touch sent a violent bolt of pleasure though her.

"Do it," he said. "Fuck yourself."

She must be out of her damned mind, because she didn't hesitate. Just thrust two fingers, wet and glistening from his mouth, into her pussy—and then she moaned helplessly, both at the feeling and the feral satisfaction on his face.

He looked down, and something flared in his eyes, so she looked too. Saw the way her pussy spread around her fingers; saw the stiff, swollen nub of her clit and the way she circled it frantically. All at once, she came. It was like bursting out of the ocean to gulp down sweet, fresh air. She shuddered in his arms and moaned through each wave of pleasure while he dragged his lips over her throat, her jaw, her cheek. Kissing her, kissing her, kissing her.

And then, when the brilliance faded, along with all the strength in her muscles, he lowered her gently to the bed. Lay beside her, caught the end of her braid, and trailed it between the valley of her breasts. Told her she was fucking beautiful. She found herself smiling giddily, breathless and mindless and humming with a new kind of pleasure.

Maybe Zach hadn't desired her, once upon a time. But he certainly did now.

ZACH WAS INHALING PURE ELATION, so high he barely knew his own name. His cock throbbed in his jeans, but he couldn't manage to care; the gasping moans Rae made when she came were all his head had room for. He remembered those moans as he bathed in the scent of her: warm skin, soft musk, lemon and sugar pancakes. She lay beside him in the intimate, vulnerable haze of *after*, and it was so close to his wildest fantasy, he could come on the fucking spot.

Instead, he rolled over, covering her body in a single, sudden move. "I want to kiss you."

She gave him that brilliant, one-sided smile, big brown eyes crinkling at the corners. "Oh, really?"

"No-one's here," he reminded her—because he'd give her whatever she needed, but *he* needed acknowledgement that deep down, this was real. "I just want to fucking kiss you."

Quietly, carefully, she murmured, "Then kiss me." As if the words were shameful, but she couldn't stop herself from saying them.

He wanted so badly to take those words and run. To trust in the shy affection he felt radiating from her. To believe that, no matter what she claimed, Rae was here for just one reason: she couldn't be anywhere else. Couldn't be *with* anyone else.

Maybe, behind the walls she built for her own safety, she hid feelings for him.

He cupped her face, running his thumb over the soft threads of her scars. Tried to tell her with his eyes what he didn't dare to say: *I won't let anyone hurt you. Not even myself.* When his lips finally touched hers, he held his breath. She slid her hands into his hair, opened her mouth for him, and he exhaled sweet relief. His tongue traced the pronounced curve of her lower lip, dipped inside, and tasted bliss. She hummed her pleasure and tasted him just as hungrily. He shuddered over her, poured himself into her, and with every desperate press of her mouth and flick of her tongue, he felt a little more superhuman.

He pulled away, breathless, and found her staring, wide-eyed, up at him. Her hand rose to cradle his face, and she whispered, "I should've known you all my life."

"From now on." The words were ripped from deep in his chest, a promise that reverberated through the room. He couldn't have explained them, but he felt them, and she must've felt them too. She grabbed his T-shirt and dragged him down and kissed him again. Then he bent his head over her throat, licking and sucking his way down to her chest. Sinking into all that bare skin. Her fucking *body.* She was so vulnerable but powerful with it; all thick, soft warmth, but she held herself like some kind of warrior. On Rae, nakedness was the sweetest armour.

Her fingers tightened in his hair, her moans growing higher the lower his hungry mouth went. When he pushed up her breast with one shaking hand and licked, licked, licked, her whole body shuddered beneath him. That was what he wanted—more of her mindless reactions. And teasing them out was no hardship. She had these sweet, suckable tits and tight little nipples like drops of chocolate, and she gasped when he flicked his tongue over one. Gasping was great. Gasping was fantastic. Next up: make her scream his name.

He ran his hand over her ribs, her waist, the curve of her hip, until he reached her underwear. "Can I take these off?"

She opened her mouth, then hesitated. "What for?"

"I have a list."

Her laughter was bright and beautiful. "That's good to know. Do you also have a condom?"

Ah, fuck. No, he did not, because up until now, sex had not been on his agenda. He sighed and bumped their foreheads together.

"I'll take that as a no," she said wryly.

"And I'll take *that* to mean you don't have one either." His dick was throwing a vicious tantrum, but he ignored it. "Oh, well. I suppose I'll have to be satisfied with licking you out until we—" He cut himself off just in time. Swallowed. Slid his gaze away from hers and cleared his throat.

Until we die. That's what he'd been going to say. But at the last moment, a little voice had warned him that she might see beneath the joke to a truth she wasn't ready for. A truth that involved him, Rae, and a boatload of commitment and gentleness and all the other things that seemed to make her sweat.

For the first time, cruel uncertainty squeezed at his gut. Hesitating with her didn't feel right. Hiding from her didn't feel right. But what could he do? He'd claimed this was all about their friendship, and now he was realising just how badly he'd lied.

As if she sensed the tension in him, her kisses slowed, then stilled. "Hey," she murmured. "Are you okay?"

"I was—thinking. I need to—" Zach took a breath and almost told her everything. That this wasn't just a favour. That he was starving for her. That he'd take down the wall around her heart, brick by brick, until he could be absolutely sure she didn't feel the same. Could she ever feel the same? He'd let himself hope so, but now that hope felt more like a childish wish.

He clamped his jaw shut and held his reckless tongue.

Softly, she asked him, "Do you want to stop?"

He almost didn't understand the words. *Did he want to stop?* Was that even English? No-one had ever asked him a question like that at a moment like this. And there was no censure in her voice, no pressure, no ominous hint that the wrong answer would ruin everything. He met her eyes and they told him secrets. She looked at him like he was precious. Did he believe her?

He must, because the tension in him slid away. "Yeah," he said. And then, because it was an option, and because having that option felt so fucking good: "Let's... let's take a break."

"Okay." She hesitated, then caught his hand and kissed his big, rough knuckles like he was something delicate and fine. The action shivered through him like sheer bliss. He thought he heard a thousand things she hadn't said— things Rae would never say, words of adoration and of trust. But maybe she spoke best through looks and touches, and maybe he was learning her language.

The tightness in his chest eased. His worries receded,

just a little. "Later," he murmured. "We'll get back to this later."

She blinked. "Are you sure?"

Surer by the second. "Yes. We should go to dinner. And," he added, shooting her a wicked grin, "we need condoms."

A shy smile curved her lips as she looked away. "Right. Condoms! And dinner. Both very important things. Um... do you mind if I take a shower before we go down?"

God, she was cute. "Of course not." Before she could leave, he reached out and caught her hand. Held tight until her gaze met his again. Told her, in a sudden rush of warmth and heart-swelling tenderness, "I'm so glad I have a friend like you, Rae. So fucking glad."

She squeezed his hand, her breaths suddenly shaky. "And I'm glad I have you."

He smiled. One day, he'd tell her something else. Something about the way she made him feel, the way her presence tugged at his heart like they were connected by invisible threads.

And maybe, just maybe, she'd tell him the same.

CHAPTER ELEVEN

RAE'S NEED tasted like blood on her tongue: coppery and helpless.

"I'm so glad I have a friend like you." She should've been pleased by that sentence, happy that sex wasn't changing the way Zach saw her. Instead, the words had felt like a bucket of cold water, dragging her from soft, dreamlike pleasure to harsh reality.

Friendship wasn't all she wanted from Zach, but it was all she could have. She needed to be alone, to be *safe*. And that was that.

They sat together in the dining hall, just like yesterday, but today Rae wore a plastic smile and felt a lump of self-loathing in her belly. She was *feeling* things, and she hated it. She'd thought that common sense would keep her safe —that she'd remember, no matter what, how dangerous love was. That she'd never forget trusting Kevin with her forever, and having that trust abused in countless ways.

But Zach's kiss had killed every hesitation, as if there'd been nothing before him and there'd be nothing after.

It wasn't true. She couldn't let it be true. When this meal was over, she would take him to bed, but she wouldn't forget reality for a second. She couldn't let herself.

God, she hoped dinner would never end.

In contrast to her misery, Zach was more cheerful than ever, playing the besotted fake boyfriend to the hilt. Every time he squeezed her hand, kissed her knuckles, or called her *sunshine* in that low, knowing voice, she flinched and ached simultaneously. Was this how it would feel, when he fucked her? Like slow, sweet poison? God, she didn't know if she could take it.

Despite her best efforts, they finished eating all too soon. Zach led her toward the exit with an air of urgency that would be flattering if she weren't terrified, but sadly, she was.

So, she did something desperate.

Rae looked left, looked right, and spotted an author she almost-sort-of-knew. Miriam was a charming, gregarious woman surrounded by a gaggle of friends, all of them clearly headed to the hotel bar. The bar was good. The bar was great. The bar could take forever. Decision made, Rae released Zach's hand, took a deep breath, and forced herself to call across the room like some kind of possessed, extroverted socialite. "Miriam!"

They hadn't spoken for at least a year, and they'd only ever been acquaintances—but, to her credit, Miriam didn't miss a beat. "Rae, darling!" she trilled, and opened her arms as if they were long-lost sisters. Air kisses were exchanged. Introductions were made. When Rae called Zach her partner, the women all looked at her as if she'd won the lottery. Little did they know that by the end of this weekend, her winnings would disappear like fairy gold.

This wasn't real. She couldn't let it be real. She couldn't look at him in case he made it real. She couldn't, she couldn't, she—

"We were just heading for a drink. I don't suppose you'd like to join us?"

Rae nodded so hard she almost snapped her own neck. *Miriam Barnes, you brilliant, beautiful fucker.* "Yes, please."

At the bar, Rae tried her best to seem like one of the girls for about ten minutes before giving it up as a bad job. She'd never done well in group situations. At home in Ravenswood, her saving grace was the fact that all of her friends were kind of... weird. Rae got weird. She meshed with weird. She *was* weird. A gaggle of sensible adults having mature and logical conversations, however, was far from her comfort zone. She slowly faded into silence and texted Hannah instead.

Even though she'd dropped Zach into this with no warning or explanation, he was handling it way better than Rae. He held court with the increasingly tipsy authors as if there was nothing else he'd rather do. But while they all cackled over some joke or other, he turned subtly away and focused on her.

God, she wished he wouldn't focus on her.

He put a warm, reassuring hand on the small of her back and leaned across the gap between their bar stools. "Are you okay?"

Rae sat ramrod straight and took a healthy gulp of wine. "I'm fine," she bit out, sounding like a pissy teenager. Her phone vibrated in her hand.

Hannah: Duke's good. You want pics?

Rae: OMG yes please.

"You don't seem fine," Zach said as she typed. His hand moved in slow, soothing circles over her back, even though they sat at an angle where no-one could see. As if he just wanted to touch her.

Maybe he does.

She squashed the pesky voice of optimism in her mind —honestly, who knew she still possessed that?—and clung to her bad mood with all the strength she could muster. "If you're trying to say I look like shit," she muttered, "just say it." Her moment of glamour last night had not been recreated today. Her mouth was bare, her outfit simple, her naptime braid frizzy and falling loose.

Without warning, Zach caught her face in his hand. She almost dropped her phone. She kept a good grip on the wine, though; wine was her precious now. With strong, sure fingers, he tilted her head until they made eye contact. His gaze was an unexpected storm, so intense she imagined lightning shattering his pupils. Carefully, clearly, he told her: "You look beautiful."

She forced herself to take a deep breath. Of course, that breath came with a lungful of his intoxicating scent, so it was less calming than it should be. She imagined his pheromones like vaporous warriors, armed and vicious, attacking her common sense with alarmingly sexy battle cries.

She was officially bonkers, and it was definitely his fault.

"If something's bothering you," he said, "you need to tell me."

"Why?"

"So I can fix it." He caught her hand and raised it to his lips. Her heart broke.

Her voice barely above a whisper, she told him, "You can't fix this."

"Then I want to be miserable with you." He turned his barstool toward hers by some long-legged magic, separating them from the group of authors they'd come in with. A few shot her amused, knowing looks before returning to their conversation. Zach caught the back of Rae's chair and dragged it closer, until they were practically on top of each other, her legs caged between his.

Her phone vibrated, and she bit her lip.

"Hannah?" he asked.

"She has Duke pictures."

"Well, don't keep me in suspense."

Rae's lips quirked into a smile, her first real one of the night. She opened the message and they bent over the phone, chuckling together at an action shot of Duke running through Nate's massive garden, his tongue flapping in the breeze and his legs pointing in different directions. He seemed to be chasing a squidgy pink ball. Judging by his trajectory, he'd missed catching it by a thousand feet and possibly faceplanted the grass, too.

"That dog was not made for athletic pursuits," Zach said, amusement twinkling through his words.

Rae snorted. "He's a gentleman of gravitas. He's dignified like his mother."

"Yeah," Zach said dryly. "Dignified."

"Watch your tone," she sniffed, and then froze, because she'd teased him. She'd teased, she'd smiled, and she'd forgotten, for a second, that she was upset. Because of him. Even though she was literally upset *because of him.*

Why did he have to be the one? The one who did this to her?

He must have noticed she was feeling pensive again, because his own smile faded. "Do you miss him?"

"Yes."

"But that's not what's bothering you," Zach said with unnerving certainty, as if he had a direct line into her head.

She wanted to hate him for being this way, for understanding her—but she couldn't, because knowing him was a gift. Her sigh released the last of her resentment and frustration. If she could see them, they would look like cherry blossoms swirling away in the wind, slowly disintegrating. Maybe she couldn't act on her emotions, but there was no use fighting them inside her own head. She adored this man, and that wouldn't go away.

He made another guess, surprising her. "Is it your mother?"

She was speechless for a moment. Then, clinging to habit and family pride, she asked, "Why would it be about my mother?"

His mouth twisted, a grim tilt that couldn't be labelled a smile. "She calls you a lot, and then you stare at the phone like you want to kill something—or maybe like something's coming to kill you."

Rae forced herself to shrug. "We don't get on."

"Then why do you always pick up the phone like you wish you could call her back?"

She felt like he'd unravelled her. He was one of those top hat magicians and the coloured hankies he tugged out of his sleeve were her rainbow of problems. Rae huffed out a laugh that sounded disturbingly like a sob.

"Hey, now," he said quickly, squeezing her hand. "We don't have to talk about this. Ignore me. Drink your wine."

This time, her laughter was a little less tragic. "You make me sound like a baby with a bottle."

"If you were a baby, your bottle would be Duke. Wine will have to do."

She managed a smile and took a sip, but the deep red tasted sour. It barely fit on her tongue, either, in between all the words crowded there. Finally, she said, "Did you ever tell anyone else about your sexuality?"

He smiled, raking a hand through his hair. "Funny thing about that is, once I told you—once I got it out—it didn't feel like some big secret anymore. I haven't gotten around to mentioning it, because it's not weighing on me like it was. But I will. In fact, I've, uh... well, there's this forum for demisexual and other ace/arospec people, and I've been a member for a while. Haven't really said anything, but I'm thinking about it. To meet people, you know? To make friends."

For a moment, the weight of her misery lifted. He looked tentatively hopeful and adorably determined, and it made her heart swell. "That's good," she murmured with a smile. "That's really good."

"Yeah."

A pause. Rae's smile gentled, then faded. "I want to tell you about my mother."

Her words took them both by surprise. The syllables huddled together as if she'd rounded them up and shoved them out into the world.

Zach nodded. "Okay. I'd like you to tell me."

"Because we're friends, so we share things," she said. *That's all.*

"We do," he replied, with a sweet sincerity that made her want to curl up in him like a blanket and hibernate for the next fifty years.

"Right. So." She rubbed her clammy palms against her jeans. The words felt thick and sticky in her mouth, her body's last attempt at preventing this cardinal sin. *You're being disloyal. Keep it in the family. Don't tell anyone, or they'll think badly of her.*

Usually, she couldn't bear that idea. But she remembered telling Zach about Billie, and the way he'd said instantly, *Do we hate her?* That *we* had rearranged something fundamental inside Rae. She could accept Zach's righteous indignation on her behalf in a way she couldn't bear anyone else's.

"I don't hate my mum," she said, just to be clear. "But she's not easy to get along with. Most days, being around her makes me feel like shit, but I can never explain why. When I try—when I ask her to stop what she's doing—I get all tongue-tied and confused, and she has an excuse for everything. Then she gets upset, and somehow, I'm the one hurting her, and by the time the conversation's over, I just, I feel like I'm going nuts."

Zach's expression was tight. "I see."

"I don't want you to say anything," she blurted. "I mean, I don't want to bitch about her. I do love her. She does love me. She's my mother."

Something about him seemed to soften, ice turning to cool water. "I know, sweetheart."

"I just... Ugh. I don't know why I'm moaning about this when I haven't done anything to change it. Sorry. This is pointless."

"It's not," he said firmly. "You want to talk, you talk. Changing her is not your responsibility."

Rae nodded and heaved out a huge breath, like she'd been underwater. She knew, logically, that he was right—and that knowledge surprised her. Usually, when she tried to talk about her mother, she ended up feeling worse. She'd told a few friends years ago, but she'd barely been able to explain. By the time she'd finished, it all sounded like harmless mother-daughter arguments.

Even now, she wanted to give Zach examples—to tell him about the times she'd been reduced to tears as a kid, a teenager, fuck it, a grown woman—but she heard Marilyn's voice telling her not to be petty and to stop bringing up the past. That voice was vicious and wrong. Rae still listened.

Zach swept his thumb over the inside of her wrist, commanding her attention again. "You don't have to tell me everything all at once. Just know, if you ever feel like talking, I'll always be here."

She nodded. Her smile was as tremulous as the hope in

her chest. "Right. Thank you." Then, trying to lighten the mood, she said, "You have to tell me a secret, now. To make it even."

He didn't respond with the easy teasing she'd hoped for. Instead, he said quietly, "Sure. I'll tell you a secret. I'll tell you about my dad." His fingertips followed the faint turquoise veins of her wrist, his eyes distant. "When I was a kid, he ran off with some woman. Just vanished. I still loved him, but I felt so guilty about it, because he'd fucked us over. All of a sudden, we were poor, Ma had to work all the time, and everyone treated her like dirt. I'd fantasise about him coming home, but somehow, I always knew he wouldn't." There was a pause before he added softly, "I missed him anyway."

If Rae was a lifelong Ravenswood resident, she might've known the bare facts of this story already. But she'd had no idea—and even if she had, she wouldn't have understood until she saw the look on Zach's face right now. She nodded slowly, put her free hand on his shoulder, and squeezed.

He looked up in a flash of grateful blue. "We figured it out, in the end. My mother is a superhero. We didn't need him. But then Nate fucked off." Zach added that without bite, more exasperated than upset. "Not that I minded—he had his own life to live and his own issues to deal with— but it was... hard. You know he never came back until Mum got sick?"

No, Rae hadn't. "Really?"

"Yeah. He had great timing, because all my friends disappeared on me at that point. Except Evan. He calls it the cancer effect. No-one wants to stick around."

"Wow." She bit her lip. "I'm starting to see a trend in your life. The universe throws awful shit your way and you just... deal with it."

Zach huffed out a laugh. "Seriously? That's the trend you see?"

"What do you see?"

He frowned, thoughtful for a moment. "I don't know. I guess... everyone leaving me behind."

Her heart fell. "Zach."

"Hey, now. Don't look so serious. Fuck 'em, right?" She could tell he regretted saying something so heavy. In fact, it occurred to her that he was *never* heavy. Usually, everything was easy with Zach. Now she wondered just how hard he worked to avoid ever being difficult.

She caught his hand in both of hers, staring down at his pale, work-roughened palm, fighting the urge to kiss it. "You know, I... I really..." *Love you. You are like no-one I've ever met, and I really fucking love you.*

The weight of the realisation cracked her ribcage open. She couldn't deny it now—no matter how much she wanted to. Her heart was painfully, wonderfully vulnerable, officially free to fly off and hurt itself again. But maybe, if she didn't react, the poor thing wouldn't notice that it belonged to him. Maybe it would stay safe and sound and oblivious. That would probably be for the best, because she loved him so completely that it felt dangerous, so wildly that the feeling overflowed like a river after a storm. Her banks had broken. The flood would bring society to a halt and damage lots of people's carpets. There would be newspaper headlines.

Zach squeezed her hand. "Rae?"

She realised that she'd practically frozen on the spot. Shit. "Sorry. Just... thought of something."

He arched a brow. "You need to write it down?"

He thought she meant a story idea. "No," she said. "I'll remember it." *For the rest of my fucking life.* "Listen, Zach. You should know..." She swallowed hard, her throat suddenly dry. For the first time in a long time, she was desperate to say something sweet to a man, something gentle and loving and open, even if the idea terrified her. Zach deserved to hear how truly wonderful he was. To know that someone adored him, and always would. Even if she couldn't say the words outright.

"I see how you deeply care for people," she began, already feeling ridiculous. "I know how huge your heart is. I feel it. You show me—you show *everyone*—with everything you do. Some people don't appreciate you, some people leave you behind, but that's because life is shitty sometimes. Not because you aren't worth it. You're worth..." She forced herself to meet Zach's eyes and was surprised by what she found there: pure vulnerability, painted in burning blue. Somehow, that gave her the courage to continue. "You're worth everything. Please don't forget it."

He tried to flash his usual smile, but it was a faint imitation of the real thing. "How could I, with you around to remind me?"

"I think I'll make that my job from now on. Reminding you." She should be panicking at her own foolish honesty, worrying that he might read love between the lines of her speech. But how could she, when, for once, Zach was the one feeling exposed? The one who needed her to be brave, who needed her to take the leap? His cheeks were flushed, his voice rough, his gaze flitting away from hers almost shyly. She caught his hand and squeezed. He squeezed right back, and when their eyes met, something precious passed between them.

Then everything about him shifted until he was carefree and playful again.

"Alright," he said firmly. "Secrets. Your turn. You know how you're a writer, so you have mystical powers and shit? Do you ever write yourself the perfect wanking material?"

She couldn't help but laugh. He asked so seriously, with just the barest hint of that dirty, flirty confidence that called to something reckless in her blood. If this was who he wanted to be right now, she'd let him—but this wouldn't be the last time they discussed his past, or his pain. She'd make sure of that.

She leaned in and whispered, "Are you seriously asking me if I write my own smut?"

"Yep." He was wearing his most self-satisfied smile, one that said he thought he'd left her speechless.

She rolled her eyes. "Fine. Yes, I do. Sherlock and Watson fanfic, specifically."

With every word, his jaw dropped further. "For real?"

"For real," she said pertly.

He looked like he was reconsidering everything he knew about reality. She barely stopped herself from giggling at the expression on his face. Then, after a deliciously long pause, he managed to ask, "Which Sherlock?"

She gave a one-shouldered shrug, feeling wonderfully mysterious. "Wouldn't you like to know?"

"Uh, yes, I really fucking would."

"Tough. That was a secret. It's your turn."

He arched one wicked brow, and the action tugged at something low in her belly. "If my secret's good enough, will you show me your fanfic?"

Absolutely not. "Maybe," she lied with unrepentant glee. "If you really blow me away."

"Okay," he grinned. That grin was dangerous. She was already bracing herself for something pants-meltingly outrageous when he leaned in and whispered, "Remember that piercing I mentioned?"

"Oh, God. Is this the kind of thing you should tell me in public?"

"I don't know." His gaze heated. "Can you handle it?"

She really wasn't sure. "This is a sex thing, isn't it?"

"Well, I don't have many secrets, Rae." He leaned back on his bar stool, the action bringing one of his legs higher between hers. Her pussy tightened reflexively. One measly orgasm with him, and she'd developed some kind of Pavlovian response. "If you want my confessions," he told her, his voice rich with a hot, liquid promise, "be ready for sex, sex, and more sex."

She snorted, trying not to seem as overheated and fidgety as she felt. Her heart pounded so violently, she was surprised he couldn't see it through her T-shirt. With an impressively convincing laugh, she said blithely, "Stop. You're awful."

He smiled, but his eyes were intense. "What's awful is sitting here in public, remembering the little kitten growl you make when you come."

Her eyes widened even as something inside her

clenched. "Be quiet," she hissed, her eyes darting around the bar.

"Why? I wish I was fucking you half as good as everyone here thinks I am."

Heat suffused her face. And... other places. Had she thought she couldn't do this anymore? That she couldn't handle his touch? She must've forgotten how desperately she wanted it. This might ruin her, in the end, but she couldn't keep her hands off her fake boyfriend.

He caught her stool and dragged her impossibly closer. His hand slid up her thigh until his thumb pressed against the tight apex of her jeans, pushing the seam hard against her clit. "You want to know a really big secret?" he asked. "I'm dying to see you come again. And once won't be enough."

There was something about him—the fervency in his eyes, in his voice—that sent a thrill of hope and terror up her spine. Because that didn't sound fake, and it didn't sound like a favour. Rae found herself wondering: if Zach's attraction was tied up in their emotional bond, what did it mean that he wanted her so badly? Could this look, this touch, so painfully intense, really come from friendship?

She should ask him. And yet, she didn't. Instead, she rocked her hips imperceptibly forward, biting her lip as the pressure against her clit increased. "Okay," she breathed.

"Good. Now, finish your wine," he said quietly, "or, better yet, leave it here and come upstairs so I can make you scream."

Why, exactly, do you want to? She swallowed down a

difficult question and a decadent moan. "You know, you can be kind of bossy."

Those midnight lashes fluttered as his gaze dropped to his hand, still pressed between her thighs. "Good thing you like it, or we might have a problem." His eyes flew back to hers. "*Do* we have a problem?"

So, so many. But her control was just a memory now. She didn't have it in her to deny herself again. "No problems here," she lied. "Unless you count the fact that you're not inside me already."

With a scrape of barstools against the floor, he was standing, dragging her up beside him. His hands gripped her hips with a possessiveness that thrilled her. He murmured in her ear, "You good?"

"I'm good." Her heart was going haywire for reasons other than the usual.

"Then let's solve that problem."

CHAPTER TWELVE

ZACH'S PLAN WAS SIMPLE: he'd leave Rae at the elevator, sprint to the nearest chemist for a lifetime's supply of condoms, then follow her upstairs and fuck her until she couldn't live without it. Or at least until she was happy again.

He had the weirdest feeling that her sadness tonight had something to do with... him. Them. The boundaries they'd both agreed to, the ones that felt like chains weighing him down. Maybe it was arrogance, maybe it was wishful thinking, but he swore she struggled under that weight too. The connection between them was on fire, and the scorch marks on his heart belonged to her. He hoped she knew it.

But she was hesitant, and he understood why. He'd already suspected that most of the people Rae loved had only ever hurt her in return. Now, after their conversation at the bar, he finally grasped the way to her heart: he needed to earn her trust before he could take anything else. Needed to show her, bit by bit, that he would never give her a reason to regret him. Thankfully, he'd already started doing that. And, since he planned to continue by treating her just right in the bedroom, he dragged her through the hotel foyer like the building was on fire.

"Should I be worried?" she asked dryly. "Like, when we get to our room, are you going to rip my clothes to shreds in a fit of manly passion? Because I really like this T-shirt."

"If you like the T-shirt," he muttered, "I'll take that off the old-fashioned way."

"So, you *are* going to rip my clothes off," she announced, triumphant.

"If you don't take them off fast enough." Speaking of *fast enough*, had everyone in this hotel conspired to get in his fucking way tonight?

"I want to think you're teasing, but you have a face like thunder. You look so furious," she whispered, "people are going to think we're running off to argue."

"Who the fuck runs off to argue?" He parted a group of boring men in boring suits with nothing but a glare and yanked her through the gap.

"I never argue in public," she said primly.

"We'll argue in public at some point." Maybe that gave too much away. Maybe it revealed how badly he wanted to make this weekend's relationship a reality. Oh fucking well.

She must have assumed he was talking in terms of their friendship, because she replied easily enough. "We will not argue in public," she insisted as they reached the elevators. "I refuse."

He stabbed the *up* button and turned, pulling her close.

Her hands slid over his shoulders, her breasts were pressed against his chest, and her pretty, startled face was close enough to kiss. "We're arguing in public right now," he told her softly.

Her cheeks darkened. "We are not. This isn't arguing."

"Yes, it is."

"No, it isn't."

He arched a brow. "Is *this* arguing?"

"You are honestly the most annoying person I've ever met."

His lips curled into a satisfied smile. "Good. That means you'll never forget me."

"Zach," she murmured. "You are not the sort of man I could forget." She laced her fingers in his hair and tugged him closer, toward her mouth—

The elevator dinged. She hesitated, shot him a faintly embarrassed smile, and pulled away. He let her go with a barely hidden groan of frustration, his eyes sliding shut for a minute, his jaw tight as he regained control. When he opened his eyes again, he expected to find Rae's mocking, whiskey gaze on him, gloating over the way she'd ruined the line of his jeans.

But she wasn't teasing him. She wasn't watching him at all. She was staring at the man standing in the elevator as if she'd seen a ghost, and he was staring right back. The guy was tall and lean, with bold, handsome features, his face all shadow and light. He had thick, greying brown hair, silver glasses on his sharp nose, and slack-jawed astonishment written all over his face. His gaze flew from Rae to Zach and back again, narrow and calculating.

His identity should've been obvious, but it still came as

a surprise when Rae set her shoulders and said with careful calm, "Hi, Kevin."

So much for disappearing to get condoms. Zach wasn't fucking moving from this spot.

Kevin stepped forward, then hesitated, running his tongue over his teeth. "Baby."

Zach stiffened. But Rae gave a tight smile and breezed past it. "How's Billie? I saw your kid last night."

That was when Zach noticed the blue, starry bag slung over Kevin's shoulder, the kind parents used to cart around the 10,000 things babies needed. He saw mums in Ravenswood with those bags all the time, walking together with their pushchairs or going to tummy class or whatever the fuck it was called.

Now Kevin patted the bag with a self-conscious smile and said, "Jason. He's growing so fast."

Zach was dying to point out that no baby should grow fast enough to be over two years old, eighteen months after a divorce, but he didn't think Rae would appreciate that.

"He's a handsome boy," she said politely, but Zach knew she was lying, because all kids looked like walnuts or dried-out marshmallows until they hit 5 and got real people faces. In fact, he and Rae had discussed that phenomenon at length over breakfast. He found her hand and squeezed. As always, she knew exactly what he was thinking; she shot him a desperate, wide-eyed look that seemed to say, *Please don't make me laugh right now.*

He bit his lip.

"This is Zach, by the way," she said, bumping her

shoulder into his—like Kevin might have missed a glowering, 6 foot 2 inches of human being.

"Hi," Kevin nodded, his eyes darting to their joined hands.

Zach grunted. Rae trod on his foot. He cleared his throat and said, "Hi."

Kevin's smile was thin-lipped and sharp-edged as he turned back to Rae. "I'm glad you're moving on," he said, like he was bestowing a magnanimous blessing. Zach just about managed to stop his jaw from dropping.

"Thanks," Rae said. "I was really worried about my cheating ex-husband's opinion, but now you've said that, I can breathe easy."

Kevin rolled his eyes. "Come on, baby. I'm trying to be nice here."

"Good for you. Are you ever coming out of that elevator, or?"

He looked down, as if he hadn't known he was standing right on the threshold, stopping the doors from closing. "We're talking. Aren't we talking?"

Rae sighed.

"I didn't expect you to be here," Kevin said. "I mean, I didn't think you'd be invited."

What the fuck? Zach stiffened, opening his mouth to tell Kevin exactly where he could shove his surprise—but Rae sank her nails into his hand in an unmistakable warning. *Don't.*

Okay; so, she wanted to handle this herself. Perfectly reasonable. Totally fine with Zach. But if she could just give him a few minutes at the end of the conversation to beat her ex into a pulp, he'd really appreciate it. He tried to make that request via a combination of telepathy and speaking looks, but it didn't seem to work. She was too busy glaring at Kevin with an intensity that should, by rights, have turned the man to dust.

"I'm a very good writer," she clipped out, which was possibly the nicest thing Zach had ever heard her say about herself. "You of all people should know that."

Kevin shrugged. "You are a good writer. But you have no head for business, for what's marketable."

"I have words, though. Lots of them," Rae said, each syllable distinct as a shot. "Do you?"

Silence. Tension simmered. Zach was simultaneously furious and proud.

Kevin's silence grew self-conscious, and Rae smiled. With painful politeness, she asked, "Now, could you move? We have somewhere to be."

Kevin's expression darkened, and his gaze slid over Zach. "How old are you?"

Rae sucked in a breath. Zach just rolled his eyes. *This motherfucker.* "I'm old enough to mind my business and keep my promises. How about you?"

Kevin's gaze narrowed and a muscle ticked at his jaw. He turned away as if Zach hadn't spoken. "Baby—"

"Stop calling her that."

"Zach," Rae muttered, "leave it."

Zach looked down at her, astonished. "Are you for real?"

"Just leave it." She pulled away from him, leaving him cold, and walked into the elevator—or rather, she tried to. But Kevin, standing there between the doors, didn't fucking move. She was forced to slide past him, discomfort all over her face as her body brushed his.

Zach clenched his jaw so hard he was surprised he didn't crack a molar. Fuck his plan and fuck the condoms, for now, anyway. He followed her into the elevator, but he didn't just slide past Kevin; he grabbed the bastard by the shirt and shoved him, bodily, into the lobby. The other man spluttered and cursed as he fell, spilling nappies and a bottle of formula out of his little dad bag. Zach was suddenly sorry for the kid who'd have to grow up with a pathetic, bullying father like this one.

The elevator doors slid shut.

And Rae exploded. "Are you out of your mind?"

He stared. She was pissed—furious. Well, he was pretty pissed off himself, so at least they matched. "What the hell are you shouting at me for?"

"You think because you're bigger than everyone else, you can go around pushing people?" she demanded, like he'd just shoved a kid off a swing.

Through gritted teeth, he corrected, "I think anyone who's man enough to get in my way is man enough to be moved."

She raked her hands through her hair, pulling hard, turning away from him as if she could hide her growl of frustration. But he saw her screwed-up, angry face reflected a thousand times in this mirrored goddamn box, and every different angle made him feel a little more like shit.

"Rae—"

"No." She swung around to face him, holding out a

hand. "Don't say my name like that, like you can just make everything—"

"Oh, so now I can't say your name, but he can call you fucking *baby* every five seconds, and I just have to—"

"Do you think I wanted you here to get into pissing contests with Kevin? Do you think no-one noticed you throwing him around like a fucking towel? I don't want attention, Zach! I don't want drama! Not right now, not at *work.*"

That hit him in the gut just as the elevator slowed and the doors eased open. A group of women in gym wear, all smiles and sweat, walked into the cloud of tension, and their chatter slowed. They shot Zach and Rae wary looks as they pressed their floor number. Rae tucked herself into a corner to make room for them, pushing her tongue against the inside of her cheek.

She was self-conscious, and it hit him like a ton of bricks that he was the one making her feel that way. He *knew* she didn't want to be talked about. She'd told him five fucking minutes ago that she refused to argue in public, for God's sake. And what had he done? Caused trouble, put his own bullshit first, and acted jealous and possessive. All because he'd come face to face with the man she'd chosen for twenty-two years, while she'd never really chosen Zach at all.

So much for his brilliant fucking plan.

The gym-goers left the elevator first, but Rae didn't move, didn't speak, when they were gone. She just stayed tucked into her corner, her eyes distant, different. Burning rather than dreamy. He had the uncomfortable thought that instead of fantasising about imaginary worlds as usual, she was currently fantasising about roasting his balls over an open fire. Fair enough. He followed her lead and kept his mouth shut until they made it to their hotel room.

As soon as the heavy door closed behind them, he said, "I'm sorry."

She sat on the bed, nodding slowly, looking anywhere but him. "Right."

"I shouldn't have done that. Any of it. And I won't do it again."

She swallowed, her fingers twisting in the still-rumpled sheets. She looked angry and anxious and a little bit lost, and the knowledge that it was his fault suffocated him. He turned away, closing his eyes, taking a breath.

He should give her space. That was usually what people wanted, right? For him to leave? And he was supposed to be giving her what she wanted, always. Plus, he was still furious, his hands itching to wrap themselves around Kevin's throat, and there were only so many ways he could deal with those urges. He strode past her and shoved a few things into his duffel, then said, "I'm going to the gym. Okay?"

"Okay," she said, still avoiding his gaze. Probably resisting the urge to murder him.

He hesitated by the door. "I've got my phone. If you need me, call me."

She nodded. But somehow, he doubted she would.

AS SOON AS ZACH LEFT, Rae picked up her phone and

dialled Hannah's number. It took three rings before that cool, familiar voice poured calm directly into her ear. "Hello?"

"Han. Hi. What are you up to?"

There was a pause. Rae knew she sounded unnerved and shaky, that her breaths were more like pants, but she prayed to every god she knew that her friend wouldn't mention it. And, because Hannah Kabbah was a blessed angel—or maybe because she knew far more about emotional wobbles than her controlled exterior suggested —she didn't.

"I'm actually in a blanket fort with Nate right now," she said, as if that was perfectly ordinary.

Rae tugged the tail of her own braid. "Is that a euphemism? Because I can definitely call back."

"It's not a euphemism. We're meditating."

In the background, she heard Nate snort. "We're counting sheep."

"That's meditation," Hannah told him sternly. "Be quiet. Close your eyes. Rae, is everything okay?"

"Tell me why you're counting sheep," Rae demanded, like a particularly invasive loon.

"We're winding down before bed. It helps Nate sleep. The blanket fort isn't strictly necessary, but the kids are really good at making them. We always meditate before bed, or we drink something hot, or I fill in my planner and check off my goals while Nate reads a magazine."

Hannah went on to describe, in detail, the issue of *Photo District News* Nate was reading this week. Then she segued into a soothing speech about Duke. He was apparently fast asleep at the bottom of Nate's daughter's bed, and had developed a marked fondness for one of the girl's stuffed rabbits, which she had graciously gifted to him. Duke was apparently carrying it around as carefully as a new-born.

By the time Hannah was done, Rae's balled fists had unclenched, her tense muscles had eased, and her heart didn't shake inside her chest with every beat. Her breaths weren't a step away from sobs anymore, and her skin didn't prickle all over. She tapped her tongue against the scar on the inside of her cheek and felt herself knitting back together.

She whispered, so Nate wouldn't hear, "Zach and I had an argument."

Hannah hummed sympathetically. "Was it bad? Is he being an arse?"

"No. I mean, he was, but he apologised. I just... I really hate arguing." It made her soul shrivel up and whimper, made her young and small and terrorised through force of habit. Even though she knew most people—especially Zach—didn't argue solely to cause pain. Even though she knew most people wouldn't rip her words and worries apart, then stitch them back together into Frankenstein's Attack. Even though.

Quietly, Hannah said, "Did you tell him that?" As if she'd heard Rae's thoughts instead of her woefully inadequate words.

"No. I couldn't. And he thought I was pissed, so he disappeared."

"What a twat."

In the background, Nate said casually, "You wouldn't happen to be talking about my brother, would you?"

"No," Hannah said. "Rae, go and find him. He's a big puppy. He'll give you a hug and make everything fine again."

Nate's voice returned. "That definitely *sounds* like my brother."

"Shut up and count your sheep. Rae, are you listening to me?"

"Yes." Rae nodded firmly. "Yes. I think you're right."

"Of course I am."

"I'll let you get back to your, er, sheep, then."

"Wonderful. Goodbye."

But when the call ended, Rae sat rooted to the bed for at least another thirty minutes, sorting through her feelings like tangled skeins of thread. Like plot strands she couldn't quite figure out how to untwist. She felt as though she'd written herself into a corner before she'd even met Zach, never dreaming that she *would* meet someone like Zach. Someone who hurt her by mistake instead of calculation, who apologised instead of manipulating, who gave more than he took and never, ever stole. Who wasn't exempt from her anxieties, but didn't exacerbate them either.

A churning stomach and sweaty palms were Rae's habitual responses to confrontation. But now they'd faded, she realised what was absent from her usual post-argument cocktail of emotions: fear. She wasn't afraid to follow Hannah's advice. She wasn't afraid to go looking for Zach. She didn't dread trying to fix things, the way she would with her mother, or Kevin, because she knew Zach would never try to hurt her.

And she had no idea how to handle that knowledge. It felt a little bit like trust.

∼

SHE FOUND him in the weights section, suspiciously alone, as if the dark cloud around him had driven other gym-goers away. She'd always hated gyms, with their salty-stale tang of other people's sweat and their shiny chrome machines that mocked her general lack of fortitude. She'd long wondered why people used places like this when they could take a nice walk instead. But as she approached Zach in his grey, low-slung joggers and the thin, white vest that displayed so much chest, she understood.

Obviously, people went to the gym to spy on works of art like him. What a eureka moment.

He was lying on a bench, pushing a barbell stacked with weights up over his chest, which perfectly fit her cartoonish ideas of what people did at gyms. At first, he seemed to be grunting with each push, but as she drew closer she realised he was talking, muttering acidly under his breath.

"*Baby.* Baby, baby, *fucking* baby." Like he wanted to rip the word to shreds and stomp on it.

Something twisted nervously inside her, but she gave that something a stern talking-to and pulled herself together. She walked into his line of sight, making enough noise that she wouldn't startle him, before speaking. "Isn't someone supposed to watch when you do that? To make sure you don't drop it and die?"

His bitter chant halted the minute he saw her. Though

his pale skin was already flushed with exertion, she could've sworn he was blushing. Still, he didn't avoid meeting her eyes. The blue fire of his gaze burned her from head to toe. He heaved the barbell higher and said, "This is about one-sixty. I'm not going to drop it and die."

"I have no idea what one-sixty is."

"Approximately one of you. But you're right; come and spot me. It occurred to me today that I should cut the macho bullshit and use my brain more often."

A smile tugged at her lips. She went to him, her nervous wreck of a heart leading the way. Placing a knee on the bench and her hands on his legs, she said, "I'm watching."

"Uh..." His heavy thigh muscles tensed under her touch. He put the weight he'd been lifting on the bar above his head, then cleared his throat. "What are you doing?"

"I'm holding you down," she said, "like when someone does sit-ups."

His laughter was rich and musical. Even though he was clearly laughing at *her*, she found herself smiling along rather than dying of mortification.

When he stopped chuckling and sat up, she said dryly, "I take it that's not what I'm supposed to do?"

"Not really." A chunk of hair had come loose from her braid, and he twirled it around his finger. "But don't stop on my account. I've got no complaints."

"You're not even lifting anymore."

"No, I'm not. Something more interesting came up." They were both straddling the bench now, face to face, her hands still on his thighs. He sighed. "I really am sorry,

Rae. I was thoughtless and selfish, and... I know I fucked up."

"I'm sorry, too. I was just trying to avoid confrontation—"

"Which you don't need to apologise for," he said firmly. "Really. You don't. Please don't."

She almost choked on her relief, not because he didn't want an explanation, but because he was so eager for things to be okay again. She'd never fixed a mistake with someone she loved without paying a pound of flesh. He was the only one who cared like this.

Just to be sure, she asked, "Are we okay?"

He met her eyes. "We're always okay, sunshine."

"Baby," she blurted, the word landing between them with a thud.

He blinked, arching his eyebrows. "Uh..."

"That's my name," she explained hurriedly, wetting her lips. "Baby Ann McRae."

He blinked again, harder. A faint smiled curved the corners of his mouth. But the last thing she expected him to say was, "*Ann?*"

"...I'm sorry?" Her second name wasn't usually the one people focused on.

"Your parents called you Baby," he said, "then decided to pair it with *Ann?*" Humour danced in his eyes now, and something else, something warm and glad. She felt a surge of connection, as if she'd taken a step toward him after weeks of standing scared and still. It should alarm her. Instead, it made her giddy.

"My dad wasn't around for the birth. He travelled a lot with the army, and Mum never wanted to follow."

Zach huffed out a laugh, shaking his head. "He must've been pissed when he came home."

"Oh, yeah. He's the one who started calling me Rae."

Zach's smile gentled. "He's gone now, right?"

She'd mentioned it before, probably. Dad had been much older than Rae's mother, but his heart attack thirty years ago had come as a surprise. "Yes," she murmured.

Zach brought one of her hands to his lips and kissed her palm. "Alright," he said. "Baby, then."

Oh, God. She winced. "Just because you know my name, doesn't mean you can use it."

His expression darkened for a moment before he carefully smoothed out his scowl. "Kevin sure as hell does."

"He was trying to piss me off. I barely let him say my name at our wedding." She wrinkled her nose at the memory.

"You really hate it that much?"

"I don't hate it," she said honestly. "It's just not mine. Not really. Anyway, you can't tell me you seriously want to call me *Baby*."

He grinned. "I want to call you a lot of things, babe."

"Don't start that shit, Zachary Davis."

"You're so grumpy." But he looked at her like she was a welcome sunrise. His thumb skated over the inside of her wrist in a movement she was starting to associate with comfort, and Zach, and that excitable dip in her stomach that happened whenever he smiled. Carefully, he asked, "Are you okay?"

That gave her pause. Hadn't they just fixed things between them? "Why wouldn't I be?"

"Seeing Kevin for the first time—I know you were nervous about it."

Huh. She had been nervous, hadn't she? Possibly seeing her ex had been high on the list of reasons why she'd dragged Zach here in the first place. But it had happened, and Kevin himself had barely fazed her. He'd looked...

Kevin had looked like the past. He'd sounded like a mistake. And once he was out of sight, his sneer had vanished just as easily from her mind. She was astonished and relieved and grateful all at once.

But all she said was, "I'm fine."

"Good."

There was a pause before she added, a little belatedly, "Sorry he was such a dick to you."

Zach arched a brow. "Was he? I barely noticed."

Her mouth curved into a reluctant smile. "I should've realised he'd ask about your age."

"Is he always so pathetic, then?"

Her mouth hung open for a delighted second before she burst out laughing. "He's bad at keeping quiet about things that bother him."

"And my age should bother Kevin because...?"

"*You* know." She rolled her eyes when Zach didn't respond. "Because I'm too old for you."

"Bullshit," he said easily.

She choked out a disbelieving laugh. "I'm sorry, what?"

"If I were too young for you"—she didn't miss the way he rearranged those words— "we wouldn't have been such good friends for so long. I'd bore you or get on your nerves. Be honest: how often do you think about the age gap between us?"

"Not that often," she mumbled, which was a tiny white lie. In reality, the answer was *never*. It just didn't seem to matter.

"See?" He looked way too pleased with himself. "Now, stop worrying about your pissy ex-husband and come here."

"Come where? I'm practically in your lap."

"But not quite." He tugged her closer, lifting her up until she was *literally* in his lap, straddling him instead of the bench. She realised, with hot cheeks and no little satis-faction, that she was being semi-scandalous in a public place. And this public place wasn't part of her new, care-free life back in Ravenswood—it was in a hotel where her old life lingered like a bad smell.

Maybe the two pieces of herself were slamming into each other, finally connecting, for better or for worse. Maybe Zach's support, as solid and unflinching as his current grip on her arse, had helped that happen.

"There," he said softly, his eyes burning into hers. "That's better."

She pressed her hands to his chest, felt his heart racing under her palm. "Much. Kevin interrupted us."

His voice deceptively mild, Zach asked, "Did he?"

"Yes." She said it firmly, almost formally, because this was a serious issue. She couldn't allow her worthless ex to derail her evening. "We were going to continue our agreed-upon—"

"*Agreed upon*," Zach cut in with a snort. "Aren't you sharp tonight." His tone was even sharper. But when he looked at her, she saw something beseeching in his eyes. "Do me a favour, sunshine," he sighed. "Don't talk about fucking favours."

If she were sensible, she would interpret that as an obvious rejection. And she would carefully ignore the rapid beat of his heart against her palm, the yearning in his voice, the way his grip on her tightened as if he couldn't let her go.

But Rae wasn't feeling sensible. She noticed everything, and she let herself enjoy it. Stopped trying to hide her own yearning, her own longing, her own tight grip on him. Holding his gaze, she said, "Alright. No favours."

He nodded curtly. Then she leaned in close, and everything about him tensed.

"Zach," she whispered, as if they were starting again. "Will you come upstairs with me?"

He pulled back to look at her face. She watched his expression shift from disbelief to sheer, shocking pleasure. Then came his smile, slow and sweet and so fucking sexy. Teasing as ever, he asked, "Upstairs? What for?"

She smiled back, a little afraid and a lot determined. "I have a list."

CHAPTER THIRTEEN

THIS TIME, Zach managed to take a detour for necessary supplies. Condoms, which he hadn't needed in a while, and a bottle of the silky, flavourless lube he actually liked —plus two Red Bulls because sleep was for people who didn't have a shot with Baby Ann McRae.

His lips twitched as he remembered her wrinkling her nose at her own name. Then, without warning, more memories followed: Rae, Rae, Rae, so fucking wonderful. The look in her eyes, burning desire and hesitant trust, when she'd spread her legs for him. The exhausted curl of her right hand after she signed all those books. The way she smiled at her own reflection when she looked especially good. How she said whatever it took to catch him by surprise, and braided her hair all pretty, and drifted away inside her own head.

What came next wasn't a realisation so much as a release: he was in love with Rae.

Zach stopped dead in the middle of a hotel corridor and breathed, "Fuck."

He should've figured this out a while ago. Hell, he had a sneaking suspicion he'd started falling for her before he'd even developed an attraction toward her. It was the kind of oblivious shit he did all the time, but right now it was extremely inconvenient. Something had shifted between them tonight, something monumental—but he was 100% sure that if he mentioned his feelings, she'd panic and pull back.

He started walking again, muttering sternly to himself. "Keep your mouth shut, Davis. Keep it together."

Love danced on the tip of his tongue.

By the time he slipped his key card into the door of their hotel room, his hands were shaking. Fear, love, and way-too-intense lust had him in their grip, and he was breathing slow and deep to calm himself down. Blood rushed in his ears like a stormy sea, every breath tasted of urgency, and his thoughts had narrowed to a single, shit-scary refrain.

If you fuck it up, this might be all you ever get.

But that wasn't true. He couldn't let himself believe it. Rae was skittish, and he understood why, but he could prove that she didn't need to be. His long-term plan involved regular orgasms and casual intimacy and the perseverance of a fucking ox, and he would make it work.

She was sitting in the glow of the bedside lamps, looking all prim and pretty in nothing but a T-shirt and her under-wear. He was arrested by the sight of her, but it took him a second to realise what was different. She'd taken her hair down, so for once, it was completely loose. No braids at the front; just a wild, brown and bronze length that was starting to frizz and curl at the ends. She watched him approach with fathomless eyes, and for a moment he felt like prey. Like she was about to sink her teeth into him in the best way possible, and he should approach with caution.

It wasn't a sensation he disliked. Quite the fucking opposite.

He put down his pharmacy bag, threw her a can of Red Bull, and said, "For later."

She gave him that familiar, one-sided smile with a brand new, sex-hungry edge. "You have the best ideas."

"I should shower."

"No, you shouldn't." She crawled across the bed, rose up on her knees, and reached for him. When he came closer, she threaded her fingers through his hair and licked a hot, electric stripe up the side of his throat. "I like you like this. It's how you look every morning on your break, when I come to see you."

Possessiveness rolled off her in waves, whether she knew it or not, and he was more than happy to bask in the heat like an animal. He wrapped an arm around her waist, pinned her to him, and drank down her gasp-turned-moan. "When you come to see me, huh? Is that what it is? I thought you were just taking walks."

"Yes," she said, one hand slipping under his vest. "That's what I meant." But there was no heat to her denial, no panic in her eyes.

"You know what I think?" he murmured, pushing his luck. "I think you've wanted me for a long time."

Her lips tilted into a wry smile. "Maybe. Way longer than you wanted me."

He frowned and caught her chin, letting her see the truth in his eyes. "Just because I didn't want you in my bed, doesn't mean I didn't want you. I was desperate to be around you, to *know* you, and I still am. I want to carry every inch of you in my head forever, because you are too precious to remain a mystery."

She swallowed, her lashes fluttering as she looked away. "Zach..."

He was fucking this up—pushing too far, too fast with the emotional declarations. He couldn't bring himself to say, *I meant that as a friend,* so he said the next best thing. "Don't freak out. I care about you, remember?"

"I remember," she whispered. But she looked so vulnerable, as if she wasn't quite sure *why.*

"Tell me something," he said, suddenly curious. "Why do so many people downstairs know you, but none of them act like your friend?"

She blinked, obviously confused by the question. He'd meant what he said; he needed to understand her. It was a compulsion, now.

Finally, with a rueful twist of her lips, she murmured, "I suppose Kevin got all our friends in the divorce. I don't think I'm the type of person others hold on to."

"Me neither," he admitted easily. "Does it bother you?"

"No. I have everyone I need."

"Do you think you could ever lose me?"

Her nails raked his chest as she curled her hand into a fist. "I think I don't want to find out."

Sharing time was officially over. He could see it in her face and feel it in the tension of her body. So, he soothed her the only way he knew how: by unleashing the full force of his lust, letting it rush out and sweep her away. Soon, she would trust him completely. For now, just a taste was enough.

∾

THE SUDDEN CHANGE in Zach felt like a storm; like the thrill of excitement as the wind whipped up and the sky grew dark with the promise of thunder and lightning. Rae had a thing for storms, always had. They drew out a mix of primal fear and violent, feral triumph. They were overwhelming and all-consuming. So was Zach.

He pushed her back onto the bed and dragged his shirt over his head in one swift movement, so fast she barely followed. In the low light, his pale skin seemed to shine. Ridges of muscle defined the slab of his chest, carved his broad shoulders, slashed a V at his hips. Then her gaze found the thick curve of his erection, clearly outlined by the grey jersey of his joggers.

"Top off," he said, but she shook her head, trying not to pant at the sight of him. At the living temptation he'd become, half-dressed like that.

"You think I'm missing the rest of your strip tease?"

"Fair point." He pushed down the joggers and his underwear all at once, then laughed softly as she went slack-jawed. Oh, Lord. She liked to look at men, but Zach… he did something strange to her. He always had.

It was the way he held himself, maybe, like some proud Greek statue from an age gone by. Like he'd never felt an ounce of shame or self-consciousness in his life. He was so casually dominant, so lazily confident, his nudity deliciously lewd yet utterly natural. She tended to focus on his chest, since it was usually bare, but now she took in his thickly muscled thighs, his lean hips, the jut of his erection.

And God, that erection... Her mouth went dry, but she wasn't sure if anticipation or outright nerves were to blame.

"Zach," she said calmly, "did you know there is a piercing in your dick?"

He looked down as if shocked. "Well, shit. How did that get there?"

This didn't seem like the moment to laugh, so she clapped a hand over her mouth—but amusement bubbled up anyway, hysterical and delighted. "I *knew* your secret piercing was a sex thing."

"Of course it is. Unsexy piercings aren't usually secrets."

"Right," she said dryly, eyeing the little ring that curved through his swollen cockhead. It was a bright, shining silver, stark against his flushed skin. "Um... does it hurt?"

"No," he said, then held up a hand. "Actually—I've changed my mind. It hurts like hell because I'm not inside you."

She bit her lip. "Oh dear."

He laughed and climbed on to the bed. "You look scared as fuck."

"I'm not," she lied. "It's just a piercing."

As if throwing him off would be that easy. "I wasn't talking about the piercing, Rae. Relax," he murmured, his fingers catching the hem of her T-shirt. "You don't need to be nervous. We'll take our time. Okay?"

"Okay. Yes. Right." The last of her words were muffled as he eased her T-shirt over her head. She'd already removed her bra, so now she was naked except for her knickers. She remembered the last time she'd sat before him like this, and the thought must have hit him too, because their eyes met and their lips curved almost simultaneously.

"Are you going to take these off for me, this time?" he whispered, fingering the lace at the edge of her underwear. When she hesitated, he ran his mouth over her jaw, his lips soft and his stubble rough. "Doesn't have to be now," he breathed into her skin, low and reassuring. "Touch me."

Rae couldn't believe she'd needed the reminder. It had been forever since she'd actually had sex—longer than the eighteen months since her divorce, anyway. Luckily, Zach seemed dedicated to reminding her how this was done. She ran her palms over the fine rasp of hair on his chest and was rewarded with his hands kneading her arse, making her clit swell and her pussy ache. She nudged the flat disc of his nipple with a fingertip, and he pushed out a breath and sucked on her lower lip. Everything inside her turned molten. His big, rough hands stroked her so softly, his mouth was so tender but hungry, and the tension was killing her.

Then her questing fingers brushed the skin just above his hip, and he shuddered. A moan escaped from somewhere deep in his chest. "Christ, Rae," he murmured, and when she looked up, she was shocked by the decadent need on his face. His eyes were bright, swallowed up by black pupils; his sharp cheekbones were flushed; his lips were swollen and parted and slick.

"Lie back," she said, the desperate thud of her heart driving each word. "I want to see what else makes you moan." When he obeyed, she settled between his thighs and licked that soft, sensitive skin above his hip. He jerked, his hands sinking into the mess of her hair, tugging until she looked up at him.

"You," he rasped, "are going to kill me. I don't know why I agreed to this."

But Rae did. She'd been trying so hard to ignore it, this knowledge, but she couldn't anymore. Wouldn't. The lines between real and fake had blurred so badly, they were barely visible—yet she didn't want to run away. Not even when she saw possession in his eyes and felt it in his touch. She realised with sudden, endless relief that she loved him more than she feared for herself. She was stronger than she'd ever been, and she chased what she wanted, and if this connection between them hurt in the end, perhaps it would be worth it.

She didn't know how to say any of that, though; simply feeling it was exhausting enough. So, she bowed her head and worshipped him, instead.

Her lips traced a teasing path across his skin while he moaned and arched and begged her for more. She smiled to herself and nuzzled his cock, barely resisting the urge to purr like a cat. He smelled like heat and salt and skin and Zach, so she flicked her tongue out to taste.

"Rae," he moaned, his hips bucking. "Don't—I'll—"

"What?" she teased. "You'll come? Really?"

"Yes," he gritted, clearly serious. "You have no idea how fucking good you look right now."

She did, actually—she could tell just by the way he watched her. But she wanted to hear him say it. She ran her cheek over every steely-soft inch of his cock, enjoying his tortured groans. "Tell me," she whispered against his skin.

The words were ripped from him, sudden and breathless. "You look like mine." Then he bit his lip bloodless, his frown agonised, as if he hadn't meant to let that slip.

She should've been horrified, but wild, rebellious pleasure bloomed inside her. On a sex-fuelled wave of defiance, she murmured, "Maybe I am."

He rose up on one elbow, his gaze darkening. Then he reached down and grasped his erection at the base—hard. His voice even harder, he ordered, "Open for me."

She did, and he lifted his hips, murmuring sweet, sordid things as he fed his cock into her throat. It was a hot, human intrusion that shot straight to her clit. She sucked hard, and he thrust up into her mouth, his hand a delicious weight on her nape, his voice cracking as he urged her on. God, she wanted him. Like this, yes—or, even better: between her thighs, filling the ache that grew inside her as his pre-come teased her tongue.

She wanted him in her life, always, wanting her right back.

"Stop," he gasped, the word abrupt, ragged. She eased back, and he sat up, dragging her into his lap. His kiss was dangerously deep, as if he wanted to devour her, or maybe to be devoured himself. His hands never stopped moving, sliding over her bare skin, the heat of his palms branding her sides, her breasts, her throat. Then he cupped her face, and the kiss turned tender in a way that made her heart break and her hips rock. *This.* This was what they were.

A second later it was over, as if he thought she couldn't handle too much. Rae was flipped onto her back, her body tingling in anticipation while Zach reached for something on the bedside table.

Her underwear felt so inconvenient, all of a sudden. Confining, even. She peeled them off and sank into the languor of the moment, teasing her plump clit with delicate fingers... Only for Zach's warmth to return, his body a comforting weight as he lay above her, his own fingers joining hers. But his were slippery, and he glided over her folds, spreading the luxurious wetness. His gaze caught hers, held. Then he pushed two fingers inside her, and she thought she might shatter. His thumb swept over her greedy bud, circling gently while his fingers fucked her nice and slow. She spread her legs wider and choked out, "More. More."

He kissed her cheek, her jaw, the corner of her mouth, and then his tongue slipped between her lips just as his fingers curved inside her. He rubbed something sensitive and sultry and *perfect,* and she came. Wrapped her arms around him, sucked on his tongue as she moaned, and came. He kept stroking, kept circling her clit, until she gasped and twisted and jerked away, the sensations too overwhelming.

But not so overwhelming that she couldn't say, "Condom." It wasn't a reminder so much as a warning: *You better be ready, because I'm about to need you again.*

She heard the rip of foil before he settled between her

thighs, his lips soft over the pulse racing at her throat. His voice was rough and rumbling and oh-so-satisfied when he murmured, "You're not nervous anymore."

She carded her fingers through the silk of his hair. "With you? I don't know how I ever was."

His weight grounded her, his breath hot against her ear. His grip on her thighs was urgent, commanding. She could feel the thick head of his cock parting her folds, but he didn't push. "Tell me you want it," he growled.

She responded without thought, far too truthfully. "I want *you*."

"So take me," he murmured against her lips. "Whenever you want. Just take me." Then, with a snap of his hips, he filled her so deep she couldn't breathe. Sparks flew from the place where he was buried, so thick and hard and hers. She tightened helplessly around him, her moans ragged, need dancing through her veins.

"Fuck," Zach hissed, his forehead pressed to hers, his breaths more like pants. "*Fuck.* You feel like heaven."

And he felt like home.

ZACH THRUST into Rae like an animal, sweat gilding his skin, her cries urging him on. Nothing could be better than this. She chanted, "Oh, fuck, *yes*," and he knew he'd never stop. She looked up at him with something like surrender, and he knew he'd never be the same. She was his. She'd always been his. He could feel every inch of her —from the soft bounce of her breasts to the roll of her hips to her thighs spread wide for him. Their bodies fit together like puzzle pieces, the same way she helped him fit into the world. Her cunt, so fucking hot and silky, tightened around him, fluttering as her breaths stuttered.

"That's right," he murmured, the words dripping satisfaction. He slid a hand between them and felt her soft folds spread around his shaft. Her clit was a lush little bead, and when he stroked it, she spasmed beneath him. He brought his lips to her ear. "Feels so fucking good when you're like this. If you come, I'll lose it."

She laughed, breathless and broken. "Don't stop. Faster."

Whatever she wanted. That's what he would give her. Not because he had to, not because it was the only way to keep her around, not because it made him useful or worthwhile or better—but because seeing her pleasure, in any context, took him to another fucking planet. He thrust hard until she melted under him. He twisted his hips, and she gasped like he'd given her the sun. He stroked her in slow, gentle circles that didn't match the punishing pace of his thrusts, and her moans became whimpers, then sobs.

When she finally broke, her cunt a hot, honeyed fist around his cock, he did exactly what he'd said he would do. He lost it. Fucked her through those dizzying spasms, choked out her name in a voice like broken glass, and lost it. Every muscle in his body stiffened as electric sensation coalesced at the base of his spine—and then pleasure ripped him apart. He forgot himself for a second. He was no-one, floating through nowhere, having the greatest orgasm in history.

When he came back, his body was limp, his arms

around Rae as they lay together on their sides. He held her tight and knew this was perfection. Didn't speak in case reality intruded. They'd spun their own world for a moment, a world where she didn't have to worry or fight old fears or push him away, and he was happy here—so happy he could barely drag himself off to deal with the condom. Returning to her a few moments later felt like coming home.

He must've dozed, in the end, because he woke up in the pitch black of true night. Rae was kissing his face, quick and sweet and frantic. "Mine," she whispered. "Mine." The word shimmered with electric honesty. He slid his hands into her hair and held her still and fit his mouth to hers. He could taste her tears.

CHAPTER FOURTEEN

ZACH WOKE up the next morning half-afraid it had all been a dream. The sunlight was warm and brilliant through the curtains, his body was deliciously exhausted, and Rae's naked arse was pressed against his dick, teasing it back to life anyway. He lay there for a while and wondered how today would go—if she'd regret the things she'd said and pull away from him. And how he'd stand it.

Then she woke up, purred, and spread her lovely legs.

In the end, he fucked her slow and sweet from behind. Worshipped her body, kissed the line of her throat, and lived and died for the way she said his name. After, he held his breath and waited for her to speak. To bring this thing between them fully into the light.

But it never happened. They didn't talk about the night before, about the touches or the tears. Instead, she kissed him tenderly on the mouth, then gave him a one-sided smile that made his heart beat faster. And if something in his mind whispered that this wasn't enough, that they needed to communicate—to finally be straight with one another—well... that whisper was easy to ignore when he had Rae to hold.

And when he had a job to do. He was still her fake boyfriend, and he remembered as they dressed for breakfast that tonight was the awards ceremony. Rae was nervous as fuck; she hid it well, but he could tell. Worry made her edgy and thoughtful and quiet. She needed his support—yet another reason to save his difficult, what-about-us questions until they got home.

She looked worn and vulnerable today in a cartoon cactus T-shirt, slight shadows cradling her eyes. But tiredness didn't stop her from typing frantically on her phone every so often—so fast and so focused that Zach knew she was spinning stories. Judging by the look of satisfaction on her face, Rae's writer's block had well and truly broken. So, as they wandered down the corridor toward the lift, he coaxed her out of nervous silence and into storytelling.

"Myra's on the examination table," Rae was saying, while Zach melted at the cautious excitement in her voice. "The stone is cold against her bare skin; her body is strung tight with the effort of keeping still. Her husband holds out a hand, and murmurs, 'Alanna. The talisman.'"

Zach interrupted just to get on her nerves, to distract her even further from the weight of their evening plans. "I've got questions about this Alanna character. Where, exactly, did she come from?"

Rae shot him an unconvincing glare. The corner of her mouth twitched, her eyes sparkled with something indefinable, and laughter danced beneath her reprimand.

"Shut up and listen to the story." They swerved out of the way of a cleaner's trolley and murmured polite greetings like normal human beings. Then they went back to irritating each other.

"I'm just wondering," Zach said reasonably. "Like, is he fucking her? Is she pure evil, or something? Who would sleep with a guy who cuts up his own wife for fun?"

"If you stop blabbing for a second," Rae said sweetly, "you'll find out."

"Sorry. Sorry! Go on."

"You're too kind." She rolled her eyes. "So. Lune holds out his hand and says, 'Alanna. The talisman.' Alanna steps out of the shadows, and Myra sees the woman completely for the first time. She doesn't look quite human, but then, neither does Myra's husband."

"What's wrong with her?" Zach asked. "Alanna, I mean."

Rae tutted. "I was getting to that."

"Well, come on. The suspense is killing me. What is she, green?"

"Of course she's not green. She's not a bloody plant."

"Beast Boy's green," Zach pointed out. "He's not a plant."

Rae wrinkled her nose. "Who the hell is Beast Boy?"

"Oh, Rae. *Rae.* You did *not* just say that." Zach clasped a hand to his chest, giving her a look of agonised betrayal. "You and me need to have a little talk about your comic book education."

She smiled slowly and murmured, "Educate me, then."

Just like that, electric heat burned away his amusement.

They took the stairs that morning, instead of the lift. There were more dark corners.

Zach spent the rest of the day stealing Rae's breathless kisses, just to feel her soften and relax in his arms. At the panel discussions they watched that afternoon, he whispered nonsense in her ear and made her laugh when she was trying to be serious. And every time, she gave him this hopeful, tentative look from the corner of her eye, as if she didn't quite believe things could be this easy, but she wanted to.

She'd get used to it. He'd make sure.

THAT EVENING, he sat on the bed in his suit, compulsively checking his watch. There wasn't much planning involved tonight; his schedule covered such complicated points as *Get ready* and *Walk downstairs*. But he was nervous, because Rae was nervous, so he found himself breaking their time into tiny pieces. If they left in five minutes, they'd have about seven minutes to wander down and find their seats, and maybe eight minutes before the event itself really got going. He'd given Rae a ten-minute warning fifteen minutes ago, because he'd known she'd be late, so altogether...

She came out of the bathroom, and her presence wiped his mind clean. Zach was facing the window, so he didn't see her. He didn't really hear her either; her bare feet were quiet against the carpet. But something in the air shifted, warmed, until he felt more comfortable in his own skin, and he knew. Then he saw her reflection in the window, and that turned out to be a good thing, because if he'd looked at her directly without warning, he might've passed the fuck out.

She was so beautiful, he still couldn't believe it sometimes.

He stood, turning to face her. Rae wore the kind of fancy, floor-length dress that he didn't have the words to describe accurately. All he could say: it was a pale blue that made her brown skin glow; it had thin straps and a low neckline shaped like a heart; its silky fabric clung to her curves, then flared out softly from her knees. Her hair was up in some fancy style with actual jewels stuck in it, as if she really was a princess. Or a queen, more like. She looked like a distant, regal, fairy-tale creature and it was doing strange things to his insides.

But she was worried about tonight. He saw it in the way she held herself, and the way her tongue pushed out her cheek. His heart squeezed because she was so fucking brilliant, yet she still doubted herself.

He spoke without thinking. "It doesn't matter if you win."

She smiled softly. "I know."

"So why are you freaking out?"

Her mouth twisted, the smile turning rueful. "Not sure. Knowing and feeling are two different things."

"But you're okay?"

She nodded. "I'm okay."

"Good." He crossed the room to take her hands, pulling her closer. When she came without hesitation, something tense inside him started to unravel. He wrapped his arms around her waist, held her a little too tight—but she held him tight, as well, her fingers twisting his shirt, creasing the fabric. He nuzzled her neck, breathed her in, and told her, "You look perfect."

"Thank you." She must have heard the love-struck fervency in his voice, but she didn't push him away. "You're not too shabby yourself."

"I know," he winked, and she laughed. Then he sobered again, because it was important that she understand something. "You know you already won, right? You came here, and you had a good time, and you took up the space you're entitled to. You won. Tell me you get that."

"I do." Humour sparked in her dark gaze, and she flashed him a smile. "Plus, I finally got laid."

Not so long ago, the way she said that might've given him pause. But he was confident, now, that she felt something for him, something real—so he just laughed, and meant it.

"I got laid by *you*," she added, making the whole thing sweeter. "Zach Davis, hottest guy on earth."

He cupped her face, desperate to kiss her, and whispered, "Flatterer."

She kept going, her eyes burning into his, as if they were trying to share something her lips couldn't bear to spill. "The hottest guy on earth and the best man I know. I have another secret: I wouldn't take anyone else."

It was like she knew exactly what to say to silence the last of his whispering demons. Tomorrow they would leave this place and all its complications behind. He would tell her everything that he'd kept locked inside his chest, and it wouldn't scare her away. Because she would feel the same.

He kissed her hard, until she laughed and warned, "Makeup." He'd hate to ruin something that had taken her so long, so he made a face and smacked her arse. Then he enjoyed the hell out of her widening eyes and her slight, shy smile.

"Soon as this ceremony ends, Rae..."

She licked her lips. "Tease."

~

THE AWARDS WERE HELD in a huge function room, rammed with so many circular, white tables that the space seemed impossibly cramped. There was a stage put up against a backdrop of blue velvet, and a screen hovered against that backdrop, currently displaying the Burning Quill logo. At the front of the stage was a podium flooded by spotlights and a little table holding a ton of awards that looked like bronze quills. The room already hummed with chatter, guests buzzing from table to table like bees in a hive.

Zach noticed more than a few eyes turning their way as they skirted through the crowd, and he knew Rae did too. He kept waiting for her to look uncomfortable, to shrink the way she sometimes did in this world. Her ex-husband's world.

Except she didn't.

The Rae in front of him, tugging him along by the hand, was the Rae he knew from Ravenswood. Head high, pace unhurried, almost obnoxiously unconcerned. When she looked for their table, her eyes slid over the gawkers like a dare: *Go on. Keep watching. Maybe I'll put on a show.*

He couldn't control his grin.

When they finally found their place on the left side of the room, not too far from the front, she sat like a queen on a throne and crossed her legs in a flash of blue silk. He dragged his chair closer to hers, slung an arm over her shoulders, and prepared for a long evening of ignoring everyone else at their table. Whispering with Rae was way better than acting like an adult, and tonight he was going to indulge himself.

"You excited?" he murmured, his lips hovering just below her ear. Right where he knew she was deliciously sensitive.

She shivered, flicked him a warning look, but couldn't hide her smile. "Stop that."

"What? This?" He brushed his lips over her skin, and she released a breathy sigh. Then she put her hand high on his thigh and squeezed.

From the corner of her mouth she whispered, "I can make tonight very difficult for you."

He didn't doubt it. Fuck, the *sight* of her was making things 'difficult'. He kissed her cheek and said ruefully, "Got it."

Her laugh was low and satisfied.

Zach shook his head, grinning, and looked up—right into the eyes of Kevin Cummings. Everything that had been soft and warm in Zach solidified, his back teeth meeting with a *clack*. He glared daggers and hoped the *Fuck off* message was clear. Rae did not need this prick staring at her all night. Although, with the mood she was in, she'd probably handle it fine.

Kevin looked away after a moment, fiddling with his shirt collar. Grey suit, maroon tie, and beside him was the wife—Billie, Zach thought—in a dress the same deep shade of red. Kid was nowhere to be found, which at this time of night was probably for the best. Zach kept half an eye on Twat and Twatter while he and Rae chatted. As the evening got underway and the emcee took to the stage, he couldn't help but notice that Kevin *and* Billie's eyes were drawn to Rae like flies to honey. Billie's most of all, her pale gaze flicking over every five goddamn seconds. She seemed almost... nervous.

What did she think Rae was going to do, storm over there and slap her? Zach rolled his eyes and looked away.

The ceremony wasn't as boring as it could've been, mostly because everyone who won made a genuinely interesting acceptance speech. Rae sat through them all with a polite smile and faraway eyes, but the tension humming through her body told him she was still on edge. And then, finally, her category came.

The emcee was an older woman with flaming red hair and a loud, sixty-a-day rasp that was charming rather than grating. She was swathed in green and black velvet, her many crystal necklaces clattering when she moved. She waved her thin arms excitedly—which was an action she executed often—and said hoarsely, "The nominees for best debut *are...*"

With each name and title, a book appeared on the screen behind her. When Zach saw Rae's, it was all he could do not to surge to his feet and cheer like a parent on a school sports day. He watched Rae's face instead and witnessed her quiet, consuming pleasure. Pride like he'd never felt before flooded his heart with warmth.

He pulled her closer and whispered in her ear, "You done good, Baby Ann."

She must've been happy as fuck, because she didn't even glare at him. Just smiled wider and murmured, "I have, haven't I?"

The emcee took a deep breath and intoned, "And, the winner is…"

Everything about Rae stilled.

"*Heartsworn* by Thomas Murray!"

Rae barely faltered, clapping loudly for the guy who'd won—a white-haired man with glasses and an awed, disbelieving expression. But Zach saw the momentary shadow in her eyes and the tiny slump of her shoulders. He bent his head to kiss one of those shoulders and said beneath the cover of applause, "I've decided awards are for losers."

She nodded solemnly. "We're too edgy to care about external validation."

"Yep."

She leaned closer, looking up at him. "Can I say something horrifyingly sappy?"

Oh, this should be good. "I would *love* for you to say something horrifyingly sappy."

"Do you promise to forget I said it as soon as the words leave my mouth?"

He grinned. "Absolutely not."

"Ugh. Fine." She took a breath and said in a teasing tone, "Maybe I won something better than an award this weekend."

The applause had faded now, so he bit back his delighted laugh. Pulled her as close as he could without dragging her onto his lap and scandalizing everyone in the room. "Jesus, sunshine. That was awful."

"I know."

"Say it again," he murmured.

"Piss off."

The announcements continued while he and Rae quietly misbehaved. She whispered to him about nominees and tried to guess the winners before they were announced. When one of her favourite authors won an award for a short story, she clapped so hard Zach worried she might hurt her hands. And through it all, she leaned toward him almost unthinkingly, as if they were connected by more than just nearness and touch. Not once did he find himself wondering how many of their interactions were real or fake. She'd practically told him. In Rae-speak, she'd just poured the contents of her heart into his lap. For the first time all weekend, he knew exactly where they stood.

Until the biggest category of the night began, almost an hour later.

By now, he was used to the emcee's drama, so he barely registered when she announced the "Best Full-Length High Fantasy nominees!" But then he noticed that Rae was holding her breath, a familiar mixture of nerves and near-excitement in her avid gaze. He started paying attention to the awards again just in time to hear the final nominee: "...And, Kevin Cummings with *Everlee*."

He saw the image on the screen, and his blood turned thick and sluggish in his veins. He knew that book. He'd seen it. It was the book he'd picked up from Rae's luggage on their first day here, the one she'd snatched out of his hands. Something cold crept over his skin. Rae watched the stage like her life depended on it, but Zach... Zach watched her face.

The emcee opened a shiny envelope and joked, "Drumroll, please!" There was a weighty pause before she beamed, crowing, "And the winner is: *Everlee* by Kevin Cummings!"

Rae bloomed with sheer joy.

It was the kind of happiness no-one else would even notice, carefully controlled and quickly suppressed. But sometimes it felt like there was a direct line between Zach's heart and Rae's hidden feelings, so he couldn't have missed it if he'd tried. Her applause was polite, and her smile was stiff, but he saw the flash of pleasure in her eyes, lighting her up inside like a firework. He knew what it meant when the edge of her mouth curled that way, the restrained excitement it signified. She was ecstatic. Beside herself. Over the fucking moon. All because Kevin had won.

She might as well have punched Zach in the gut.

He straightened in his seat, swallowed hard, and tried to explain this away. Tried to tell himself, for the thousandth time, that he knew this or he sensed that. Except, even when he wracked his mind, he couldn't find a damned scrap of knowledge about Rae that would explain such a reaction.

Well. Except for one awful possibility. Maybe, for whatever reason, she still wasn't over Kevin.

The idea was ridiculous, until it wasn't. Zach's memories shifted, took on another dimension, as if he'd never seen the full story until now. From the start, Rae had been worried about bumping into her ex and his new wife. She'd latched on to the fake boyfriend idea with surprising ease. The one time they'd actually met Kevin, she'd come out of the situation furious with Zach rather than her shitty ex. And now, here she was, losing it over the guy's book. Which, apparently, she carried around with her like some kind of lucky charm.

Understanding was an icy trickle down Zach's spine. Finally, he realised just how foolish he'd been. Rae had said from the start that she wasn't interested in relationships, but he'd pushed and pushed and pushed, with actions if not with words. He'd decided they had some unspoken connection, that she was simply skittish, and he was—what, *fixing* her? Healing all her wounds with the magic of good sex and conversation? God, what fucking arrogance. What absolute delusion. She'd probably given up trying to smack him over the head with the truth. Must have decided it was easier to let him build fantasies around friendship and fucking.

Except... Zach dragged his thoughts under control with an iron fist, forcing himself not to get carried away. Tonight, Rae had made it clear that she wanted him in more ways than one. Maybe there hadn't been any confessions of love, but he knew her, and he knew what she'd meant. So, he wouldn't lose his shit and make assumptions. He'd stop fucking around, sit her down, and ask her. They'd finally talk like actual adults, and he would know for sure what this thing was.

The thought, sensible and logical as it may be, didn't make him feel any better. Didn't soothe the hot, prickling well of his panic or stop worries racing through his mind.

He tried to reassure himself, to remember that Kevin was a toxic, controlling prick, and that last night in bed, Rae had been so different. But what did *different* really mean? This was the problem. Zach had *almost*s and *possibly*s and sex-soaked hints; Rae and Kevin had an entire marriage. A shitty marriage, from the sound of things—but love didn't always make sense. Sometimes saplings survived in wastelands.

And sometimes hope wasn't enough.

SOMETHING WAS WRONG WITH ZACH.

Rae's shoulders were cold and bare where his arm should rest. Her side missed the press of his body. Her mood dipped without regular shots of his smile. During the final hour of the ceremony, he clapped with robotic stiffness and held himself distant from her, while she worried and watched the clock. A handful of hours ago, she'd believed that this ceremony would be the worst kind of torture. And now, it was—but not for the reasons she'd expected.

In fact, concern for Zach aside, she felt kind of... powerful tonight. Maybe it was the stern pep talk she'd given herself in the bathroom before coming down. The one where she'd decided it was time to be truly brave, to tell Zach outright that she adored him, that she wanted to build something real and romantic with him. Something that felt impossible but might actually work.

Or maybe her iron spine came from the ceremony itself, and the knowledge that she'd made it. That she deserved to be here, and that this world wasn't Kevin's—it was hers.

Whatever the reason, she was eager to grab her happiness, and that happiness was Zach. So, when the ceremony wound up, she rushed her way through conversation with Neil and a few other writers. Congratulated acquaintances, accepted consolations, and clutched Zach's cool, stiff hand as if they could communicate through their skin. It didn't work.

She was so desperate to fix whatever had turned him to stone, she couldn't even wait to drag him upstairs. Instead, she tugged him into a semi-private alcove, turning away from the crowd to cup his cheek. "What's wrong?"

He tilted his head, just enough to shake her off. The movement was so subtle it might have been an accident, but something in her chest constricted.

"Nothing's wrong," he said, but he was a terrible liar. It might've been funny if fear weren't scuttling over her like spiders.

"Clearly it's something," she said, moving closer. But he flinched away, and she froze. Froze, curled up inside, and died. Still, she managed to speak calmly through sheer force of will. "You're upset. Please tell me why."

"This is your night," he murmured. "We'll do this another time. Tomorrow."

For a moment, she thought that he knew—but of course he didn't. He couldn't. "Oh, come on. It's not like I won." She laughed, and meant it, because the fact didn't bother her. Not anymore.

But Zach sighed, shook his head, and said, "Exactly," as

if she were seconds from a tragic breakdown. For heaven's sake.

"It doesn't matter what tonight is," she frowned. "You can't put your feelings on hold to avoid disrupting other people. Or maybe you can, but you shouldn't, and I don't want you to. Please, Zach. Tell me what's wrong."

An expression she couldn't quite read passed over his face, something indefinable but achingly sad. Then he asked, "Are you still in love with Kevin?"

She jerked back, shocked. "No, I'm not. Why would you say that?"

"You have his book." Zach's voice was quiet but powerful, like the hiss of explosive gas from a broken pipe. "I saw it. You tried to hide it, remember? But I know it's in your suitcase, and I saw how happy you were when he won—"

"No," Rae interrupted through numb lips. "No." But she could see he didn't believe her. She wanted to shout, *How could you think I give a damn about Kevin when I'm in love with you?* But then she remembered the crowd.

Oh, God, the crowd.

Why had she pushed? Her horrified gaze slid out toward the mass of people that filled the room. Already, a few groups eyed them curiously. Something inside her shrivelled up.

"Rae," Zach said. "This thing between us—I know I came here as a favour, but when I touched you, I meant it. And I told myself you meant it, too. The truth is, I... I'm not attracted to you just because we're friends. I have feelings for you. I've been making a lot of excuses to stay silent about that, to avoid demanding something you can't give. I've never wanted to push you. But I can't explain this away." He watched her with burning, hopeful eyes, as if she might leap in and fix his confusion with just a few words. Christ, he'd just confessed to having *feelings* for her. This was the perfect moment to admit everything, to finally be honest with him and with herself.

But the declarations she'd practiced in the bathroom mirror were frozen on her lips, scared off by the excruciating exposure of this situation. She hadn't been prepared for conflict, or for Zach to drag at secrets she couldn't possibly share—never mind for his confession, as wonderful as it was. Her heart pounded, her palms began to sweat, and she felt familiar panic lap at her mind like waves against the shore.

"If you don't still care about Kevin, why do you have his book?" Zach asked, soft but urgent. "I need you to tell me. Can you do that?"

She heard the words he'd never say, the ones she deserved. *Can you do that single fucking thing for me? It's not like you've done anything else.*

She wanted to. So badly. But then, over Zach's shoulder, she caught sight of Kevin moving through the room, grinning wide and shaking hands, accepting congratulations. The past seemed so close all of a sudden.

"I can't," she whispered. "Not right now. Can't you—just—trust me?"

Zach's gaze remained wary, but something about him seemed to unfurl, as if his soul were turning toward hers again. He asked in turn, "Do you trust me?"

She laughed, high-pitched and a little hysterical. She didn't mean to; it just happened, a reflexive response to a

219

preposterous question. Of course Rae didn't trust him—she *loved* him. The two things never mixed.

But Zach clearly didn't see the humour. She watched him ice over before her eyes, cold, cold, cold. Her laughter died in her throat, and she realised all at once how badly she was fucking this up. *As always.*

He spoke quietly, his voice hard. "You won't ever trust me, will you?"

"I—" She hadn't thought about it. She couldn't think about it. "I don't know. It's not that simple. But Zach, if you just—"

"No." The word was sharp, like it had burst out of him without permission. Then he repeated, softer, slower. "No, Rae. I think I've been fooling myself this weekend. Filling in all your gaps. But I don't want to be that person anymore."

The gentleness in his voice knocked the air out of her lungs. *Filling in her gaps.* That sounded about right—and she had so fucking many. Must be so exhausting. But still, selfishly, she whispered, "Please."

"I'm leaving," he said. "Tonight. I think that's for the best."

CHAPTER FIFTEEN

HEADING home had been the smartest choice.

So what if Rae had seemed so alone, standing separate amongst a crowd as she watched Zach walk away? And so what if he'd thought he glimpsed pain in those helpless, hypnotic eyes? Of course she was hurt. They cared about each other—but clearly not enough, and Zach was exhausted by the constant imbalance in his relationships. He'd shoved down his feelings, rage or despair or discomfort, for so many people, just to make them happy. But he refused to hide love or longing. He refused to accept lust and affection without trust. He refused to *make* himself right for Rae. Not because she wasn't important enough, but because she was everything.

It hurt too much.

So, he had made a clean break. And yet, three days later, Zach didn't feel clean at all. He was blazing with anger at nothing in particular, or maybe at himself. His mind was all jagged edges, torn-up bits and pieces of the man he wanted to be. He stood under his shower's scalding hot spray after a long day at work, muscles screaming almost as loud as his head. While the water ran into his eyes, he stared blankly at the tiles and tried not to think about Rae.

Rae, Rae, Rae.

Maybe he should've noticed that she had feelings for Kevin. Maybe, if he'd pulled his head out of his arse—no, out of *her* arse—for five seconds, he would've.

He twisted the shower off a bit harder than necessary, ignoring the screech of his shitty, old plumbing. The floorboards creaked as he dried off and got dressed, reminding him of Rae's horror at his 'serial killer house'. The memory made him want to smile, which made him want to fucking cry. He was a fool. He was a mess. He was in love, and he was furious about it. So furious that he simply stood for a moment, staring at nothing, wondering how to handle this.

His first thought was to calm down, take deep breaths, and let the moment pass. But it had been days now, and this 'moment' wasn't passing at all. In fact, he didn't want it to. Sitting with it, *feeling* it, felt raw and real and right.

And he had a feeling that talking about it might feel even better.

He was moving before the thought had fully formed. Striding over to his bedside table, picking up his phone, navigating to a much-observed and never-contributed-to forum whose black and purple display had grown so familiar over the months. Before he could think better of it, Zach hit 'Create' to start a brand-new thread. Then, his chest heaving with the quickening breaths he'd barely even noticed, he stared down at the screen.

Title, it said. *Type here,* it said.

What the fuck did he want to say?

The words came out eventually, halting and laboured —but that didn't matter, because once it was over, it was over. He'd typed out the truth, and it didn't look any less honest just because his hands had been shaking as he'd done it.

I'm Angry

I fell in love. She hurt me. What do I do now? I don't know, and I'm not in the mood to figure it out.

He pressed *Send*, then squeezed his eyes shut and gritted his teeth against a sudden rush of nervous energy. Had he seriously just done that? Yes. Yes, he had.

Well, fuck it. Might as well comment on the DC thread, too.

Zach sat on his bed, found the thread, and finally let himself comment the way he'd long wanted to. Just slid in as if he had a right to be there, offering his opinion on the Netflix adaptation of *Teen Titans* (which was surprisingly good). Because he *did* have a right to be there. Taking up that kind of space, even just online, felt almost perfect. He found himself smiling slightly for the first time in a while, imagining how he'd tell Rae—

No. No, he wouldn't tell Rae. He couldn't tell her anything. And just like that, some of his pleasure dimmed.

He missed her. He missed her so much that when the slow, haunting chime of his doorbell rang five minutes later, he let himself imagine it was Rae. That she'd come over to say something, anything, the *perfect* thing—the thing that would prove him wrong. She'd throw herself into his arms and whisper magic words in his ear, and then maybe she'd propose because she was just that overwhelmed by her feelings for him. He'd say yes, and Duke would be the ring bearer at their wedding, and she'd wear a thousand tiny braids in her hair.

It was an excellent fantasy that lasted about as long as it took Zach to jog down the stairs, open his door, and find his brother and his best mate on the doorstep.

"Oh," he said, disappointed but not particularly surprised. "It's you."

Nate rolled his eyes and shoved his way into the house, grim as a big, pale crow. Evan followed with a smile and a warm, "Alright, mate?"

"What do you want?" Zach asked, trying to sound less dead inside. It was something he'd been working on over the last few days, ever since that late-night, last-minute train back from Manchester. He hadn't gotten the hang of it yet.

Nate stared at him for a moment, then nodded at Evan. "You were right. He's all… grey."

"I know," Evan said sadly. "And he hasn't been sneaking off to meet Rae every morning."

Oh, for fuck's sake. "I don't sneak. And if I'm grey," he glared at his brother, "it's because we're both ridiculously pale and I haven't been taking my vitamins. Go away."

Instead of obeying like a good sibling, Nate wandered off into the living room, Evan bringing up the rear like a labrador with a disturbing independent streak.

Zach wondered how Duke was doing, then shut down that train of thought before he could wonder how *Rae* was doing, or if she missed him. It didn't matter if she missed him. He couldn't be around her anymore. He was working really hard on not being in love with her, and he knew for a fact that if he saw her smile or heard her voice, all his efforts would be wasted.

Of course, Ravenswood was a small town, and they shared the same friends, so he was probably doomed. Maybe he should give up and accept his fate: eternally unrequited adoration. Zach sighed, followed Nate and Evan into the living room, and sank into his favourite armchair like a sack of bones and despair.

Evan's brows rose. "I'm glad we came. Obviously, we're not a moment too soon."

"What are you talking about?" Zach asked, then muttered, "Actually, I don't care. Piss off."

"This is an intervention," Nate said in his Firm and Fatherly voice. It didn't work on his kids, and it wasn't working on Zach, either.

"Piss. Off."

Nate's expression softened, a worried crease appearing between his brows. "Zach. Do you need help?"

Fuck. That wasn't a question Zach could brush off, because he and Nate had promised each other—with good reason—to always answer it honestly, so he forced himself to breathe. To sort through his emotions. He found a tempest inside himself, all rage and pain and soul-deep disappointment, but that was it. He was heartbroken, but he wasn't depressed, so he wasn't in any particular danger.

"No," he said. "I don't need help."

Nate didn't ask if he meant it. Just nodded. "Alright. You fucked up with Rae, huh?"

You fucked up with Rae. Zach gritted his teeth and willed himself not to blow. Or at least, to keep a lid on the explosion, same way he always did. But maybe keeping a lid on it had left him with charred insides. Maybe someone else should feel the fucking heat for a change.

Before he could think better of it, he said sharply, "Because this has to be my fault, right?"

Nate blinked, clearly brought up short. Evan leapt into the silence, always the peacekeeper, shooting Nate a warning glare. "No. Of course not. Why don't you tell us what happened?"

But the calming voice didn't work. There was a tide of anger rising in Zach, bitter and harsh and eternally unspoken. He'd held it back for so long, just in case too much temper drove people away. In case it made everyone —even his brother—disappear again.

Well, fuck that. It wasn't Zach's job to make anyone hang around. And he wasn't to blame if they left.

"You know what's wrong with me?" he asked, rising to his feet. "What's wrong with me is I'm fucking *furious.*"

Nate blinked, sitting up straight. "With—me? What did I—?"

"With everything." The words weren't supposed to come out as a shout, but they did, bouncing off the house's high, cobwebbed ceilings. The slight echo felt like support. Which, in turn, reminded Zach of Rae.

When he spoke again, he was quieter, but every word burned. "I'm pissed at all my so-called fucking friends for disappearing when I needed them. I'm pissed at Callie Michaelson for loitering outside work when she needed her car fixed, even though I hadn't seen her in months. I'm pissed at both of you" —he jabbed a finger at Evan, who looked confused and horrified all at once— "for bugging me to hook up with someone. Even though I know you meant well, and you're trying to be supportive, and it's not your fault that you don't know I'm demisexual."

Snapping out each word felt like bleeding the poison from Zach's veins, filling him with an odd, giddy sort of relief. He was finally doing it. He was releasing everything that festered inside him, pouring it somewhere other than a hunk of molten metal, and his world hadn't collapsed yet.

Quite the opposite, actually. Despite his aching heart, despite his misery, Zach was flying. Soaring. Free.

Evan, sounding mildly dazed, said, "Demiwhat?"

Still irritable, Zach muttered, "And I'm pissed I'll always have to fucking explain that." But then he remembered the person he *didn't* have to explain it to, and that made everything worse. The fire in him evaporated, and he sat down again, so hard it jarred his bones. Under his breath, he said finally, "I'm pissed that I'm in love with Rae, and she's still in love with her ex."

There was a moment of dumbfounded silence before Evan beamed, "You're in love with Rae?"

Almost at the same time, Nate scowled, "Rae's in love with her ex?"

It was weird; the first of those sentences hit Zach right, a humming note of truth, while the second grated on him like the scream of steel on steel. He opened his mouth to say "Yes," anyway, but he couldn't. He just couldn't.

"Are you sure?" Nate went on, his scepticism obvious. "Because according to Hannah, Rae hates her ex's guts."

"Yeah, well," Zach bit out. "Hannah's smart, but she's not a bloody mind reader. Things are... complicated."

"Did she *tell* you she loved him?" Evan asked, reasonable as ever.

"Rae's not so good at saying things out loud." Although it hit Zach suddenly that she had, in fact, said something out loud on that horrible night. Repeatedly.

"*No.*"

He'd asked if she was in love with Kevin, and she'd said no.

Zach swallowed and sat up straight. He heard his brother say something, but he couldn't focus on the words. His mind was stuck on the night of the ceremony, a night that blurred with hurt and frustration and distrust. He hadn't believed Rae's denial, had dismissed it instantly, but now he polished murky details until they shone like gems, and remembered...

The shock in her voice, as if she couldn't believe what he was saying. The vehemence. And her obvious, tongue-tied discomfort, which he'd put down to their awkward conversation. Only now did it occur to him that Rae hated to argue in public.

He'd been so preoccupied that he'd forgotten that. Again.

"Hey." Nate raised his voice, cutting through Zach's concentration. "Are you listening to me?"

"No."

That gave the other man pause. "Uh... are you sure you're okay?"

Zach repeated, "No."

Nate and Evan shared a look.

He ignored it. Possibility was dawning in him like some toxic sun. He shouldn't stare directly at the light, but he had a suspicion that refused to let go, and he owed it to himself to prove or disprove it. Surely, he deserved that much.

Slowly, Zach said, "I need you guys to leave. I have something to do."

Nate snorted. "I'm not leaving. You just dropped more than a few bombs on us, and I want to make sure you're—"

"Listen," Zach cut in, because he had something urgent to deal with. "I need you to go."

"Zach—"

"By the way," he added, "demisexuality is a way of feeling attraction that's on the asexual spectrum. I'm demi, and I don't give a fuck what you think about that. Even if —especially if—you don't think it's real, or that it matters. But I trust you, and neither of you are arseholes, so I'm 99% positive everything's going to be fine. If you could both fuck off and Google it, so I don't have to play teacher, and maybe text me to let me know you're not gonna be dicks, that'd be amazing. Thanks." He strode across the room, grabbed both speechless men by the arm, and dragged them with surprising ease toward the door. Apparently, they were too astonished to put up much a fight.

"Zach," Evan tried, "do you think we could all just talk—"

"Later. I promise, later. I'm busy."

"Wait," Nate said. "Just so you know, I don't give a fuck

if you're demi... uh, demisexual. I don't know what it is yet, but I know I support you. Okay?"

Zach met his brother's eyes, a slight smile curving his lips. "Okay."

"Me, too," Evan added.

"Good. Now piss off." Zach shoved them out of the door with a quick goodbye, then went to grab his wallet and keys. He needed to buy a book.

But, before he could leave the house, his phone vibrated in his back pocket. He pulled it out and saw a notification that stopped him in his tracks. Someone had replied to his thread, the one about Rae.

WonderWomxn81: Been there. I know it's hard to believe, but everything will be okay in the end. <3

He stared at the message for long moments, a bitter-sweet smile curving his lips. For some reason, this calm support from a distant stranger meant a hell of a lot. Maybe because the stranger, whoever they were, got it. Maybe because that stranger didn't have to remain one. After a while, the *bittersweet* part of Zach's pleasure faded, leaving plain old satisfaction and a brand-new strength behind.

Perhaps reading Kevin's book would unlock some grand mystery that brought Zach and Rae back together. But if it didn't—if he never truly had her, and this was really it—well. He'd survive.

Remembering that helped.

RAE WANTED to find Zach and fix things. She did. Maybe

she even could. But she'd decided, after four days spent working through the thorny tangle of her own fear, that she shouldn't.

Their argument had started with a misunderstanding, but that in itself proved she wasn't right for him. If she were, she could've stopped things before they went too far. Could've overcome all her layers of anxiety and taken control of the situation. If Rae was the kind of woman Zach needed, she would've whispered her secret in his ear, and said without hesitation that she trusted him, that she returned his feelings, and everything would've been fine.

But she hadn't.

The most galling part of it all was knowing that she *did* trust Zach. After hours of lying awake in their hotel room with tears streaming down her cheeks, the realisation had arrived to crush what was left of her heart. She trusted Zach Davis like no-one else—which was why she'd made him her fake boyfriend in the first place, why she'd shared her secrets and her desire with him—but the feeling was so unnatural and unexpected that she'd never even recognised it.

Which described her problem in a nutshell, didn't it? She was a mess of hesitation, and he was the kind of man who loved unreservedly. She kept too many parts of herself locked up safe, but sometimes *safe* was another word for *trapped*. She'd grown to rely on her cage, and until she was ready to change that, she should stay away from him.

Still, for the thousandth time in a handful of days, she found herself staring at his name in her phone, wondering if it would be so wrong to call.

Rae sighed, put the phone down, and bent to tangle her fingers in Duke's silky fur. He rolled his teddy bear eyes up at her, sympathy glimmering in their depths, or possibly condemnation. Her interpretation depended on her mood.

"Take pity," she said. "I am just a sad and lonely dog mum."

Duke huffed and pushed his wet nose into her palm. His sweetness made her smile, but it didn't make her whole again, didn't even slap a bandage on her many wounds. That wasn't Duke's fault, or anyone else's. Rae had changed. Become just that bit more tragic, she supposed. Must be a side-effect of feeling love slip through your fingers like sand.

"I should put some of this melodrama to use," she told Duke, letting go of his fur with one last, wistful pat. She was sitting at her desk, determined to be productive and creative and brilliant. She still had her stories, after all, and they would never leave. In fact, her current misery was perfect for a scene she had planned, one involving betrayal by a lifelong friend and blood-spattered, tear-stained cheeks. She could do this, at least. Her wits were sharp, her talent was unmatched, and oh, for Christ's sake, her phone was ringing. Hadn't she turned it off?

Irritated, she snatched it up and answered without checking the display. "Hello?"

"Baby! *Finally*. I hope you don't always answer the phone like that, dear. It's not very charming."

Rae's stomach dropped out of her body, smashed a hole through the floor, and sank into her shiny new house's foundations. Shit. Shit, shit, shit.

It was her mother.

Maybe Duke heard that grating, upbeat trill, because he stood and put his big head in Rae's lap. She slid her fingers into his fur again and took a deep breath. "Hi, Mum."

"I don't suppose there's any point asking where you've been," Marilyn sighed. "Honestly, anyone would think I had no daughter!"

The words made Rae's gut clench. She'd heard them too many times, thrown like grenades in an argument, to see them as anything other than a honeyed threat.

"Sorry." She waited for more veiled barbs, for the inevitable escalation, but Marilyn just tutted. She must be in a good mood. Perhaps this would be one of their happy moments, a conversation where nothing particularly terrible happened and Rae forgot to hate her mother. That would be nice. That would be just what she needed, right now.

"Well, never mind," Marilyn said, and Rae's heart gave a hopeful little hop. "How are you, my dear? How's work? What have you been up to?"

"Work's good, thank you. The convention was last weekend—I don't know if you remember. I didn't win anything, but it was actually quite—"

"That's nice, darling. It's been a nightmare over here, of course, an absolute nightmare."

Rae rolled her lips inward, swallowing her words. "Oh, right. Really?"

"Yes. Your father—"

"Not my father," Rae murmured for the thousandth time.

"—*insisted* we get up early for some awful nature ramble, and you'll never guess what happened."

There was a pause.

"Well, go on," Marilyn said sharply. "Guess."

Rae cleared her throat, running her tongue nervously over the scar inside her cheek. "Ah... you got lost?"

"No."

"You twisted an ankle?"

"*No,*" Marilyn said, sounding deeply irritated. "Honestly, Baby, it's like conversing with a dead thing. If you don't have time to talk to your own mother, just say so."

And here were the warning signs. Marilyn seemed to live off confrontation like a leech fattened by discord. When Rae was younger, her mother's unrelenting arguments had been a devastating tornado, closing Rae's throat and making her palms sweat. She'd never quite gotten over that childhood fear.

But, for some reason, it was oddly absent today. There was no room for it. She was too busy being pissed off. "For God's sake, Mum, just tell me."

There was a wounded gasp. An ominous silence. And then it began. "Was there any need for that tone?"

Rae took a breath and said patiently, "I don't have a tone."

"Of course you don't, because it's never you, is it? It's always someone else's fault."

Her heart pounded its way up her throat. "Mum—"

"One of these days," Marilyn went on sadly, "you'll realise just how much I put up with. You were a difficult child, and now you're a difficult woman. It's as if you don't want anyone to love you. I mean, bad enough that you ruined your face—"

Ruined? Rae curled her hands into fists, her nails decorating her palms with crescent moons.

"—but you had a wonderful husband who stayed with you anyway. He was so devoted! Except, you just can't help yourself, can you? You're so excruciatingly *miserable*. I'm not surprised he needed a little freedom, in the end."

Rae squeezed the phone so hard her fingers paled. "That's enough, Mother."

"Now look at the mess you're in. You're not young and beautiful anymore, you know. Who's going to overlook your—your *ways*? It's high time you realised you aren't nearly as wonderful as you think you are."

Snap. The sound was almost audible. For a moment, Rae thought she'd broken her phone. Then she realised that razor-edged twang had been the death of her stretched-thin patience.

"That's *enough*, Mother." Her voice was harder than it had ever been during a conversation like this. Usually, she could barely speak, was too busy fighting shocked tears, her mind curling in on itself to hide from each verbal blow. But not today.

"Baby! Don't shout at me," Marilyn gasped, a slight wobble in her voice.

So many times, that wobble had convinced Rae she was a monster. That she, not her mother, was the problem with their relationship. That whenever she spoke out, she ruined things. And that belief, in turn, was why Rae had let Kevin control her, stifle her, drain her dry; it had seemed safer than the alternative. She'd been taught so thoroughly that standing up for herself was an act of aggression, it had taken her forty fucking years to figure out who she really was.

The realisation shimmered through her like an awakening. Her mother, Kevin—they were both so manipulative in such similar ways, and no-one had ever given her the tools to see it, never mind to defend herself. That was the problem. Not trust, but trusting the wrong people. Hadn't she learned, after laughing with Hannah and drinks at the Unicorn and kissing the man she loved, what closeness should be?

She had. It might take her a while and a whole lot of help to remember, sometimes. But she knew. Underneath the fear, she knew.

So, she set her shoulders, lifted her chin, and fought back. "You don't get to behave like this, Mother. You don't get to hurt the people who care about you. Not me, anyway, because I'm not going to let you."

Marilyn made a faint, strangled sound. "Baby Ann. What on earth are you talking about?"

"You know what I'm talking about," Rae snapped, then thought for a moment. "Or maybe you really, genuinely don't. In which case, that's sad, but it doesn't make this okay. And it's not my job to bear the brunt of your fucked up-ness. If that makes me a bad daughter, so be it. Because you are a bad mother."

The words seemed to hover in the air, as if she could reach out and snatch them back. As if she could recall the blasphemy safely into her mouth. But she didn't want to, because it was true. She released a pent-up breath, and her tense muscles loosened. The weight in her belly faded away. It was fucking true.

"Well," Marilyn huffed, part-wounded, part-raging. "*Well!*"

In a second, she'd recover from this shock, and then she'd launch some clever, scathing attack. It might slice Rae to pieces, or it might bounce off her new protective shield. They'd never know, because Rae didn't wait for it to come. She ended the call with a tap, but that didn't seem final enough, so she threw her phone at the wall for good measure.

It hit the plaster with a *thunk* and landed on the floor with a clatter. She stared dully, her chest heaving, her mind tingling like a numb limb coming back to life. Duke lifted his mammoth head from her lap and licked her wrist.

"Thanks, honey," she breathed. "I'm okay." And it almost felt true.

But not quite. Because deep down, she wasn't okay, never had been. Rae lived in a constant state of fearful defiance, always waiting for someone to lash out and hurt her, to use her as a whipping post, to throw her love back in her face. And that wasn't okay at all.

She stood and wiped her clammy palms on her jeans. Duke stayed by her side as she crossed the room to inspect the chip in her study's paint and the lovely new crack on her phone screen. "Real mature, McRae," she muttered to herself. But she didn't care about the phone. She was too busy worrying about all the other things she might have broken.

Precious, beloved things.

Duke whined and butted his head against Rae's thigh.

She looked down, but she didn't see him. She saw Zach's face, the way it had crumpled when she'd laughed, then hardened as he'd turned away. As he'd protected himself.

From her.

She remembered every excuse she'd made to avoid letting him in, and she wanted to kick herself. She'd spent the last few days actively avoiding him instead of rushing to explain, nursing her own scarred-over wounds instead of healing the fresh ones she'd inflicted on him.

Her love should be worth more than that.

"Duke," she said. "We're going for a walk."

CHAPTER SIXTEEN

ZACH'S TALL, thin, detached house really did look like the haunt of several vengeful phantoms. Rae wouldn't be surprised to find the bones of a serial-killer-slash-cannibal hidden in the attic. A thing like that would certainly explain the creepy aura that settled over the house's grimy, white-painted exterior like fog.

Though she'd been joking, weeks ago, when she'd refused to go to Zach's house, it didn't seem particularly funny now. Rae tightened her grip on Duke's lead as they approached. The place was giving her bad vibes—or maybe that was just her heart-pounding fear that Zach would take one look at her and slam the door in her face.

She'd deserve it. And she'd take it, along with anything else he wanted to dish out. She kept remembering little moments from their weekend together, moments when the truth of his feelings had been in his eyes, and she'd turned deliberately away. She'd been so terrified to trust him, but he had trusted her. Right until the end, against all the odds, he'd quietly, steadily trusted her. And she'd hurt him in return.

She rang the bell and waited as it hummed ominously. Then the door swung open, and there he was.

If she weren't so anxious, she'd melt at the sight of him: mouth-wateringly sexy, almost obnoxiously built, and shirtless. So thoroughly Zach, and so wonderfully familiar—except for the way his eyes widened when he saw her. And for the book in his hand.

Now *Rae's* eyes widened, her throat tightening, her fingers fiddling nervously with Duke's lead. Why the hell was Zach holding *Everlee*? Everything she'd planned to say flew out of her mind like a flock of startled pigeons.

Luckily, he spoke first, staring at her like she was some kind of alien. "Rae," he said, his voice faint with surprise, hoarse with something she couldn't quite identify. "You came. You came to the haunted serial killer house."

She wanted to smile, but she couldn't quite manage it, not when everything was so wrong between them. Still, she huffed out a humourless laugh and said, "Of course I did. You're here."

Something about him softened almost imperceptibly. He stepped back, holding the door wider, and said, "Come in. I promise there aren't any ghosts."

She did as he asked and was pleased when Duke followed without hesitation. Maybe the house wasn't as haunted as it looked. Then Zach shut the door behind them and held up the book, its iridescent cover flashing in the light. She almost winced at the sight of it.

His tone painfully neutral, he said, "I really hope you're here to tell me about this."

She swallowed hard. Of course he'd be direct. In her mind, she'd imagined things going more smoothly: he'd wait in polite silence while she recited her perfect speech, then offer her a fortifying cup of tea. After some deliberation, he might, perhaps, possibly, forgive her and love her despite her many flaws.

In reality, they stood in his draughty old hallway while he arched a dark brow in her direction. She supposed this was to be expected; apologies shouldn't be comfortable experiences for the one who'd done wrong.

"Yes," she said. "I came to talk about the book, and to explain that I'm not in love with Kevin."

"Talk," Zach repeated slowly, his expression impassive. "As in, you want to communicate. Out loud. Explicitly. Yeah?"

She could tell, by the weight of each word as they landed, that this question was important. She nodded. "Absolutely. All of that. So much." Was she overselling it? Maybe, but another reassurance bubbled over. "That's exactly what I want."

Zach almost smiled, a flash of warmth brightening his gaze. "Okay. Good." Then he waved the book and added without warning, "You wrote this, didn't you?"

For a moment, Rae was speechless—but she'd promised to talk. So, she pulled herself together and said, "Yes. Yes, I did."

ON PAGE 37, *Everlee's* hero faced off a god and told it,

politely but firmly, to fuck off. That was the moment Zach's sneaking suspicions had finally solidified.

He might've heard echoes of Rae's fantastic mind much earlier, only he'd been thrown off by the main characters' clichéd personalities. Honestly, the overdone story setup could've been lifted from any boring, white, male fantasy of the last twenty-five years—but once shit actually started happening, he saw Rae everywhere.

Which had finally convinced him that Rae didn't love her ex. In fact, after watching him win a coveted award for a book *she'd* written, she must hate the fucker. But questions still buried themselves in Zach's chest like poisoned arrows: why was Kevin's name on Rae's book? Why hadn't she told Zach the truth? And would the answers to this mystery change anything about their relationship?

Probably not, he told himself sternly. But useless hope crept into his heart, anyway.

"Come on," he said, after fussing over a demanding Duke. "Let's go and sit down."

All three of them padded into the living room where Zach had spent most of his free time yesterday, devouring this book. He wasn't the fastest reader—as much as he enjoyed it—but he was almost finished now. He supposed he could've stopped reading after the first fifty pages, but he hadn't wanted to. The ghost of Rae's voice trapped within the ink made him feel closer to her, soothing the hollow emptiness left behind by her absence.

And now she was here, completely ruining all his attempts at stoicism. When she curled up on the sofa with Duke, Zach chose the armchair, as far away as possible.

His hands were hungry for her, but he didn't trust them. He and Rae had spent one endless weekend touching each other without truth, communicating with something other than words—and look at the mess it had gotten them into. This time, she would talk, and he would listen.

She was beautiful today, from her scraped-back ponytail to the push of her tongue against her scarred cheek. As always, she hadn't dressed properly for the harsh spring weather, but he squashed the urge to take her reddened hands. If she was cold, she could warm herself up. That wasn't his job anymore.

She bit her lip, then said quietly, "I've decided it's best to explain everything at once."

Usually, Zach was the one explaining for other people, fixing rifts he hadn't caused and excusing shitty behaviour. But he didn't do that anymore, and apparently, with Rae, he didn't need to. Suddenly, she was all too happy to chat.

Well, *happy* might be overstating the matter. In fact, she looked vaguely sick—but she was talking, all the same. And an irrepressible part of his mind whispered, *She's doing this for me.*

"I'm not supposed to tell anyone this," she said, "but I should've told you. I'm going to tell you. Even though it makes me sound weak."

Without a second thought, he told her, "You could never be weak."

The look she gave him seemed to say, *And yet, I have been.* Then she began.

"In the last years of our marriage," she said, "Kevin was always angry. It reminded me of home. It made me nervous. The more he pushed me away, the more I wanted to please him." She gave a wry, one-sided smile and stroked Duke absently. "But, surprise, surprise, I never could."

Zach clamped his jaw tight, swallowing his response. No matter the circumstances, he couldn't help but rage for her. The people she loved just kept hurting her, and it made him want to rip heads from bodies.

"I thought maybe the problem was work," she went on. "He was behind on a deadline, and he wouldn't let me help. Usually, we'd talk through ideas, and I'd smooth out choppy scenes for him, but not this time."

"Wait," Zach scowled. "So, he made you do his work for him?"

Rae chuckled. "No, he didn't make me. I'd always wanted to be a writer, but agents and editors said I had no potential audience. I guess Kevin caught the writing bug from me, but he was actually successful. I wanted to help. It was fun, and I was excited for him."

Excited. Zach thought most people would be slightly jealous, too, but not Rae. She was the type to get swept away on a wave of happiness for someone she loved—and Kevin, he could already tell, was the type to take advantage of that.

"I had all these manuscripts lying around," Rae said softly. "His deadline got closer, his moods got worse, and I just wanted to make everything better. So, I gave him a story, told him to use the idea as a framework. I never dreamed he'd rip the whole thing word for word. Of course, there were some changes: he made the heroine a hero. Made her white. Kept a few of my side characters, replaced the rest. The book sold almost instantly. His advance was £500,000."

Zach closed his eyes for a moment, wrestling with his fury.

Rae didn't sound furious, though. She sounded wryly amused, like she was telling the story of some teenage mistake, distant enough to laugh about. "I didn't read *Everlee* until it was published. He kept getting all these accolades for his 'diverse' cast, and I got curious." She shook her head, chuckling. "Christ, that first read was a shock. When I confronted him, he wasn't even sorry. He said my version hadn't been marketable, and anyway, I'd given him permission—which was true, I suppose. I gave him the story. But..."

"But you trusted him," Zach finished. "You trusted him to use it the way you intended. Not to stick his name on it and sell your words behind your back."

"Yes," Rae nodded. "Exactly. I told him that I wanted a divorce, and he said, 'Good, I'm fucking Billie anyway.'"

She said the words matter-of-factly, but holy shit, that had to hurt. Badly. Even now. Zach got up, his ideas about distance and control abandoned, to sit beside her. She leaned into him without hesitation, and he told his heart to calm the fuck down as he held her close.

There was a gentle silence before he said, "I really don't know why you won't let me murder him."

Rae laughed, the sound dancing through his blood. "Because I don't think you'd enjoy prison. And because I want you here with me more than I want him dead—or otherwise injured," she added quickly, like she was covering all her bases.

Zach couldn't help himself; he dropped a kiss on her forehead, quick and light. She looked up at him with something like hope in her eyes, and that sparked *his* hope, and suddenly the room was glowing so bright he could barely see.

"The divorce was messy," she said, "and you know I hate messy. In the end I gave him an ultimatum: give me everything I wanted—and I wanted a *lot*—or I'd tell the world what he'd done. And it worked. But the thing is, I was bluffing. I didn't want to tell anyone, then or now, because I know how these things work. Most people don't care about plagiarism or ethics as much as they care about power. Calling him out would damage me way more than it damaged him, and the drama... the drama would have made me miserable." She rolled her lips inwards, her mouth a grim line. "I suppose you think that makes me a coward."

Zach frowned. "No. I think the whole story is fucking awful, but you chose the path that was best for you, and that's its own kind of bravery."

She exhaled hard, as if she were relieved by his answer. "Yes," she said firmly. "That's what I think, too. Kevin agreed to my deal, and I officially gave up all rights to the content."

"That's fucked. That's just... so fucked." The unfairness of it was eating him alive, so he couldn't imagine what it did to her.

But she shook her head, smiling slightly. "You know what? I don't mind. *Everlee* is his most popular book ever, and it came from me. Every award he accepts is mine. Every accolade. Every sale. All that magic came from my head, and I can recreate it any time I want. Watching my book succeed under his name is what gave me the confidence to start writing again."

Then her smile gained a vicious edge that made Zach want to grin. "But even if my career never touches Kevin's, the fact is, I'm the better writer. And he knows it." She laughed, and the sound was sheer delight. "That's the fucking thing, Zach—people are constantly telling him, 'Rae's better than you!' but he's the only one who can hear it. And he has to *smile*. He has to look happy about it!" She laughed harder, and this time, Zach joined in. He couldn't help himself. Because when she put it that way... it still wasn't right. Not at all. But it was really fucking funny.

After a while, though, she sobered. They were leaning against each other on the sofa, his arm over her shoulders, and she nestled closer.

"Zach," she whispered. "I'm sorry."

He held his breath.

"I'm sorry about everything. That weekend—I lied to you in so many ways because I was scared. I didn't want to trust you, I didn't think I could, so I pushed you away. I already regretted that. I'd planned to apologise after the awards ceremony, and to tell you the truth about... about my feelings for you."

Her feelings for him. The words felt so surreal, he almost missed the rest of her speech—almost. But not quite.

"Then," she said, squeezing her eyes shut. "*God, then I just*—I fucked everything up. I panicked and I treated you like... like you were someone else. I took my own shit out on you, and I shouldn't have. But I promise you, I never will again." She opened her eyes, her gaze drilling into him. "Zach, I swear. I never will again."

The words held an earth-shaking finality. He nodded slowly, the swell of hope inside him growing even further, the last of his hurt starting to ease away. "I believe you, sunshine."

But she still wasn't done. "I need to tell you the truth, now. I know I pretended we were nothing, but honestly, Zach, we're everything. *You're* everything. And I want to be with you, for real. Even if it terrifies me. I mean—that is—" She faltered, her gaze flitting away. "If you want to. I don't know if you…"

"Hey." He caught her chin, turning her to face him. Even that slight connection sent pleasure zinging up his spine. No, more than simple pleasure; this was comfort, this was faith, this was a love so deep, it must be stitched into his DNA by now. So fierce she must feel it in him, must see it in his eyes. God knew he wasn't trying to hide it. Not anymore.

"I think you know I want to," he said softly. Understatement of the fucking year. "If you can tell me that weekend was real, and that we'll always be honest moving forward—yeah, I want to."

"I promise," she said instantly. "I'll try, Zach. I will try so hard for you. And…" She raked her teeth over her bottom lip. "Yes. We both know that weekend was real."

He felt himself smiling, broad and impossible to control. "I'll try, too, sunshine. No more faking. Or pretending to be faking. Or whatever the fuck we were doing. We're both terrible liars, anyway."

Finally, she laughed, her hand coming to rest over his chest—over his heart. "We are, aren't we?"

"Oh, yeah. And shitty communicators, but we'll work on that."

"Me, you mean."

"No. Us. It's always *us*, now. Do you trust me?"

She didn't reply right away, and Zach told himself to relax. To wait. Then, slowly, her hand glided from his chest, up his throat, to cradle his jaw. He held his breath because this moment felt breakable, impossible, precious. Like everything was coming together. Like they could do this, and they wouldn't let anything stop them.

She swept a thumb over his cheek. Leaned in close, until he was surrounded by her sweet, bright scent and still-cold skin. Her whisper warmed his lips. "I do. I do trust you." Then she kissed him. It was the slightest pressure, but it lit him up inside, crackling through him like pure power. Pulling away, she murmured, "I love you, Zach. I don't care about anything else. I love you, and you're mine, and if anything gets in the way of that—including me—I'll deal with it. Quickly." She added with a scowl.

He would've laughed at the vicious determination in her voice, but he was too busy floating up to cloud fucking nine. He ran his thumb over her smiling mouth, his own grin so wide it shouldn't have fit on his face. The brightest happiness he'd ever felt flew through his blood like a rocket. He dragged her into his lap, ignoring Duke's suspicious look, and held her so tight his arms ached.

She slid her hands into his hair and yanked him impossibly closer. Then their lips met, and everything was right again. Sheer bliss. Pure intimacy. Tender, shivering touches that ruined him utterly.

"I love you, too," he breathed against her skin. His voice cracked as he spoke. "It's changed me, loving you. I can't accept bullshit anymore because you've given me so fucking much. You make me feel..." He broke off. "You make me feel like myself."

She blinked rapidly, her words choked by unshed tears. "That's what you deserve. That's how it should be. And the way you look at me—I want to be worthy of that. Of you. I promise, I will be."

"You already are." He kissed her cheek, her throat, the curve where her neck met her shoulder. Again and again, so she'd never forget, never be afraid. "I love you. I love you. I love you."

"Zach," she murmured, soft and longing. He looked up to find her lashes fluttering, her eyes turned midnight. He wanted to make them darker still. Wanted to feel her come apart for him, to make love honestly and to have her do the same.

He held her, and stood, and carried her to bed.

ZACH'S SHEETS smelled like him. By the time he laid her gently on top of them, Rae was shaking, overwhelmed by need and by breathless relief. He must've sensed how surreal this all seemed to her, because he lay by her side and whispered gentle reassurance in her ear until she could believe that this was it. This was her life. This was her love. It really could be so simple, and so good.

When she was calm, he started to take off her clothes.

He was slow, slow, slow, but achingly steady, as if a natural disaster wouldn't stop him. He stripped off her T-shirt and ran his hands up the curve of her spine, the breadth of her shoulder blades. He pushed down her jeans and underwear, stroking the tender crease where her arse curved into the back of her thigh. When she whimpered, he kissed her throat, hot and wet with an electric flick of tongue.

It broke something in her. She rose up on her knees and snatched at his clothes, and she wasn't slow or steady at all. But he didn't seem to mind.

He did, however, take over again when they were both naked. "Let me taste you," he murmured, his voice rough, his hands insistent. "Let me."

As if she would argue.

Her pulse leapt as she lay back. He ran a possessive palm over her thigh, spreading her wide for him. His eyes were heavy-lidded, his breath warm against her sex. "Such a pretty cunt."

She rolled her hips, anticipation thrumming through her clit. "Do something."

He pressed a chaste kiss to her hip bone.

"Oh my God, Zach, I swear I'll strangle you."

His laughter was low and rich. She felt each puff of air, right before she felt his tongue.

Good Lord, that was good, so good she almost sobbed. His tongue laved her swollen flesh, slick and slow, sending sparks through her blood. He moaned against her pussy and the vibrations rolled through her, melting her into a puddle of lust. His thumbs parted her folds, and his next torturous lick massaged her needy clit. She almost flew off the bed.

"Fuck," she gasped. "Yes. There. Please."

Countless times in the past, Zach had playfully ignored her wishes just to hear her growl. Thank God he was too sensible to start that shit in bed. He licked her clit like it was his job, swirling his tongue around the sensitive bud, sucking and stroking, making her dizzy—literally dizzy— with heart-racing pleasure. She bit her lip as her vision darkened at the edges. Ignored it. Gasped recklessly, "*More*."

He gave it to her, gripping her hips to hold her still and pushing his face into her slippery, aching cunt, making a mess of her. His moans grew louder and the bed bounced a little, until she realised that he was rocking his hips against the mattress—working his cock without hands. As if the taste of her turned him on so much he couldn't stop himself. Maybe it was that possibility that snapped the band of delicious tension inside her. Maybe it was his open hunger, so rough and needy and unrestrained, that made her come.

She almost screamed, it was so sudden and intense. Shockwaves of pleasure ripped through her until her ears rang, but through it all, she felt Zach's hands on her, and she loved their weight.

Languid and dazed, her heart slowing, she murmured, "I liked that."

Zach laughed. "I appreciate the verbal confirmation."

"Look at us communicating," she said wryly.

"Like a dream." He moved to lie over her, every rough-hewn inch of him pressed boldly against her body, the perfection of his smile filling her vision. She felt his thick erection pushing against her belly, that wicked piercing so different from his soft skin and crisp hair. She'd only just come, but her pussy tightened in anticipation of his swollen shaft. Her hips rolled without permission, rubbing against him, and he growled and bit his own lip.

"Fuck, Rae. Tell me you want me."

"So much." Her voice was shattered, but her lust rang out loud and clear. Their eyes met, and it was such a relief not to hide. "I want you so much in every way, and I have you, and I'm not letting you go."

He groaned and thrust against her belly, his pre-come silky on her skin. He smelled like salt and desperation. "That was pretty fucking romantic, sunshine. Are you coming down with something?"

"Impatience."

"I've got you," he rasped. And then again, a few minutes later, his fingers slick and sure as he prepared her for his cock. "I've got you, love." Tight, wet circles over her needy clit; long, thick fingers buried inside her. His jaw was tight, his control palpable, but she wanted the storm hiding inside him.

"Please," she whispered. "I need you. I need you."

He let her go and rolled on a condom.

Remembering the slow, blissful morning they'd shared last weekend, Rae lay on her side, her back against his chest. He grasped her thigh with a shaking hand and spread her legs. His breaths were laboured, his heart pounding so hard she felt it against her spine. Then the head of his cock nudged her entrance from behind.

She could barely speak. Even her moans were breathless. But she managed to say, "Now. Please. You're mine. And I'm yours."

He groaned as if the words were a touch. Then he thrust hard, rocked deep, and took her completely. His arms were iron bars around her, and each stroke of his cock unravelled her mind. She clutched at his tense forearms and gasped, sobbed, begged for more. He sank his teeth into her shoulder and gave it to her.

He gave her everything.

Rae's second orgasm was a lightning-bolt blow to her nerve endings, a wave of beautiful devastation. Behind her, Zach choked out a moan, one hand gripping her hip to hold her still. "Jesus," he gasped. "*Fuck*, you feel so good, squeezing my dick. Rae—"

She felt the moment he came, too, his whole body spasming behind her, his voice cutting out and his cock pulsing between her thighs. As soon as he finished, he rolled her over and kissed her like his life depended on it.

Later, when she was dazed and satisfied, and he'd dealt with the condom, she said, because she felt like it, "I really, really love you."

"And I really, really love you."

This was peace. Pure and simple.

He gathered her close and kissed the top of her head, holding her for a while. Then he broke the comfortable silence to say, "Nice of Duke to stay downstairs through all of that."

Rae snorted, clapping a hand to her mouth. "Shut up."

"I'm just saying. Very considerate."

"You're ridiculous." She poked his ribs. He poked back. She pulled his hair. He smacked her arse and bent his head to lick her nipple. After a moment, she was gasping, "Alright, okay. You win."

He pushed her onto her back. Bent over her breast again with obvious intent. "You're damn right I do."

Pleasure shivered through her, but somehow, she kept her wits. "Do you know what this is?"

He looked up, releasing her breast. He must've seen something serious in her face, because he caught her hand and twined their fingers together. "What is it, sunshine?"

"This is a happy ending."

His eyes shone with satisfaction. "Oh. Shit. You're right."

EPILOGUE

TWO YEARS LATER

It was a sweltering Friday night in August, and the Unicorn's beer garden was full of disapproving stares. Baby Ann McRae, infamously gauche divorcée, had recently increased her scandalous behaviour. Bad enough that she'd started sleeping with the town trollop, a man twelve years younger and ten times prettier than she was. Even worse that they'd moved in together, living in obnoxious sin, as if they truly didn't care what the Ravenswood gossips said. Now they'd gone and fucking done it, they really, really had. Because Rae's left hand, the one currently skating through Zach's dark hair, sported an emerald and sapphire engagement ring so bright you could see it from space.

Despicable, all those razor-sharp eyes seemed to say.

Delicious, Rae thought at the sight of Zach's smile. She leaned in to kiss it.

He turned as if he'd read her mind, curling an arm

around her shoulders, dragging her close, kissing her hard. By the time they finished, Nate was rolling his eyes in a way that didn't quite match his delighted grin, and Ruth was looking vaguely horrified.

But the poor woman couldn't be too grossed-out, since she managed to complain a moment later. "Do you realise how horrendous it is that we are *all* engaged? At the same time? As if we planned it, like... like *sorority* sisters?"

Evan's look of triumph hadn't faded for months. Even now, it sharpened as he winked at his fiancée. "I think it's cute."

"You would," Ruth muttered, but she fingered the fine, silver necklace where her engagement ring hung, and her eyes seemed to smile while her mouth stayed disapproving.

"I agree," Hannah said. "It's cute." When all eyes turned to her in astonishment, she arched her perfectly shaped brows. "What? It is."

"That's it," Ruth snorted. "The world is ending. The apocalypse is now."

"It's a shame Laura and Samir are already married," Evan mused. "We could've planned a four-way wedding."

"We could've planned a *what*?!"

While the rest of the table wound Ruth up, Rae put her head on Zach's shoulder and breathed in the scent of happiness: lemonade and red wine, hot, languid summer, and Zach. Her love. Molten iron, dappled sunlight, and cool certainty.

He pressed a kiss to her forehead and murmured. "Penny for your thoughts."

She smiled. "You can have them for free."

The End

AUTHOR'S NOTE

So, that's it! The Ravenswood series is over. No, I'm not crying, *you're* crying. Or something. Whatever. Let's move on.

Writing this series has been absolutely incredible, and reader responses have been even better. Every time I get an email from someone who relates to Ruth or Laura or Hannah, I tear up and sparkle at the same time. I really hope you love Rae just as much as all the other Ravenswood outcasts—and I already know you guys adore Zach. You've been waiting for his story long enough!

Speaking of Zach: writing a demisexual character was a wonderful and very important experience for me. I have to thank Em Ali and Xan West again for their advice and support. Any issues with representation are entirely my own. In writing Zach, it felt especially vital that I gave him space to be angry—not just about the way people mistreat him, but also about society's treatment of his identity.

Ace-spectrum individuals are often brushed off, ignored, or have their marginalisation downplayed, so I wanted to decimate that. I hope Zach's perspective will help any allosexual readers to remember that we all have different experiences, and nothing should ever be assumed.

And now, I suppose, this is goodbye. I'm so sorry to leave this small town behind, but excited for what's to come. Thank you for taking this rollercoaster ride with me.

Love and biscuits,

Talia

ABOUT THE AUTHOR

Talia Hibbert is an award-winning, Black British author who lives in a bedroom full of books. Supposedly, there is a world beyond that room, but she has yet to drum up enough interest to investigate.

She writes sexy, diverse romance because she believes that people of marginalised identities need honest and positive representation. She also rambles intermittently about the romance genre online. Her interests include makeup, junk food, and unnecessary sarcasm.

Talia loves hearing from readers. Follow her social media to connect, or email her directly at hello@taliahibbert.com.